Shadows In The Night

ISBN: 1-4392-5874-0
ISBN-13: 9781439258743

To order additional copies, please contact us.
BookSurge
www.booksurge.com
1-866-308-6235
orders@booksurge.com

Shadows In The Night

#12 'Hawkman Series'

Betty Sullivan La Pierre

Cover Design by Author, Paul Musgrove

2009

Dedication

TO MY MOTHER, CHARLIE EVELYN SULLIVAN,

AND HER DEAR FRIEND,

UNA MAE BOSSMAN

Others in 'The Hawkman Series by

BETTY SULLIVAN LA PIERRE
www.bettysullivanlapierre.com

THE ENEMY STALKS
DOUBLE TROUBLE
THE SILENT SCREAM
DIRTY DIAMONDS
BLACKOUT
DIAMONDS aren't FOREVER
CAUSE FOR MURDER
ANGELS IN DISGUISE
IN FOR THE KILL
GRAVE WEB
THE LURE OF THE WITCH

Also by Betty Sullivan La Pierre

MURDER.COM
THE DEADLY THORN

I want to thank, Yvonne Knepper, Community Marketing Director, of the beautiful CYPRESS PLACE Senior Living, at 1200 & 1220 Cypress Lane, Ventura, California, for the patience and help in explaining to me the way this beautiful home is run. It helped me so much in laying the foundation for this story.

I also want to thank, Dorothy Robert, a resident of the Independent Living Section of Cypress Place for allowing me to take her picture for the cover of this book.

chapter

ONE

Monday morning Hawkman arrived at the office in Medford, and had just put the coffee on to brew when he heard a loud banging. It sounded like it came from the stairwell. When it quit, he figured the noise had traveled from somewhere on the block. Then it started again and he swore he could feel the vibration in the floor. His curiosity finally got the best of him and he opened the door. An old man with flighty white hair, dressed in a long black over-coat, stood at the bottom of the steps with his cane raised to strike the bannister.

"Hey, what's going on?" Hawkman yelled.

The fellow shaded his eyes and looked up. "I should have called you on the phone. I can't climb stairs, and I don't have the time or energy to go find another private investigator. I need to talk. So you're going to have to come down here."

Hawkman grinned. "Sure. Want some coffee?"

The old fellow leaned on the staff and nodded. "Sounds good."

"Cream or sugar?"

"Black."

After pouring a couple of cups, Hawkman went down the stairs and handed him a steaming mug. The old codger sat on one of the lower steps, so Hawkman leaned against the hand rail, and studied his face. "What's your name?"

"George Hampton."

Hawkman held out his hand. "Pleasure meeting you, Mr. Hampton."

After they shook, he looked up at Hawkman with sparkling, yet faded blue eyes. "Let's not start that formal stuff; call me George. I know you as Hawkman." He raised the mug, took a sip of the hot liquid and continued. "Granted, it's your nickname. Your real tag is Tom Casey, but I like Hawkman better, so that's what I intend to call ya." He pointed to the sign at the top of the stairs. "I've kept my eye on you ever since you came into this town and hung your shingle above the doughnut shop."

Hawkman suppressed a smile. "How come I don't know you?"

George raised his bushy eyebrows. "Never needed your services until now."

"What can I do for you?"

"I want you to investigate some murders at Maggie's senior home."

"Never heard of the place," Hawkman said, scratching his sideburn. "Is it around here?"

"No, no, that's not its name. My wife lives there and her name is Maggie."

"Sorry, I misunderstood."

"It's called, Morning Glory Haven."

"Oh, yes, I know the place. It's on the outskirts of town, near the hills and right behind that new mall. Beautiful area."

"Yeah, it's the right home for Maggie. She's been there three years, come the first of next year, and she loves it. After she fell and broke her hip, it never healed right because of her arthritis, and she couldn't drive anymore. Then she got pneumonia. Just about lost her. Once she got over the worst part, she needed to get out and go places. I knew I couldn't take her everywhere she wanted to go with my bad knees and back, so after much discussion, we decided she needed to be where she'd have people and things going on all the time." He wiped his eyes with the back of his sleeve. "I go see her every day. I sure miss her."

"I'm sure you do," Hawkman said, sitting down on the stair next to George.

"The house is way too quiet. If it weren't for my dog, Pesky, and the television, I'd go stark raving mad."

"Tell me about this murder. I don't recall reading anything about it in the paper."

George shook his head, then pointed a crooked finger at Hawkman's nose. "You won't either. When you're at one of these old folks' home, they just blame death on age, and say you died of natural causes. Well, I don't buy it." He angrily slapped his thigh.

Hawkman felt a cool autumn breeze whirl around his shoulders. "Are you warm enough? We could get in my SUV."

He waved a hand. "Naw, I'm fine." Repositioning his body, he pulled the coat around his chest. "Sybil Patterson and Maggie were best friends. They shared a two bedroom unit at the haven, and did everything together. It really helped me, knowing Maggie was happy. Then yesterday morning they found Sybil dead in her bed. No apparent reason. Maggie had played a game of cards with her the night before and said she was fine."

"What did the doctor say?"

He glared angrily at Hawkman. "They'll tell you anything. Said she had a bad heart and it just finally gave out. I don't believe it and Maggie is hesitant about accepting the diagnosis as Sybil had never shown symptoms of a heart problem." He let out a loud sigh. "I'm about ready to pull my wife out of there, but she says there's no way she'd leave."

"You said there were other murders."

"Yeah, a couple just recently and no telling how many I don't know about."

"What were their names?"

"The first was old Fred Horn. I'd see him walking the halls and paying visits to all the ladies. I used to tease him and tell him to stay away from my Maggie. He'd laugh and tell me since I was there all the time, I really put a damper on his flirting."

"How did he die?"

"The very next day, when I went to see Maggie, she told me Fred had passed away in his sleep. It really seemed farfetched as the man had been walking the halls, fully dressed, and joking with everyone he saw. He sure didn't act sick."

"Who else passed away, making you question a natural death?"

"My checkers buddy, Eddie Parker. He went last week, and I really miss the guy and our nightly games. We'd meet in Maggie's room every evening after supper. She'd have the table all set up for us and then retire to the chair in the corner and do her knitting. She really enjoyed us laughing and carrying on."

"Did he go the same way?"

"Yep, in his sleep. Don't you see a pattern here?"

"Sounds suspicious. Do you know if autopsies were done?"

George shook his fluff of white hair. "I don't know, but I really doubt it. These people were all old, and like I said, death is expected in these places."

"This sounds like it could be complicated. If I do take this case and discover foul play, I'll have to bring in the police."

"I understand. I just fear for my Maggie. I don't want to go visit her some morning and find her dead in the bed." He turned and gazed into Hawkman's face. "I'd like her watched from the time she gets up until nightfall. I usually go in the morning, stay a couple of hours, go back later and have dinner with her, then remain until she goes to sleep. I can't be by her side all day, because I do have responsibilities at the house. Plus, she doesn't want me hanging around constantly."

"I could arrange for someone to be there on the hours you're not available, but it would cost you a pretty penny."

"Cost doesn't bother me. I'd do anything to keep my sweetheart alive."

Hawkman rubbed the back of his neck. "If you want to hire me, I need to get your signature on a contract and explain the terms."

"I don't need no signed paper; a handshake will do."

"I appreciate it, but legally I have to present you with the document. It protects us both."

Hampton sighed in resignation. "If you insist."

"I won't put you through the agony of climbing the stairs. Instead, I'll get everything ready and bring it to your house. You set up a convenient time in the next day or two."

George checked his watch. "How about tomorrow morning at ten?"

"Sound good. It'll give me time to round up all the items." He took a pen from his pocket and a small pad of paper he always carried. "What's your address and phone number?"

After writing down the information, Hawkman stood and helped Mr. Hampton stand. George gripped the bannister, then lifted his cane from the railing.

"You okay?" Hawkman asked.

"Yeah, just have to let everything get back in sync before I take a step; otherwise I'd fall flat on my face." He sniffed the air. "What's that delicious smell?"

Hawkman pointed toward the doughnut shop. "Clyde fires up those ovens about this time in the morning and bakes his pastries for the day."

"Oh, my, I'm surprised you're not as fat as a butterball with such a business sitting just below your office."

"It's not easy," Hawkman chuckled.

"I think I might stop by and pick up a treat before going to see Maggie. She'd like that."

"I can guarantee they're delicious."

Hawkman watched George's slow, swinging gait, clunking his cane against the concrete with each step, as he swung around the corner toward the shop.

chapter

TWO

Hawkman jogged back up the stairs, and sat down at the desk. He shoved up his eye patch and rubbed his hands across his face. Leaning back in the chair, he flipped it down to shield his bad eye, then let his mind wander back many years. When he'd worked for the Agency, he'd never had to venture into a senior home to look for a murderer. The ones he'd stalked were usually much younger and vicious. Enemies still emerged from time to time, and he had to always be on guard.

He vividly recalled the time he went after the thugs who'd killed his first wife with a car bomb. A good whack on the head with a tire iron had caused him the eye problem.

When the optical injury couldn't be corrected, the Agency wouldn't allow him to work in the field, so he decided to retire. He went to Copco Lake with a new identity and formed his private investigator business.

However, it didn't take long for one of his nemeses to find him, and a pursuit occurred. It involved Jennifer, his present wife, and he feared for their lives, but together they brought the man down quickly. Many years passed before he had to deal with the second adversary who entered his life.

He took a deep breath, dismissed those memories and leaned forward. Pulling a folder from the drawer, he set up a file for the Hamptons, and wrote on the outside the address and phone number George had supplied. He noted the old fellow lived in a high income part of town, which surprised him, due to his appearance. Maybe money wasn't a problem. You never knew about these old codgers, and definitely can't judge them by their clothes. He jotted down Morning Glory Haven, and the names of the three dead people George had mentioned. Sensing the leg work involved in this case, he figured a big challenge lay ahead. He'd first have to interview the family members of each of the deceased. Many times the residents of these selected establishments chose to stay near familiar territory even though their sons or daughters might live clear across the country. He could only pray he'd luck out.

George appeared serious about surveillance on his wife. The expense would be phenomenal as he'd have to pay top wages for this type of service. Hawkman would present Hampton with the estimated price and continue from there. Gathering up the needed contract and other forms,

Hawkman slipped them into a large brown envelope which he placed on the desk.

***

Since Hawkman's office was in Medford, Oregon, a good hour and a half drive from Copco Lake, he left home early the next morning. Hampton had mentioned a dog named Pesky and he felt it would be a courteous gesture to pick up some doggie treats at a pet shop. He didn't have any trouble making up to canines and usually they'd mind his commands, unlike Jennifer's little scamp, Miss Marple. He chuckled to himself when he thought of the cat and how she tried to get by him with her antics.

Studying the different sized treats in the shop, and not knowing the weight of the animal, he chose medium sized biscuits. He then stopped by the office, picked up the brown envelope, and headed for George Hampton's place. As he drove through the upper class area, he couldn't help but admire the beauty of the architecture. Some house plots had tall fences with big pillars at intervals; others were surrounded with beautiful sculptured shrubs. There were two and three stories with a few single level homes scattered among them. When he reached the address, it didn't surprise him to find a lovely one story dwelling. George suffered from knee and back problems, so the choice made sense. The man must have money, because property here cost big bucks.

Hawkman turned into a circular driveway lined on both sides with a large white chain fence connected to short pillars every ten or so feet. He parked in front of the entry, got out and walked up a short aggregate sidewalk which led up a couple of steps to a porch that extended the width of the house. The front door made of highly polished oak with a beautiful beveled glass insert glistened in the sun. He pushed the bell and could hear chimes ringing through the house. A dog barked and when George finally got to the door, an energetic golden retriever, tail wagging, bounded out, and ran around Hawkman's legs.

"What a beautiful animal."

"Pesky, behave yourself," George said, then gestured for Hawkman to come in. "Please forgive her. She loves company and gets very excited when anyone visits. Afraid she's not much of a watch dog. I think she'd get in the car with anyone who offered her a goody."

Hampton led Hawkman into a huge den that took his breath away. The walls were covered in rich dark panelling, and beautifully framed paintings of hunting scenes hung on both sides. A huge flat screen television almost covered one end, flanked with stands holding different types and lengths of fishing rods. The furniture was big, heavy duty, but covered with plush leather. The whole area definitely had a masculine touch.

"This is a man's dream room," Hawkman said.

George stood leaning on his cane, smiling. "Thank you. As you can probably tell, I added my two cents worth in getting it decorated. Have a seat."

Pesky had followed them in and eyed their guest with big begging eyes.

"I think she smells the treats I've brought."

George let out a hearty laugh. "Well, for heaven's sake, don't make her suffer. Give them to her."

Hawkman pulled the bag from his pocket and before he could take one out of the package, George butted in. "Make her do a trick. She can do about anything you ask."

Hawkman tested her with certain commands and the dog proved her worth of receiving all the goodies. When finished, she went to the rug on one side of the room and lay down.

"Smart and very friendly dog. I like her."

"I enjoy her company very much. Especially, since Maggie's not here."

Hawkman placed his arms on his knees. "Forgive me for asking, but it looks like you have plenty of money. Why didn't you just hire a driver and a nurse to take care of your wife, instead of putting her in a home?"

George shook his head. "Maggie going into Morning Glory Haven was not my idea. She insisted."

"With all this luxury, why would she want to go?"

"We weren't born with it. It took lots of work from both of us to get to this stage in our lives. We married young and worked hard. Then one day Maggie and I decided to start our own company. She couldn't have children, so we struggled together to build our fortune. When I sold out, it brought us enough to live very comfortably for the rest of our lives. However, Maggie never got over the feeling of being poor. She said she'd worked out the expenses. It would take four or five house servants to take care of things, and she never liked the idea of having strangers running around our home. So she figured going into the independent living place would be half the price. The driver, food and entertainment were all included in the fee. I couldn't talk her out of it."

"Do you think she'll return one of these days?"

George sighed. "I don't know. She really enjoys all the people who surround her and she's staying pretty healthy. The doctor says her condition is about the same." He waved a hand in front of him. "I don't think she'll ever come home."

"I'm assuming you were serious about keeping a watch over her during the hours you weren't there, until we decide it's safe. What about the nights?"

"Yes, I'm serious about having someone there during the day. It won't be necessary at night, as she can lock the door. Since Sybil passed away, I've told the staff I want Maggie in a one bedroom unit. It's about five hundred dollars a month cheaper. They'll move her into one when it's available."

"Remember I warned you, the cost is exorbitant when I have to bring in an extra man to do this type of work. I can come in some of the days, but I have other cases and need to give time to those."

"I understand." George said. "What do you have in mind?"

"We need to set up a schedule."

"Okay, I can be there at eight in the morning and stay until noon. I can usually run my errands in three or four hours." He raised his hands and let them drop on his thighs with a thud. "Takes me longer with these danged knees. I'll make sure I'm back by six o'clock to take Maggie to the dining room. Would that work?"

Hawkman jotted down the information. "Yes, I think so. Once I line up one of my guys, we should meet at your wife's room so she can be introduced to me and the one who will be sharing her day. Then my man can get familiar with her routine. We'll need to check with the head of the place and get his approval. He may not take to strangers lingering around your wife. It could make for an uneasiness."

"No, problem. I'll handle that end."

"Does Maggie know what you're up to?"

"Not yet. I plan to tell her tonight."

"How do you think she'll take it?"

"Oh, she'll have a fit. This is one time I'll stand my ground and not give in. When she realizes I mean business, she'll simmer right down, give me a kiss and a hug for loving her so much."

Hawkman opened the brown envelope and removed the papers. "Here's the contract, and the extra page I typed up for the service of another person. I'll need a down payment to get started."

Hampton took a pair of reading glasses out of his pocket and read through the agreement. "This is a very good, and easy to understand." He signed both copies, then worked his way to the edge of the couch, pushed himself up with the armrest and latched onto his cane. "Let me get my checkbook and we'll start this process rolling."

Hawkman wondered why the man had never gotten his knees fixed. He definitely had the money. Of course, he didn't know George Hampton's medical condition and doubted he'd ever get it out of him. Hampton returned in a few minutes and handed him a check.

"Will this do for now? I can always write another when the money runs out."

Hawkman glanced at the sum of five thousand dollars. "This should do us for quite a spell. All depends on how long this case will drag on. I'll get in touch with you when I line everything up."

Hampton pointed a finger. "I expect to hear from you tomorrow."

chapter

THREE

Hawkman deposited the check at the bank, stopped at a fast food drive thru, grabbed a hamburger and drink, then drove to the office. His mind churned with the first orders of business on this case. He needed to contact one of the two retired police officers, Kevin Louis or Stan Erwin, who usually helped him out. It would be interesting to hear their reaction to watching an older woman in a senior's home. For sure, the job wouldn't appeal to them, but the pay might.

He pulled into the alley, parked and climbed the stairs carefully so as not to spill the soda. When the aroma of pastries wrapped around his nose, he mumbled to himself, "Wonder which has the most calories, my lunch or a bear claw?"

Once inside, he sat down at the desk and unwrapped the sandwich. As he ate, the thought rolled around in his mind that George Hampton might have gone over the top in assuming murders had taken place. People were usually old and some sickly when placed in these homes. Many needed twenty-four hour care, and would spend their last days in this type of environment. He looked forward to seeing the facility.

Once Hampton got permission from the management to allow him to do his job, it'd be interesting to see how the staff of Morning Glory Haven liked their routine being interrupted by a one-eyed investigator hovering around one of their female residents. He figured George would float a few bucks in front of the top guys and the plan would probably go down okay. Money always seemed to talk.

After finishing his lunch, he pulled the yellow tablet containing his notes in front of him and dialed Kevin Louis, then punched on the speaker phone.

"Hello."

"Hey, Kev, Hawkman here. How's life treating you?"

"It could be better. Had to take my pickup in for repairs and it cost me an arm and a leg. I hope you're calling to offer me a job. I could use a little extra dough right now."

Hawkman chuckled. "You must be living right, as that's exactly why I'm contacting you. The pay is good."

"Well, so far it sounds interesting, but when you beat around the bush, I get antsy."

Hawkman laughed, then explained the situation, the salary and what Kevin's role would be. "Does that sound intriguing?"

"Not at all, but I'll take it. When do I start?"

"We'll meet at Morning Glory Haven tomorrow evening so you can meet George and Maggie Hampton. I'll get back to you about the time."

"Sounds good."

Hawkman hung up, drummed his fingers on the desk and smiled to himself. "Yep, money talks," he said aloud.

He pulled the phone directory from the drawer in his desk and looked up the number of Morning Glory Haven, wrote it on the folder, then picked up the receiver.

"Yes, could you put me through to Fred Horn's room, please."

He listened a moment.

"Oh, no, this can't be true. I'm an old service buddy of his just passing through town, and thought I'd pay him a visit. Can you give me the name of his nearest kin so I can contact them and give my condolences?"

Hawkman jotted down the daughter's name and phone number.

"Thank you so much. This really makes me sad. I'd so hoped to see him."

He hung up and leaned back in his chair. It surprised him to get the information so easily. Maybe because the guy had died, they figured there wouldn't be any threat to the home.

Not wanting to try the same method to get information about Eddie Parker, he decided to let George take on that job as they were checkers buddies, and the staff knew they were close. The same with Sybil Patterson. Since she shared a unit with Maggie, they probably confided in one another. If not, Maggie had the advantage of finding out her former roommate's nearest relative more quickly than he could.

He also needed to get a list of the staff. It would be big. He had no idea how many residents the place held, but the buildings spread over acres of land. Some of the employees had to be there twenty-four hours every day, ranging from professionals, aides, to the guys or gals who mop the floors and keep the bathrooms clean. If George's accusations were correct, any one of them could be a killer, and they all had access to the rooms. He doubted the management would turn the names over to a private investigator, due to the privacy act, and he certainly didn't have any evidence show-ing foul play, so a subpoena was out of the question. He might have to do a little snooping during odd hours.

He glanced at the name of Fred Horn's daughter. Susan Palmer lived in Ashland, Oregon. At least she lived close by and not in another state. Just as he slid the meager notes into the folder, the phone rang. He reached over and punched on the speaker. "Tom Casey, Private Investigator"

"Mr. Casey, I'm so glad I caught you. This is George Hampton. I'm visiting Maggie right now and she's having a fit. Says she won't consent to my plan unless she can meet you tonight. Is there a chance you could drop by here on your way home?"

"Sure, I can be there within thirty minutes."

"Whew, what a relief. See you soon."

Hawkman grinned as he hung up. What will Maggie think of a private investigator with an eye-patch, who wears a cowboy hat, jeans and boots to work? Too bad he didn't live closer. He'd drop by and pick up Pretty Girl, then walk into her room with the falcon perched on his arm. He chuckled as he stood, placed the file in his briefcase, slipped the recorder into his pocket, and headed out the door.

When Hawkman arrived at Morning Glory Haven, he realized he didn't know Maggie's room number. He was very impressed with the outside appearance as he strolled into a large open foyer that looked like an elegant living room. A woman was working at an oak desk, her head bent over a bulky ledger. He stopped and observed a nurse pushing a man in a wheelchair toward an elevator.

After several moments, he crossed the room toward the person at the desk. She wore a suit, instead of a white uniform, and looked more business oriented. When he stopped in front of her, she glanced up and her eyes widened.

"Uh, may I help you?"

"Yes, I'm looking for Maggie Hampton's room."

She started to thumb through the papers on her desk, then laughed. "I'm sorry, she's not in this section. This is the assisted living group. Maggie is in the independent building." She pulled another book toward her. "Mrs. Hampton was just moved into a one bedroom unit on the second floor, room 202. She pointed toward a double glass door. "Go through there to the next building. The elevator is on your right. Is she expecting you?"

"Yes." Hawkman touched the brim of his hat. "Thank you." He walked briskly through the doors into a beautiful area lined with river rocks, a large fish pond and a waterfall splashing down a stepping stone structure. Luscious green plants surrounded the border. He couldn't help but stop and admire the sight before him.

Going through the next set of swinging doors, he walked into a lovely alcove furnished with overstuffed couches and an oak coffee table. A large fireplace and high hearth took up one wall. Straight ahead and facing him was a huge comfortable living area with a colorful jukebox in the corner. Several round tables with white iron cushioned chairs filled the right side of the room. To the left, a large couch and a couple of leather mini sofas separated by another oak coffee table, also faced a fireplace. The walls were lined with colorful paintings, and vessels filled with real flowers of different hues were scattered throughout the room. It surprised him to see the space empty; then it dawned on him it was near dinner time. More than likely, everyone had gathered in the dining room.

He quickly located the elevator and took it to the second floor. Stepping out on the carpet, he glanced at the door numbers and soon found Mrs. Hampton's quarters. He flipped on the voice activated recorder in his pocket and softly knocked. George opened the door and ushered him inside.

"Maggie, this is Tom Casey, the private investigator I told you about."

She held a vase of flowers in one hand as she maneuvered her walker toward the table in front of the large window overlooking the fishpond. She glanced his way. "I'll be right with you. I just moved into this smaller unit and it's taking me a while to get things the way I want them."

"It's very pleasant," Hawkman said, as he glanced around the interior. The doors were open where he could see into a large bathroom, and a bedroom big enough for a king size bed along with two bedside tables on each side.

Maggie moved toward him and stopped within a foot of his body and glared up into his face. "So you're a private investigator. Bet you scare the hell out of anyone who approaches you."

Hawkman stared down at the frail woman. She wore a dark green pantsuit which emphasized her sparkling hazel eyes. Her short, thin silver hair clung softly to her head, but separated over small ears adorned with tiny emerald earrings. Artfully applied make-up with a touch of soft pink lipstick gave her a delicate appearance. She raised her hand.

"A pleasure meeting you, Mr. Casey. May I call you Hawkman, like George does?"

He took hold of the small fingers. "Of course."

She gestured toward the chair. "Please take this seat. I have many questions."

"I hope I have all the answers," he said, sitting down.

She plopped on the couch, folded and pushed her walker to the side, then pointed to his eye-patch. "Is that for show or for real?"

He smiled. "It's for real. Due to an old injury, I have difficulty processing light in the eye."

"Maybe one of these days you can tell me the story."

"Sure."

Maggie glared at her husband. "Right now, I have a problem with George hiring a private investigator without my knowledge. We both have reservations about the causes of death of our friends, but we're not sure if they were murdered or died of old age."

"I understand. All I can promise, is we'll look into all possibilities."

"George says you have a man who will watch over me when he's not here."

"Yes, I've hired him already."

She let out a sigh. "I really don't like the idea of strange men hanging around my place. No telling what kind of scuttlebutt will soar through these halls."

"I don't think any rumors that emerge will hurt your reputation. You can always squish them with the rebuttal that you've had threats on your life and we're your bodyguards."

Her face lit up with a big smile. "Oh, you're good. I like the thought." She rose and took hold of her walker. "Don't mind me. I have to stroll around occasionally or else my hip aches."

George moved to her side.

She gave him a gentle shove. "I don't need any help. Just get out of my way."

After Maggie scooted around the perimeter of the room a couple of times, she flopped down on an overstuffed chair and chuckled. "Gives me a bit of exercise too."

chapter

FOUR

Maggie glanced at the watch pendant hanging around her neck. "George, don't let me forget to take my medicine."

"You want me to get it now? he asked, starting to stand.

"Of course not, we have a guest," she grumbled. "It just makes me sleepy and I'd prefer to be alert."

He frowned. "If you don't take your medications regularly, it throws you off schedule."

"I doubt thirty minutes is going to make a hoot of a difference," she replied curtly.

George nodded.

Hawkman watched the two with interest, then turned his attention to Maggie. "Do you take medication every night?"

"Oh, yes," she said. "I've missed the ending of many movies because of it. I should change my schedule. I mean, who cares what time I go to sleep or wake up. It's not like I've got an appointment. I can eat anytime because the dining room opens at seven in the morning and serves anything you want all day. I really like this place. It's clean, orderly and the staff's efficient."

"It certainly has lovely grounds." Hawkman said.

"The next time you're here, I'll take you on a tour. There's a billiard room, a place to watch movies on a big screen, puzzles to work and events happening all the time. They even have bingo."

"Interesting. I'd like to walk around the area." He pointed out the window to the structure across the way. "I didn't realize I'd come in the wrong way. The woman told me that first building houses the assisted living group, and you lived over here in the independent wing. So what's the difference between the two?"

"The people living in the assisted quarters need twenty-four hour care, so there is staff available night and day. In the independent living group, we've just gotten to the point in our lives where we don't want all the responsibilities of trimming lawns and the upkeep of a home, but are very capable of taking care of ourselves." She gestured toward a door. "However, there's an emergency pull cord in the bathroom if we need help. It's the one I pulled when I couldn't wake Sybil. The staff rushed up here and called 911. We don't have any medical assistance on this side, so none of the personnel touch us if we fall for fear they might do more damage. They'll cover us with a blanket and stay until the paramedics get here. Which usually only takes minutes."

"At least there's help available to call in case you need it." Hawkman glanced at Maggie, then again pointed out the window. "I noticed even another extension on the other side. What's that building?"

"It houses people with Alzheimer's. There's no way they can leave without the staff knowing. Each patient has a wristwatch they always wear. It's rigged so it sends a message if they pass through one of the doors they're not supposed to. Then employees can also keep track of them in case they get past the line." She threw up her hands. "A real state of the art contraption if you ask me."

"Very interesting," Hawkman said, and then changed the subject. "I don't want to tire you out, but there's a couple of questions I'd like to ask you about your friend, Sybil."

"I'm doing fine. Go ahead."

"How well did you know her?"

"We were friends before we came to this place. After her husband passed away, her health declined to the point she was afraid to drive, and it became too much for her to take care of their huge two story house. Sybil's children wanted to share their homes throughout the year, but she didn't want to be traveling all over the country every six months. She and I talked about this place after I'd broken my hip." Maggie scowled, "The break wasn't so bad, but the pneumonia and having this horrible arthritis about did me in. No way could I ask George to drive me all over the place. Here they have a bus that will take you wherever you want to go, plus they have all the arts and crafts I love to do.

So Sybil and I examined different places, but fell in love with this one; decided to check in together and be roommates. Then she ups and dies on me after almost three years. The doctors said her heart gave out. I miss her so much." She peered into Hawkman's face with moist eyes. "Sybil never mentioned a heart problem."

"Are any of her children nearby?" Hawkman asked.

Maggie pulled a tissue from the box on the coffee table and dabbed her cheeks. "One son lives in Klamath Falls. The other children live out of state."

"What's the boy's name?"

She pointed across the room to a small desk built into the wall. "George, look in the first drawer and hand me my address book." She tapped her temple. "I think his name is Jason, but let me check for sure."

George handed her the small tome and sat back down. Maggie thumbed through the pages.

"Yes, here it is." She read off the name, address and phone number. Then she lowered her lids into a questioning gaze. "Don't you want to write this down? Surely you can't remember all this stuff."

"I have a confession," Hawkman said, pulling the recorder from his pocket. "I don't like to take notes."

She shut the book and broke into laughter. "George, you've hired the right man. I like him, and if any one can find the truth, I think he can do it." She reached over and patted Hawkman on the knee. "You're my kind of cowboy."

"Thank you, Mrs. Hampton. I can't promise we'll find a killer, but will do my best to put your minds at ease."

She waved a hand. "Please drop the 'Mrs. Hampton' bit, I'm not that old. Just call me Maggie."

Hawkman stood. "Maggie, I think I've overstayed my visit, but I plan returning tomorrow evening with the man I've hired for your approval. What's a good time for us to come?"

"Around six thirty. I'll make sure I've had my dinner by then."

He turned toward George. "I hope you'll have had a talk with the management, so we can start the surveillance no later than Friday."

"I have an appointment at ten in the morning."

"If they don't agree with the plan, we might find it a bit difficult to move around without their permission."

George made a face and waved a hand. "Don't worry. It's in the bag."

Hawkman headed for the door. "I'll see you tomorrow evening." Stopping, he turned and pointed at Maggie. "Don't forget to take your medicine."

She flitted her fingers in the air and chuckled. "Oh, my, you sound like George."

When Hawkman passed the recreation room, several people had gathered and a few were playing a game of cards. He paused and decided to cross over to the front door, to see where he should park next time. Cars in the parking lot were in special slots, each with a reserved sign in front. He spotted a two year old Cadillac and figured that it just might be George's. Strolling across the parking lot, he meandered over to the rear of the car and could see the writing on the placard which read, 'Reserved for Hampton'. He smiled as he went back through the building and across the open alcove displaying the fish pond. The lights glistened off the waterfall, but it felt too chilly for anyone to be outside. He walked through the assisted living area and out the door where he'd parked his SUV.

Once inside his vehicle, he gave Jennifer a call and let her know he'd be late. She sounded exhilarated, as she knew he'd started a new case, and wanted to know the details. He hadn't enlightened her previously, so promised to tell her all about it when he arrived home.

Driving toward Copco Lake, Hawkman's mind drifted to Maggie Hampton. Quite a live wire mentally, but he could see her body had deteriorated and understood why she felt George couldn't take care of her needs. She had the freedom to come and go as she pleased, but Hawkman felt she had no desire to leave the Morning Glory Haven comforts. He'd come to the conclusion that both the Hamptons' minds were sharp and he doubted their fears were false. It made him eager to dig into the lives of those now deceased. He'd need medical histories and hoped he could acquire them through their children, instead of having to go though Detective Williams to legally obtain the records.

He planned to spend time at the facility so he could meet the staff and other residents. It might make it a little easier to find out about individuals and eliminate certain ones as being suspects.

He came to the bridge over the Klamath River and could see the lights shining through the windows of the house. His wife seldom turned in before eleven, which meant he had a good hour of being questioned before bedtime.

When he pushed open the door, Jennifer jumped up from her computer and greeted him. "I can hardly wait to hear about your new case."

Hawkman laughed. "May I put my briefcase down and grab a beer?"

She grinned. "Only if you hurry."

They retired to the living room, and Miss Marple, their Ragdoll cat, leaped into his lap. "So what do you want, you little monster?" he asked, running his hand down her furry back.

"I think she's tired of me. I had to scold her several times today."

"Uh, oh, our little pest has been a naughty girl."

"Forget about her; she's not going to tell you a thing."

Hawkman threw back his head and guffawed. "Okay, so what do you want to know?"

"What does this new case involve?"

"Possible murders at Morning Glory Haven."

She straightened in her chair. "You've got to be kidding."

"Nope."

"You're going to be talking with a group of people who can't hear, have a hard time getting around and won't remember what happened fifteen minutes ago." She rolled her eyes. "Boy, you've taken on a doozy."

He raised his brows and turned down the corners of his mouth. "You mean you don't want to help me out? You might be surprised."

She shook her head vigorously. "I think I'll pass."

"What if it gets intriguing?"

Jennifer played her fingers across her chin and looked thoughtful. "Well, I might change my mind."

chapter

FIVE

Thursday morning Hawkman arrived at his office, poured a cup of coffee, sat down at the desk and picked up the receiver. He reached Kevin and instructed him to be at the parking lot of Morning Glory Haven at six-fifteen. He'd show him up to Maggie's room where they'd meet the Hamptons. Afterwards, they could roam the halls and get the lay of the building.

He then punched on the speaker phone so he'd have his hands free to take notes and dialed Susan Palmer's number.

"Hello."

"Is this Susan Palmer, the daughter of the late Fred Horn?"

"Yes, it is. Who's this?"

"My name's Tom Casey, a private investigator in Medford. I've been hired by George Hampton to look into the untimely deaths of some of the patients who resided at Morning Glory Haven. He mentioned your father, so I wondered if you have a moment to answer some questions."

"I met Mr. Hampton and his lovely wife, Maggie. This is really uncanny. I had many problems with my father's death. I'd just visited him the day before he died and we'd gone for a walk. He was cheerful and full of life. It really shocked me when I got the call the next day. I've had all sorts of doubts about his sudden death."

"Did you have an autopsy done?"

"No, we didn't. The doctor said his heart gave out. We accepted the diagnosis, as he'd had some minor strokes right after mother died. I wanted him to come live with me, but he wouldn't think of it. That's one of the reasons we talked to him about moving into Morning Glory Haven. When he accepted, we felt much more comfortable knowing he wouldn't have to drive unless he wanted, as transportation was available. Also help was only a few steps away if he needed it. We were very impressed with the facility. It was ranked one of the highest in the state, so we felt good about it being close to familiar surroundings and his friends. Also, if the time came when he needed twenty-four hour care, all we had to do was move him to the next building."

"I understand and, yes, I agree it's a lovely place. Who was the doctor in charge of your father?"

"His regular cardiologist is a woman, Dr. Eva Paulson. Dad told me, after going into the home, even with his normal appointments, she'd stop by about once a month or send one of her colleagues, just to see how he was doing. He really liked her and so did we. He didn't care too much for the associate. His name was Dr. Jeff Grahm."

"Did your father take medication on a regular basis?"

"Yes, and as far as I know he was very good about it. He was also diabetic and kept good control over his blood sugar."

"I won't keep you any longer. I'm sure questions are going to arise as I dig deeper into the investigation. May I call you back?"

"Absolutely, Mr. Casey, I'm thrilled you're looking into these untimely deaths. Please thank Mr. and Mrs. Hampton for hiring you."

"I sure will. Nice talking to you."

Hawkman tapped the desk with his fingers after hanging up. Glancing at his notes, he pulled the phone directory from the drawer and looked up Dr. Jeff Grahm. Mrs. Palmer didn't mention if he was a cardiologist. When he located the doctor's name, he found he had a private practice and was only listed as a MD. She spoke as if Grahm was an assistant to Dr. Paulson. He'd check this out, and circled the doctor's name.

Flipping through the pages, he hunted for Dr. Eva Paulson. He didn't find her under physicians, so assumed she was affiliated with one of the local hospitals. Scanning the residential section, he discovered several Paulsons, but nothing under Eva. Her personal phone might have been listed under her husband's name.

He thumbed through the notes he'd taken off the recorder after the visit with Maggie. He doubted Jason Patterson, Sybil's son, would be home, but decided to try. After punching in the number Maggie had given, he listened to it ring several times before an answering machine came on. Hawkman left a message, explaining who he was, the purpose of the call, and asked if he'd please contact him as soon as possible.

Tonight he'd talk with George Hampton about any information he might have on his checkers buddy, Eddie Parker. He also hoped Hampton had good luck with the management meeting. If all went well, it would make the job of interviewing the staff a lot easier. He'd also like to find out how many deaths had occurred at the home in the past six months.

At this point he felt stymied by how little he could do until he had more freedom and information. He looked forward to the meeting this evening and hoped to hear Hampton had made progress.

He kept himself busy during the afternoon by updating his books and getting checks written for bills. Before he knew it, time had rolled by and he found himself hurrying to get out of the office to meet Kevin.

Hawkman pulled into the parking lot at Morning Glory Haven and spotted his colleague, arms folded across his chest, leaning against his pickup. He parked nearby and strolled over.

"Are you ready for this exciting venture?" Hawkman asked.

Kevin guffawed and the two men entered the lobby of the building. Hawkman pointed out the living room and the recreation room with juke box. He led Kevin to the elevator, then down the second floor hallway to Maggie's door where he knocked lightly.

George invited them in and pulled up a couple of extra chairs. "Have a seat and we'll get this meeting under way."

Maggie soon came out of the bedroom, scooting the walker. Her fancy white pant suit decorated with sequins down the front, around the cuffs on both arms and legs, gave the appearance of an attire one would wear to the opera. Even her white flat heeled shoes had rhinestones embedded around the toes in a unique pattern. She gave a sparkling smile as Hawkman introduced Kevin. "My goodness, what a handsome young man. I don't think I'll mind being looked after by you two, for sure."

"Thank you, ma'am. You're not so bad yourself," Kevin said.

George laughed. "Don't pay a bit of attention to her. She loves to flirt and is full of baloney."

Hawkman turned toward George. "Did you have a meeting with management?"

"Yes, I talked with the Executive Director, Mr. Robert Mackle, who in turn put in a call to the owner. Not wanting him to feel we were putting the home under scrutiny, I did as you suggested, and told him Maggie and I had received threatening phone calls, so I'd hired you to watch over my wife. At first, they were a bit anxious, but I think I satisfied their concerns by telling them I couldn't be here all day, and didn't want her left unguarded.

"Great. Will they notify the staff to cooperate with us?"

George nodded. "Mr. Mackle asked if you and your assistant could drop by their weekly staff meeting this evening." He glanced at his watch. "In fact, they might be gathering right now. He wants to introduce you, so his people won't wonder where the strange men came from. I told him you'd be there."

"Good," Hawkman said. "Did they put any restrictions on us?"

"A couple. They asked you not to wear uniforms or carry a weapon. He felt if the residents saw men with guns, it would make them nervous."

"The no uniform request is fine, but we're licensed to carry our firearms and there might be a need for them. They'll be concealed, so it shouldn't cause any problems."

"If you desire, you can explain the situation to Mr. Mackle, as I know you don't go without yours," George said, winking.

Hawkman pushed his hat back with his index finger. "What he doesn't know won't hurt him."

About that time, a soft knock sounded. The woman Hawkman had seen downstairs, stood at the door. "Mr. Hampton, may I talk to you a moment, please."

He excused himself and conversed with her for a few moments, then turned toward the men. "Would you guys please come with me?"

Hawkman, Kevin, and George followed the woman to the elevator, then down a long hallway on the main floor to the end where they turned into a room with a sign on the door, which read, 'Conference'.

All heads turned toward the two men. Expressions were wary and some even appeared frightened.

chapter

SIX

Mr. Mackle introduced George Hampton as Maggie's spouse, then turned the meeting over to him. George in turn explained the story he and Hawkman had concocted, then presented Tom Casey, the private detective he'd hired to keep an eye on his wife. Hawkman brought Kevin to the front and told how he, himself, or George would always be with Maggie.

"Until we get acquainted with the staff, we'll stop anyone from entering Mrs. Hampton's room, and ask for identification. I notice most of you wear name tags, which will help a lot. It will take us a few days to recognize the regular employees; but once that's accomplished, things should get back to normal and hopefully, we'll blend into your daily routine. We'd like your cooperation and patience while we provide Mrs. Hampton with protection. Thank you."

Hawkman stepped back and Mr. Mackle thanked him. The men left the conference area and headed back to Maggie's room. Hawkman flipped on his recorder as they again sat around the living room and discussed the plan.

"Kevin will start the surveillance at noon Friday and stay until six, or until George arrives," Hawkman said. "I'll take the alternate days, but you might see me around at other times, as I'll need to question the staff."

George turned to Maggie. "Does that sound okay to you?"

She sighed. "I guess. So much for privacy. I'm afraid this is going to get very old."

Hawkman turned to her husband. "Tell me about your checkers buddy, Eddie Parker. Did he have family in the area?"

He screwed up his face and put a finger in his ear. "I don't remember him ever talking about his family."

Maggie slapped his thigh. "Oh, George, he talked about his old maid sister all the time."

He furrowed his brow. "I don't remember him saying a word about such a thing."

She waved a hand. "Talk about getting senile, you're at the top of the hill and sliding down fast. Why, he talked about her constantly. You were too interested in getting into the checkers game. He called her Gracie. She'd visit him about once a week and he brought her in to meet me one of those times."

George looked surprised. "Really? Where was I?"

She glanced up at the ceiling and rolled her eyes. "In another world, I guess, or you could've been sitting right here."

"Maggie, did Eddie and Gracie have the same last name, or were they stepsister and brother?" Hawkman asked.

"Of course, they had the same last name," she said indignantly. "In our day, parents weren't out screwing around like they do today. All kids came from the same two parents."

"Just thought I'd ask," he said. "Does she live in Medford?"

"I couldn't tell you, but I'd assume nearby, because she did come often."

"Did Eddie have any children?"

George raised his hand. "No, that I do know. His fiance was killed in a freak accident on her parent's farm years ago, and he never got over her."

Maggie pointed a finger at Hawkman. "I think Eddie and Gracie shared a home. It got to the point where she couldn't take care of both of them, so he made the decision to move in here."

Wrinkling his forehead, George stared at his wife. "How do you know so much about my checkers buddy?"

She flitted her fingers. "I'm a social butterfly. I don't stay in bed all day and get sores on my butt. I like to get out, walk around and talk to people. Eddie liked to do the same thing, so we'd walk the halls together."

George's face turned red. "Why that old fart. Making out with my wife while I'm not here. How come you never told me about these rendezvous?"

"You two can discuss your marital problems later," Hawkman said, chuckling. "Right now I need to ask a few questions."

"Sorry," George said, and glanced at Kevin. "We get carried away. We do it mostly in fun. So what do you need to know?"

"Maggie, how often is your apartment cleaned?"

"Once a week."

"Does an outside firm do this?"

"No, they're in-house people."

"How about laundry facilities?"

"I have my own washer and dryer." She pointed to a small closet next to the refrigerator. "They also have a laundry room for those who don't have appliances. In this area, we take care of ourselves. That's why it's called Independent Living."

"Understood. What about mail?"

"We have our own mail boxes in a designated area. Now, in Assisted Living, they have volunteers who come in and help with those little jobs. I've seen them scurrying back and forth. I believe they're called pixies. They take the mail to the residents, as some can't do much walking. They also do odd jobs for the nurses."

Hawkman nodded. "Kevin or I will not allow anyone into your room unless you give the okay. We will also accompany you on your walks or any other function you want to attend. George says you like to play bingo. If we spot a problem, we might ask you not to drink or eat anything until we can check it out."

She frowned. "I'll agree, but I don't like it."

"That's the way it has to be if you want protection."
Hawkman glanced at his watch and stood. It's getting late,
so we'll leave you now. I'll check in with you tomorrow."

"Thank you," Maggie said.

chapter

SEVEN

As Kevin and Hawkman moved down the hallway toward the elevator, a little hunched backed woman strolled by. She stopped, narrowed her eyes and shook a finger in the air. "What are you two men doing coming out of Maggie's room behind closed doors? Does George know about you two? You ought to be ashamed of yourselves. Just wait until I tell him."

Before either one could open their mouths to respond, she walked away, shaking her head. They stepped into the elevator, chuckling.

"I don't think you'll find this job very boring," Hawkman said, as the door slid shut.

"Mrs. Hampton appears to be a spitfire. I'm sure she'll see to it I stay on my toes," Kevin said, as they walked out the front door to their vehicles. "This is really a lovely place. I wouldn't mind living here."

"I'd hoped we'd get a guided tour of all the amenities, but time grew late and I didn't want to tire Maggie out. She said something about a workout room, movies, puzzles and all sorts of entertainment. Everything is here for their enjoyment. Maybe she'll take you around and show it off."

"I'm sure it isn't cheap."

"I don't know, but maybe I'll get some idea of the cost when I speak with the Business Manager, which I hope to do tomorrow," Hawkman said, as they parted ways to their respected vehicles.

***

Hawkman arrived at Morning Glory Haven around eight-thirty Friday morning. His gaze took in all the people traveling the hallway, then shared the elevator with a couple, and nodded at a few others as he headed toward Maggie's apartment. He knocked, but didn't receive an answer and decided to find the dining room. Going back to the first floor, he stopped a man in the corridor, and asked for directions to the cafeteria.

The man laughed. "I can tell you're a visitor. It's not called a cafeteria; it's a full fledged dining room." He waved a hand. "Follow me, I'll show you."

When they reached the entry, Hawkman couldn't believe what he saw. The room had dozens of tables covered with colorful cloths, and fully set place settings with fabric napkins. The food smelled delicious, and everything appeared sparkling clean. The whole area emitted an air of elegance.

When he spotted Maggie and George at a far corner table, he turned to the fellow who'd helped him and touched the brim of his hat. "Thank you. I see the people I want."

The man smiled, gave a salute, and left.

George saw him coming, and pointed to an extra chair. "Good morning. Have a seat."

"How are things going with you two?" Hawkman asked, as he joined them.

"Have you had breakfast?" Maggie asked.

"Yes, thank you. This is really a beautiful dining room."

"It's open all day and you can have any meal you want at any hour."

"Maggie had a rough night," George interjected.

She slapped him on the arm. "Oh, George, he's not interested in my dreams."

"What happened?" Hawkman asked with concern.

"She had a horrible nightmare and howled so loud it awoke people across the hall. They immediately called 911 and the paramedics had to break the lock to get into the room, because they couldn't get Maggie to answer the door. When they finally got in, she'd awakened herself and couldn't figure out why they were beside her bed."

"It scared me so, I didn't know what to do. So I screamed again." She giggled. "It's kind of funny now, but it sure wasn't at four this morning. I'm really quite embarrassed, Mr. Casey. The strange thing is I didn't even know I had yelled so loud."

"Happens in dreams. Just glad to see you're okay. Did the door get fixed? I didn't notice any damage when I went up?"

"The handyman put in a new identical lock before we left for breakfast."

"Have you ever had an incident like this before?" Hawkman asked.

"Never. I think that's what frightened everyone. They had no idea why I was making such a ruckus."

"Has your night medication been changed?"

She shook her head. "No."

Hawkman rose and patted her shoulder. "I'm glad everything turned out all right. Now I've got to go do some poking around. I'll talk with you two later."

She grinned. "I wish I could go snooping with you."

Hawkman shook his head. "We can't let them know what we're doing. If you tailed me around, I'm afraid it would be a giveaway."

Leaving the Hamptons to finish their meal, he turned the corner into the lobby area, and noticed a woman come in the front door with a badge on her jacket. He watched her walk down the hall and enter a door labeled 'Business Manager'. Standing at the front desk, he waited patiently for the person who staffed this position. Finally a woman came around the corner with a handful of folders. After placing them on the surface, she glanced up and smiled.

"Can I help you, Mr. Casey? If you wonder how I know your name, I was at the meeting. I'm Julie."

"Pleasure to meet you, Julie. Could you tell me the name of your Business Manager and what the person does?"

"Lisa Montgomery. She keeps all the records of the residents of the Independent section from the day they check into Morning Glory Haven to the day they leave. It includes their nearest relatives, any special instructions and a little of their health history."

He pointed toward the door he'd seen her enter. "Is that her office?"

"Yes."

"Do you think she might have a minute to see me?"

"I'll sure check"

"Thank you."

She scurried around the corner, then returned within a few seconds. "She'd be happy to see you. You may go right in."

When he entered the large office, Lisa stood at one of the several filing cabinets lining the walls. She had on two inch heels, but they still didn't make her look much over five feet tall. Her pastel blue suit's straight lines helped melt away some of the pounds she had around her middle. The short pixie style of her frosted brown hair flattered her face with soft curls, and the gentle smile she presented, put him at ease.

"Hello, Mr. Casey. I've been expecting you to drop in. Please have a seat."

"Really?" he asked as he took the chair in front of her desk.

"At the meeting, when I heard the Hamptons had received threatening calls, I assumed you'd want to check and see if other patrons had similar problems."

Hawkman rested an arm on the desk. "Are you open for employment? I could use a woman with your uncanny scrutiny."

She laughed. "No, I've got all I can handle with this job."

"You are absolutely right about my being curious. Also, I'd like to know about the deaths that have taken place in the home the last six months, which include three of the Hamptons' friends."

"Really? What does that have to do with threatening phone calls?"

"I'd like to find out if any of those people received such calls."

"I don't know how I can help you there, other than give you the names of their next of kin."

"That's excellent. Can we start on this today?"

"Sure."

He removed the small recorder from his pocket. "Would you mind if I recorded our conversation? I'm not good at taking notes."

"Fine with me. I use one, and decipher from it later when I have time."

Hawkman felt like this woman might be of help in gathering information for the case. "First, how many deaths have taken place in the past half year?"

She pulled a large ledger to the center of the desk and flipped it open. Running her finger down the columns, she glanced up at him with a frown. "I hadn't counted these up lately, and don't like what I see."

"Oh?"

"There have been seven residents who have passed away in the last six months."

"Is that high?"

"Definitely. I remember it went through my mind that we had numerous openings come up in just a short time. Of course, there are always some who don't like our facility and want to leave or find it too expensive for their budgets. Sometimes it gets so busy I miss things, which is no excuse on my part."

"You're human, and there are occasions when life becomes a challenge just to keep up."

She looked at him over the rim of her reading glasses. "You're very kind, but my boss might not be so understanding when I bring this to his attention months later."

"Let's look into these deaths."

chapter

EIGHT

Knowing he wouldn't have time to decipher the recording before talking to Maggie and George, Hawkman removed a small pad of paper from his pocket along with a pen. He could fill in the blanks later.

"Ms. Montgomery, would you be allowed to give me the phone numbers of the next of kin of these individuals?"

"Please, call me Lisa. We were told to cooperate with you, and I really don't see a problem. The children or spouses would be able to give you more details than I'm allowed to indulge, and probably more than I know."

"Let's start with the one who passed away six months ago. I'm going to jot down the names and phone numbers in case I have a chance to call them before I get to the recorder."

"Okay, you ready?"

"Yes."

"Marion Carter. It appears she only has one child, a son. His name is Jerry Carter. I have his address, would you like it too?"

"Yes, addresses would be very helpful."

Hawkman jotted down the particulars.

"Faith Lambert passed away the same month. She has two children: a daughter, named Janis Hamel, who lives here in Medford and a son, William Lambert, who resides in Texas. The next month Jacob Thompson died. He has two daughters. Lillian Nichols lives in Grants Pass, and Nancy Walker, lives in Klamath Falls." After giving the data, she continued. "Ronald White's records list his only survivor as his wife, Edna. She lives in Medford."

Lisa read off the last three, which Hawkman recognized as the friends George had quoted. She filled in the information he didn't have.

When she finished, he glanced up from his notes.

"That's quite a list."

"Yes, and it bothers me very much."

"Did the same doctor look after these people?"

"That's classified information. Each resident in the Independent Living area takes care of his or her own medical problems, so you'd have to get such information from relatives."

"Do you have records of their health problems and medications?

"Also classified."

"Who manages the work schedules of the employees and outside contracts?"

"Perry Foster is our Staff Coordinator. His office is next door."

Hawkman rose and extended his arm. "I've taken enough of your time. You have quite a complicated job. I really appreciate your help. I might need your assistance periodically and hope it will be all right to drop by."

She stood and shook his hand. "No problem. It was a pleasure. I just hope there's no one in our organization threatening the Hamptons, or frightening any of our residents. It's scary to think about."

"Hopefully, it won't take long to get to the bottom of the problem. Have a good day and thank you again."

Hawkman left her office, flipped off his recorder, and journeyed back to Maggie's room where he found her and George watching a television program.

"How are you feeling, Maggie, after that stir you caused during the night?"

George laughed. "Leave it to my ball of fire to get noticed."

Maggie gave him a playful swat on the shoulder. "I don't like that kind of attention."

He pointed a finger at her. "Not only that, but I've already heard from a couple of your women friends telling me about strange men lingering around your room."

"Good grief, nosey old ladies. So I'm having an affair. What business is it of theirs?"

Hawkman raised a hand. "I need to interrupt this conversation and ask some questions."

Both turned their heads toward him, as he sat down on the overstuffed chair. He took the notepad from his pocket. "I've discovered seven deaths have occurred in this home during the past six months. The woman in charge of records is disturbed by this fact. I'm going to read the names of the deceased and would like you to tell me if you knew any of these people."

The Hamptons gave Hawkman their full attention.

"Marion Carter."

"Yes, I knew her," Maggie said.

George shook his head. "The name doesn't ring a bell."

She gave him a disgusted look. "Of course, you knew her. She loved to sing songs and would have everyone joining in."

He snapped his fingers. "I remember her now. The tiny mite of a woman with only one leg. She rolled around in her wheelchair, always laughing and spreading cheer wherever she stopped."

"Yes, she's the one."

"I wondered where she went."

"Probably heaven."

"Did you know her well?" Hawkman asked.

"No, but everyone adored her. She was always the life of the party."

"How did she lose her leg?" Hawkman asked.

Maggie tapped her cheek. "I really don't know. I think she'd lost it before coming into the home. My guess would be diabetes."

"Okay, how about Faith Lambert."

George raised his hand. "I remember her. A real dud. Complained all the time; we hated to have her around.

Strange I can remember her name and couldn't remember Marion's, who loved life and sparkled all the time. I guess the complainers seem to attract more attention."

"Did either of you know her well?"

"No," Maggie said. "We avoided her at all cost. No one wants to be depressed, but that woman brought a black cloud wherever she went."

"Jacob Thompson?"

"Strange man," Maggie said. "He'd stand outside your door and when you opened it, you almost jumped out of your skin. I shooed him away several times. Even George told him to 'get lost' one day."

"What did you know about him?"

"Not much," George said. "I think he was harmless, or he wouldn't have been in this wing. He could carry on a decent conversation, if you caught him at the right time. He just wasn't one you wanted hanging around. You never knew when his mood would go sour."

"Ronald White."

Maggie pointed a finger in the air. "A very sweet man. His wife Edna is a doll. She still comes around occasionally and says 'hello' to everyone. We were very saddened to hear about his death."

"Yeah, I miss old Ron too. We used to talk football. I think he knew every player on the professional teams for the past twenty years. I'd go down to his room to watch a game and Edna would come to Maggie's to watch the soap operas or a movie." George nodded. "Yeah, he's missed."

"Do you know if they had any children?" Hawkman asked. "Ms. Montgomery had no record of any."

"No, they didn't," Maggie said. "Edna couldn't have babies and they thought about adopting, but never got around to it before they were too old. They both had full time jobs and didn't want to give up their luxuries to raise a family." She shrugged. "Some people just aren't meant to raise children. At least Edna was honest about it."

"When these people died, did you hear any rumors about their deaths?"

"Nothing out of the ordinary. Except they all died in their sleep of so called heart failure," Maggie said, raising her hands and letting them flop down on her thighs.

Hawkman raised a brow. "You heard this about all of them?"

Maggie nodded. "Yes, now that I think about it."

"Who said these things?"

"Mostly the residents who were their friends."

"Did you know if any of them had heart conditions?"

"We know Ronald did," George said. "Edna felt more comfortable for him to live in an area where there were people. They lived out in the country with no one around for miles. This way, if he collapsed or had a problem, she felt he could get immediate help. Money was no issue with them."

"The next three names are those of your friends, so I won't need to go into those." Hawkman stood. "I'm off to talk to a few more people. Have a good day."

chapter

NINE

Hawkman ambled down the hallway greeting the people who crossed his path with a nod and a verbal hello. He figured, once they got used to his presence, he'd stop and chat. Right now, his eye-patch, cowboy hat and size might intimidate them, especially the women.

In hopes Perry Foster had returned from lunch, he stepped out of the elevator, rounded the corner, and headed for the man's office. He stopped at the door past Lisa's office, which also said Management, flipped on his recorder and knocked.

"Come in," a male voice called.

Hawkman stepped inside, but saw no one at the desk. He stood for a few moments and could hear the noise of a printer spitting out paper from an adjoining room. "Hello," he called. "Is this Perry Foster's office?"

"You've found him. I'll be right with you," the voice called.

When the man hustled to his desk and sat down, Hawkman noted he appeared to be in his mid fifties, about five foot six inches, and must have weighed over two hundred pounds. He wore a brown suit, which showed its age by the slick looking fabric. The buttons on his dress shirt bulged to the point they could snap off at the next deep breath. His bald head glowed under the fluorescent lighting and a sheen of sweat glistened on his flabby jowls.

Foster quickly finished the task on his computer, then glanced at Hawkman with a big toothy smile, and extended his hand. "Hello, Mr. Casey. I'm glad you came to the staff meeting and explained what you're doing here. Very interesting project you've undertaken. I hope you don't find anyone at Morning Glory Haven threatening our sweet Maggie." He gestured toward the chair in front of his desk. "Have a seat. Mr. Mackle instructed us to cooperate with your investigation as much as we could. So what can I do for you?"

"Ms. Montgomery tells me you schedule the employees' work shifts and take care of the outside contracts."

"True. Since we require round the clock staff in the Assistant Living and Alzheimer's sections to be on duty, it can get mighty trying at times."

"I can imagine. Right now, I'm more interested in the Independent Living quarters and the people you've hired in the last six months, plus outside companies who take care of the cleaning of the building, food preparation, and any other groups who aren't connected with the personnel payroll."

Mr. Foster rose and went to a filing cabinet situated behind his chair. After thumbing through several files, he pulled out a couple and plopped them on his desk.

"Before we get started," Hawkman said. "I'd like you to know I'm recording this information. I get a more accurate account of what's being said. Besides, I hate taking notes."

Perry laughed. "That's a great idea. I've been thinking about getting one of those little contraptions to take to meetings. I hate writing all the stuff down too."

"It definitely saves time."

"Our food preparation is in-house with our own cooking staff. Also, we have our own cleaning crew. They all go through rigid background checks. We want no felons in our employment."

"I've seen your dining room. It's really modern and appears very well run."

"Thank you. We're very proud of this facility. Have you seen the recreation rooms or noted the entertainment sponsored by us? It's usually posted on the bulletin board."

"No, but I'd like a tour."

"Remind me before you leave and I'll have one of our Marketing Directors show you around. Now, back to your question. The only outside business we use is for the ground's maintenance."

"Do you have much of a turnover in employees?"

"Surprisingly, no. Most of our help has been here ever since Morning Glory Haven opened."

"How long have you been in operation?"

"Five years. Our popularity has gone through the roof, and we now have a waiting list for apartments. Not only in this building, but in the other two wings as well."

"Do you have many complaints about your service?"

Perry raised his brows. "Mr. Casey, I can tell you haven't been around old folks much. If they can scream about something, they do. We've always got a bunch running in after the cleaning crew have been in there apartments to tell us they didn't do something right or such and such has been stolen, which I might add, we eventually find in their rooms. So yes, we get complaints, but nothing major."

"I can see you have your hands full." He leaned forward and placed an elbow on the desk. "Would someone be able to steal any poisonous substance from the cleaning crew?"

"I really doubt it since there are usually two people working side by side, but I guess it could be done."

"I'm assuming the gardeners never come inside."

"Right, they come once a week and maintain the grounds. We receive the bill on a monthly basis. The lawnmowers and blowers are very noisy, so we recommend they come in the middle of the day when most of the residents are awake."

"How about the laundry facilities?"

"The resident's apartments are wired for washer and dryers if people so desire to have their own. We also have a laundry room, but everyone supplies their own detergents, or whatever they need. So nothing is left once they've finished with the appliances."

Hawkman stood and extended his hand. "Mr. Foster, I've taken enough of your time and want to thank you for your cooperation and information. It has saved me hours of work, and I appreciate it."

"You're more than welcome." Perry stood. "Let me get in touch with our Marketing Directors and see if one of them is free to take you on a tour." He picked up a mobile unit and punched in a number. After speaking into it for several seconds, he placed it back on his desk and glanced up at Hawkman. "Don Jackson will be more than happy to take you for a tour of our wing. He should be here in just a few minutes. If you'd like, you can wait here or out in the lovely lobby area where there's a couch."

"Thank you. I'll go sit on the sofa, so you can get back to work." Hawkman left the office and headed for the large waiting room with it's lovely furnishings. So far the friendliness of this place impressed him. The people he'd talked to seemed to be more than willing to help in this investigation. Maggie had told him some things, and Foster had verified her comments.

He meandered around the room checking the contents and noticed the bulletin board on a three legged easel near the door. Reading the events, he could see why Maggie liked this place. Something for everyone, even a cocktail hour with a pianist.

chapter

TEN

Hawkman had just moved from in front of the bulletin board when a well-dressed man of about forty-five walked up. He held a mobile unit and a folder in his hand.

"Hello, you're Mr. Casey, right?"

"Yes, I am."

"My name is Don Jackson. Mr. Foster says you'd like a tour of the facilities."

"I hope this isn't cutting in on your work time."

He smiled. "Not at all. In fact, it's my job. I know why you're here, as I attended the meeting when you were introduced. I hope there's no problem with our staff."

"I don't suspect there is. But I'd like to see the lay of the land."

"Okay, let's get started. As we walk, I'll tell you about Morning Glory Haven. We have seventy-six units, which include private studios, and one or two bedroom apartments. They have kitchenettes and the residents may bring in their own microwaves. Also, in each apartment is a spacious common living area."

"I've seen Mrs. Hampton's and it's lovely."

He waved a hand toward the large room with a jukebox. "This is our social lounge. People can gather and visit or play a game of cards. It can also be transformed into a small auditorium."

Hawkman followed him into another area.

"Here's the billiards room."

Walking around the table, Hawkman ran his fingers along the felt edge. "Hey, this is luxurious. I wouldn't mind living here myself."

Don laughed. "It's a wonderful place. Our residents are very happy."

"I can certainly see why."

He opened another door. "Here's our fitness center with the latest equipment; each machine is pressure fixed so the elderly have no problem operating them." He explained how this was done and pointed out the seats on the equipment so the residents didn't have to stand for any length of time.

Hawkman scratched his sideburn as he studied the room and ran a hand over some of the metal. "Wow, I'm impressed."

"I'm sure you've observed our beautiful landscaped garden, courtyard and walkways."

"Yes."

"There's a Bistro area at the end of the social lounge, which has twenty-four hour coffee, snacks and refreshments. Then there's our dining room, where meals are prepared fresh, and it's open all day. The residents may eat at any hour they chose."

"Mrs. Hampton told me that was her favorite place."

"She's not the only one," Don said as they continued down the corridor. "I'm sure you noticed the elegant fireplace in the sitting area, along with a grand piano. Occasionally, one of the residents will play, or we hire someone in for special functions. There are always events scheduled."

"What about telephone and cable?"

"The apartments are wired for those services, and it's up to the residents if they want to pay for them. There's also a small closet for a washer and dryer in some of the units. We do have a laundry room, for those who don't care to have the appliances in their apartments."

On the second floor, Don pointed to an individual working on a jigsaw puzzle in a small alcove, then he gestured toward the computer center. We also have a nicely stocked library with cushioned chairs and tables on the first floor.

"We have daily activities as well as special events; you probably noted the announcements on the bulletin board. We also have scheduled transportation for those who are no longer driving. There's normally a guest suite available for visitors, or for those who just want to try the place out before committing. You might have noticed we're situated right behind a mall. People can walk over and shop anytime."

They ended up back where they'd begun the tour. Hawkman put out his hand. "Thank you, Mr. Jackson. This is quite a place. I can see why you don't have many vacancies."

"I enjoyed taking you around." He handed Hawkman a folder. "This tells you more about Morning Glory Haven and the cost. If you have any questions, my card is in the file. Just give me a call."

"Before you go, tell me about those mobile phones I see most of your staff carrying."

He held his up. "It makes it a lot easier to stay in contact, and in case there's an emergency, no one has to come looking for us."

"Great idea," Hawkman said. "What happens when there is one? How do you get into the apartment?"

"Those on duty have a master key. We can at least open the door, if no one can let us in. We stay with the person, after calling 911, but never touch them if they've fallen, as we don't have those skills, and could do them damage. We can place a blanket over their body, but we let the paramedics do their job."

"What if someone falls at night?"

"The alarm goes straight to the emergency line. They have a special code to enter the Independent building."

"Sounds like you have all situations covered."

"We try."

When the two men parted, Hawkman left the building and since it was still early, he decided to go back to the office where he could decipher the recordings he'd taken while talking with management. Possibly this weekend, he could contact some of the deceased's' kin.

When he pulled into the parking lot, he licked his lips. A bear claw with a cup of coffee would sure taste good. He hoped Clyde hadn't closed, and hurried toward the donut shop. The lights were still on, and the bronze bell clattered as he opened the door. A big smile creased the face of the baker.

"Oh, you're one lucky man. All pastries are half off."

Hawkman smiled as he pulled money from his jeans pocket. "In that case, I'll take two." He carried his prizes upstairs and put on the coffee pot. While waiting for it to brew, he plugged the recorder into the wall socket to recharge.

He settled behind the desk and moved a yellow legal pad toward him, took a big bite of a bear claw and washed it down with a swig of coffee. "Aaah, that's good," he said out loud.

Punching on the recorder, he went through the interviews of Lisa Montgomery and Perry Foster. When he finished writing down the needed information, he read through the notes. Fred Horn's personal physician, Dr. Eva Paulson, might well be worth a visit to determine what she thought about her patient's death. It would be interesting to find out more information on those who'd previously passed. He hoped the relatives would be cooperative.

Hawkman gathered up his notes, and put them into a folder, which he then slid into his briefcase. When he left the office, he met Clyde as he came around the corner of the building.

"Hey, you're working late tonight."

The baker stopped and smiled. "Needed to clean the ovens, and it always takes longer when I decide to mop the sticky floors."

"Sounds like a messy job to me."

He nodded. "Appears you're working overtime too."

"Yep, new case," Hawkman said. "Have a good evening."

Both men waved and walked toward their vehicles.

Driving home, Hawkman went over the people involved in this case and wondered if anything would come of it. It seemed odd to have murders in an old folks home where the patients were destined to spend their last days. The world is a strange place, he mused.

He felt the tension leave his body as he rolled over the bridge and could see his house. Jennifer had every light on. She usually sat at her computer, but it looked like tonight, something had taken precedence. He drove into the garage and strolled in the front door. The smell of meat baking swirled around his nose.

"My word, what's going on? I've never seen so many cooking utensils out at one time in this house."

A dish towel flung over her shoulder, she moved a pan to the pile in the sink and lifted a large fancy bowl from the cabinet. "Hi, honey. Remember, I told you there had been a death in the Perlick family, and many people have journeyed to their home. A group of us got together and decided to take turns furnishing a dinner for a few days, until the company slows down. I'm fixing it for tomorrow."

"That's a very kind gesture from all of you."

"You know Carole would do it for us."

"Yes, she would." He placed his briefcase on the counter and sniffed the air. "It sure smells good. What are you fixing for these lucky people?"

She counted off on her fingers. "I decided on ham, baked beans and potato salad."

He frowned. "So it's all going down the street? I love your potato salad and baked beans, not to mention ham."

Patting him on the shoulder, she grinned. "Don't worry, I'm making extra, so there will be plenty for us to have for our meal on Sunday."

His sad expression dissolved. "Great, it will give me something to think about besides eccentric old people."

She raised her brows. "Shame on you. We'll be old one of these days."

He rocked back on his heels and looked at her mischievously. "Didn't you tell me when I took on this case that it'd be a doozy? I'd be talking with a bunch of people who couldn't hear, have a hard time getting around and wouldn't remember what happened fifteen minutes ago."

Her cheeks turned pink. "Well, I really didn't mean it. However, you still might have trouble getting reliable information."

The timer dinged and she turned off the burner under a big pot of potatoes, put on a couple of mitts and carried it over to the sink where she poured the white cut up vegetables into a colander to drain, then checked the oven. She placed a big butcher block on the counter, then lifted out the pan containing a huge ham, and set it on the board to cool.

"I can't stand to see all this food in here when I can't have any. I'm going back to my office." He lifted his briefcase off the counter.

"Expect Miss Marple to join you. Her nose is really out of joint because I won't allow her in here while I'm cooking."

He glanced behind him and sure enough their pet cat was at his heels. "Come on, little nosey. You're welcome to join me tonight. We're being punished something terrible." Hawkman grabbed the toy stuffed bunny from the floor, then he and Miss Marple disappeared down the hallway.

***

Saturday morning, Hawkman arose quietly, so Jennifer could sleep. He had no idea how long she'd stayed up. When he hit the sack, he could still hear her banging around in the kitchen. He grabbed his jeans and a clean shirt out of the closet, then stopped at the guest bathroom to dress. When he went to the kitchen, Miss Marple stood in front of her empty bowl and let out a yowl.

He put a finger to his lips. "Shush, you silly feline. I'll get you some food. No sense in waking up your mistress. She had enough on her mind last night without worrying about you. Anyway, you need to lose some weight." Reaching down, he stroked her back as he poured some dry food into the bowl. "I must say though, you are a pretty animal."

While a pot of coffee brewed, he had a bowl of dry cereal and milk. He needed to get to Morning Glory Haven, as they were having a couple of events today and he wanted the residents to get used to seeing him and Kevin with Maggie. Then he hoped to reach some of the sons or daughters of the deceased.

He rinsed out the bowl, and fixed a small thermos of coffee, leaving the rest for Jennifer. Tiptoeing back to his office, he picked up his briefcase and started to shut the door when he noticed the cat's toy on the carpet. He picked it up and tossed it into the living room as he passed. She bounced on it like a tiger after its prey. Smiling to himself at the sight, he scribbled a quick note to Jennifer and left it on the counter, then softly closed the front door.

Driving toward Medford, he planned his day. The bingo games at Morning Glory would begin at one this afternoon. Then tonight at six-thirty they had a magician scheduled. He doubted the events would use the same room. He planned to attend with Maggie, if she felt like going to them both. He'd have time this morning to try and reach some of the relatives.

Soon he arrived in the alley behind his office, parked and jogged up the steps. He unlocked the door, then set the briefcase next to the computer and noticed an envelope on the floor in front of the mail slot. He quickly scanned Kevin's report, which didn't indicate any unusual goings on, and Maggie had showed him a good time. Chuckling, he folded the sheet of paper and put it into his valise. So far, no clues were evident at Morning Glory Haven. He then removed the Hampton file and sat down at the desk.

The first name on his list was the beloved Marion Carter with only one leg. Her son lived on the East coast. More than likely, this number belonged to a cell phone; so hopefully, he'd be able to reach Jerry Carter without much of a problem. He picked up the receiver, punched in the digits, then pushed the speaker button. Flipping over a sheet on his tablet while waiting, he readied himself to take a few notes.

"Jerry Carter speaking."

"Hello, Mr. Carter, my name's Tom Casey. I'm a private investigator looking into deaths that have occurred at the Morning Glory Haven. I believe your mother passed away while a resident there."

"Uh, yes. Is there a problem?"

"Nothing we've uncovered yet. George and Maggie Hampton have hired me because they feel uncomfortable about three of their friends who have died, so I'm going back a little farther in time to see if there were any questions about others."

"I met the Hamptons. Very pleasant people. Mother had no serious health problems that we knew about, so her death came as a shock. Of course, we miss her. She was always so positive."

"I understand she was loved and always laughing."

His voice caught. "I wanted her to come live with me, but she insisted on staying in the area she knew. I could understand, so we put her in the best home there. I tried to come out and see her at least three times a year. I'd scheduled a visit the week after she passed away."

"I'm sorry. I know this is hard on you. But if you don't mind answering a few questions, it would help my investigation."

"Of course."

"Did you have an autopsy done?"

"No, the doctor said her heart gave out and she died peacefully in her sleep."

"Did she have her own personal physician?"

"Yes, but once she went into the home, she felt like going to see him on a regular basis would be too expensive, even though I told her I'd pay for it. Parents can be very stubborn. However, he did drop by and see her occasionally."

"What was his name?"

"Dr. Phil Hart. I believe he's associated with Mercy Hospital."

"Do you know if she ever saw any other doctor?"

"Not that I'm aware of."

"Would your mother have changed doctors for any reason?"

"Only if he was cheaper."

"I see. Thank you, Mr. Carter. This information helps a lot. If I have any more questions, may I call you again?"

"Certainly, any time. I pray you don't find any foul play."

"Me, too."

chapter

ELEVEN

Hawkman sat back in the chair and tapped the pencil on his desk. Then he leaned forward and circled the name Dr. Phil Hart at Mercy Hospital. Checking the list of the deceased, Faith Lambert appeared next, a woman not well-liked by the residents of Morning Glory Haven. He'd soon find out how the family felt.

Punching the speaker button, he dialed her daughter, Janis Hamel, and after five rings, a breathless woman answered.

"Hello," she panted.

"I'm calling for Janis Hamel."

"Speaking."

Hawkman identified himself, and explained his mission. "May I ask you a few questions about your mother's death?"

"You can ask all you want, but I'm glad she's gone. She drove my brother and me nuts."

Not expecting such a response, it took him a moment to regain his composure. "Could you tell me the cause of her death?"

"Old age and crankiness. The woman hated life and everything about it. She bitched and complained until no one wanted to be around her. Even as kids we could hardly wait to get out of the house."

"Surely something physical occurred, like a heart attack or an ailment of sorts. Did she have diabetes or any other malady?"

"Yes, she had diabetes, but the doctor said her heart stopped. She died in her sleep."

"Who was her doctor?"

"I don't remember his name."

"Were you concerned about the sudden death of your mother?"

"Are you kidding. We were all relieved."

"So, you probably didn't have an autopsy done?"

"No way. We could hardly wait to bury her."

"Thank you for your time, Ms. Hamel."

"You're welcome. Bye."

After hanging up, Hawkman stared at the phone for several seconds, then took a deep breath and jotted 'forget this one' alongside her name. As he arose from his chair to pour another cup of hot coffee, he wondered if Mrs. Lambert's kids could have done her in. He just couldn't fathom a mother being so hated by her own children.

Leaving it on speaker, he dialed the number of Lillian Nichols in Grants Pass, Oregon, one of Jacob Thompson's daughters. A young male voice answered.

"May I speak with Lillian Nichols please?"

"Who's calling?"

"Private Investigator, Tom Casey."

"Just a moment."

Hawkman could hear the boy yelling, "Mom, a private investigator wants to talk to you."

"Who?" a woman asked, as footsteps approached the phone. "Hello."

"Is this Lillian Nichols?"

"Yes, who are you?"

Hawkman again went through the dialog of explaining his purpose.

"I've talked with the Hamptons several times when Dad and I would take a walk around the building. So tell me again why they've hired a private investigator."

"They're concerned about the recent untimely deaths of three of their friends. I'm going back a little farther in time to see if the families of others who have passed away were anxious over their losses."

"Dad suffered from heart problems, so it didn't shock us too badly. We were thankful he passed away peacefully in his sleep. Of course, we never imagine our parents leaving us. When Mom went, it devastated the whole family. Dad was never the same after she died. He just seemed to lose all hope and became quite depressed. We couldn't seem to bring him out of it. Neither Nancy, my sister, nor I, could talk him into coming to live with us. We thought it might help to be around his grandkids. He wouldn't have any part of it and decided he wanted to live at Morning Glory Haven. Unfortunately, it didn't seem to lift him out of the slump."

"I understand. It must have been hard, and I hate to freshen the ache, but could I ask you a few questions?"

"Sure."

"Did your dad have a private physician who attended him?"

"No, he'd just make an appointment with any of the heart specialist at the hospital and go see them."

"Did those doctors confirm his problem?"

"Yes. So when we got him situated at Morning Glory Haven, I talked with one of the physicians he'd seen. He assured me he'd keep an eye on dad. Now whether he did or not, I have no idea. Dad was very private about his health."

"Did you request an autopsy?"

"No, we didn't think it necessary."

"I want to thank you, Ms. Nichols, for your time. If I have any more questions, may I call you?"

"Certainly. I'd like to hear back from you also. It's disturbing to think there might be a problem at Morning Glory Haven."

"We have no evidence of any wrong doing. I will definitely let you know if we find anything."

"I'd appreciate it. Have a great day."

"You, too."

Hawkman checked his watch and had enough time to call one more person. He again pushed the speaker button and dialed the wife of Ronald White.

"Hello."

"Is this Mrs. Edna White?"

"Yes, and if you're a salesman I don't want any."

He chuckled. "No, I'm a private investigator hired by George and Maggie Hampton."

"Oh, my goodness, why do they need you? Has something happened?"

"They're concerned about some of the untimely deaths of their friends and have brought me in to see if anything is awry."

"You mean at the home?"

"Yes, but we haven't found any problems so far."

"Well, that's a relief."

"Tell me about your husband, Ronald."

"He made me put him in Morning Glory Haven, because he knew I couldn't take care of him. I didn't want him to go, but he insisted. He said we were getting old, didn't have the energy or stamina we used to have, and he didn't want me to go downhill because of him." She sniffed. "I miss him so much."

"I'm sure you do. What ailment did he have?"

"He had lymphoma. The cancer didn't seem to affect him, but the chemotherapy knocked him for a loop, because of the diabetes. He'd be sick for days."

"Wouldn't he have gotten over it?"

"The doctor thought he would. However, months passed after the treatments and he didn't get much better. He felt he was strong enough to handle his own problems, but he knew it would worry me constantly. At Morning Glory, he didn't have to drive to get where he wanted to go." She laughed. "To tell you the truth after we visited there, he figured he'd get a lot better food too."

"So did his doctor think putting him in the home was the best thing?"

"Yes, he thought it a good idea for both our sakes. It's a very pleasant place and Ron loved it. I figured it wouldn't be long before I'd join him. He and George Hampton had so much fun. When I'd go spend the day, those two guys would watch sports on the television and I'd join Maggie. We'd watch a movie or play cards at her apartment."

"I imagine your oncologist kept a good eye on your husband."

"I guess he did. Ron would make a trip to see him about once a month. The doctor didn't think he could take any more treatments."

"What's the oncologist's name?"

"Dr. Stephen Riley out of Mercy Hospital."

"Did your husband die of the cancer?"

"No, his heart gave out. Guess it just couldn't handle the diabetes and cancer. He passed away peacefully in his sleep."

"You didn't by any chance have an autopsy done?"

"No, didn't see any need."

chapter

TWELVE

Hawkman took a deep breath after ending his call with Mrs. White. No autopsies done on any of these people. He could understand their passing would be anticipated at some point, as they were getting older. The relatives didn't question the doctor's listed cause of death in any of these cases. Now, with this background, he felt more comfortable approaching the three relatives of the Hamptons' friends. He placed the notes in the briefcase, checked his watch, and headed for Morning Glory Haven.

When he reached the parking lot, he left the files in the vehicle under the driver's seat, locked up and hurried toward the front door. Maggie had just turned the corner, scooting the walker, as George leisurely walked at her side.

She glanced up and smiled. "I didn't think you'd make it."

Hawkman fell in alongside. "Why, I wouldn't miss this adventure. Not sure I remember much, but you two can help me."

Maggie stopped in her tracks. "You've actually played bingo before?"

"Oh, yeah, but it's been about five years when I worked on a case."

"Really?" George said, as they continued slowly toward the entertainment center. "What in the world happened at a bingo hall that would require a private investigator?"

"A young woman never returned home from a night of fun. Her dad hired me to find her."

"Did you?" Maggie asked.

"Yep. Safe and sound. A scary ordeal though."

"How do you keep track of all your cases?"

"I code name them. Like the bingo hall one, I call Blackout."

"When you have time, I'd like to hear some of the other names," Maggie said, as they entered the large room filled with tables.

Heads turned and attention focused on the tall cowboy with the eye-patch.

"You're certainly getting a lot of attention," Maggie smirked. "Okay, ladies, focus your eyes to the front. He's mine."

Twitters of laughter filled the air.

They strolled down an aisle, stopped at a table, paid two dollars for a packet of papers, then hunted for a place to sit. The room soon filled to capacity. A large bingo machine took up one end of the room and stood on a slightly elevated stage, high enough so everyone could see the caller.

Once situated at the table, Hawkman noticed they had free coffee and figured this would give him an opportunity to roam around before the games began. "You guys want some Java?"

"None for me," Maggie said, as she took a bottle of water from her bingo bag. "I get the jitters if I drink too much caffeine. I have my water."

"I'll have a cup," George said. "Black, please."

Hawkman rose and moseyed around the long way, studying the patrons as he went. A small table occupied one corner where a woman sold daubers, candy bars and assorted chips. He soon returned to the group with two plastic cups of coffee and sat down next to Maggie.

The noise level had gone up several decibels, almost to the point of hurting one's ears. It seemed most people felt they had to yell at one another to make sure the other person heard them. When the noise level lowered, George pushed a blue dauber toward Hawkman.

"You'll need one of these." He pointed toward the stage area. "The caller's here, so we'll be starting any minute."

"Good luck, guys." Maggie said, as she placed a miniature elephant on the table.

"What's that for?" Hawkman asked.

"Gives me good luck."

He grinned, as he watched the man flip on the machine.

"Okay, everyone ready?" the caller asked.

"Yeah!" they all yelled.

When the session ended, Hawkman walked back to Maggie's apartment with the couple. "Do they have the magician's show in the same place?"

"No, it will be in the big room with the jukebox. They set up a small portable stage so the entertainer is high enough for everyone to see. Makes it more like a small auditorium," George said.

"This place sure has much to offer," Hawkman said. "No wonder you enjoy being here, Maggie."

"It should have a lot of stuff. It's expensive enough," George said.

"I agree. I saw a breakdown of the costs."

"I'm going to rest awhile," Maggie said, heading for the bedroom.

"You feeling okay?" Hawkman asked.

"I'm fine, just a bit pooped. I'll see you tonight."

"Shall I meet you downstairs where the show will be held?"

"That'll be fine. No need for you to come all the way up here. I don't think we'll miss you. You definitely stand out in the crowd."

"Okay, see you two tonight." He strolled out of the room and ambled down the hallway. A couple of women stood against the wall not far from Maggie's quarters and stared at him. They had their hands in front of their mouths, talking as if he could read their lips. He touched his hat. "Hello, ladies."

One of them pointed. "Mister. What's your name?"

He stopped. "Tom Casey."

"Why are all you strange men coming and going out of Maggie's room?"

"We're her bodyguards."

Her eyes grew wide. "Why does she need someone to protect her?"

"Nothing for you to worry about. It doesn't affect anyone here, so please, don't let our presence disturb you." He stepped closer. "What are your names?"

"I'm Jessica, but everyone calls me Jessie, and this is Margy."

"Have a good day." Turning on his heel, he strolled to the elevator, then left the building.

Hawkman parked in the alley behind his office, grabbed the briefcase from under the seat and hurried up the steps. Once inside, he went over his notes and shook his head. The people were all diabetic and each had died of heart failure. It sort of made sense as diabetes was not a disease you could ignore. He'd found nothing to make him suspicious of anyone at the Independent Living place. However, since George had hired him to look into the deaths of their friends, if foul play was involved at the facility he couldn't eliminate the risk of Maggie's life being in danger.

He worked on trying to organize his notes until about thirty minutes before the magic show, then headed out the door. Driving toward the home, he thought about what the magician might be like. This place had definitely gone all out to make the life of the residents not only comfortable, but enjoyable. No wonder Maggie didn't want to go home. She had everything at her fingertips.

He pulled into the parking lot and it surprised him to see it almost full. Several cars trailed behind him, so he quickly found a slot before they were all taken. Checking his watch, he still had close to ten minutes before show time.

He observed the people as they climbed out of their cars and headed for the entrance. Several children accompanied the adults. A pleasant outing for them; not only would they be able to see their grandparents, but would also be entertained. Good psychology, he thought.

Hawkman climbed out of his vehicle and ambled toward the entry. When he walked inside, a line of people weaved down the hallway toward a small table with a person selling tickets. The room had been roped off and people entered once they'd bought in. He didn't see the Hamptons, so decided to go up to the second floor. When the elevator door slid open, the Hamptons were waiting and stepped inside.

"I didn't realize these were public shows," Hawkman said, moving over.

"They aren't," Maggie said. "Only family members of the residents can attend and we're allowed to bring a guest. Of course, we have to pay for them. Hope you brought some money."

"I'm covered. How much?"

George pulled out his wallet as they strolled to the end of the line. "Five dollars a head, and three for children under twelve."

Hawkman gestured toward the crowd. "From the looks of this large group, the expenses should be covered."

"They usually get a good turnout on these types of shows," George said. "Kids love a magician, and Saturday is a good time to come see grandma or grandpa."

The line moved swiftly, and they found good seats almost immediately. Hawkman noted they had a stage and a spot light from the ceiling, along with large speakers on each side. He leaned toward the Hamptons. "This is a great setup. Bet it cost a small fortune to buy all these props."

George nodded. "Believe me, we pay for it."

The lights dimmed and the show began. The magician did an excellent job. He held everyone's attention by telling funny stories along with doing tricks, and involving the audience which kept the younger set in stitches. After the performance, Hawkman walked the couple back to Maggie's apartment.

"I really enjoyed myself," he said. "The guy was good. He even had me laughing at his antics."

Maggie flopped down on one of the small couches in her cozy living room. "Their entertainment here is usually excellent. I don't think we've seen a show yet we didn't like. In the warmer months they have all sorts of festivals between the buildings around the fish pond. Very pleasant."

"No wonder there's a waiting list for this place. I'm sure the word has gotten around about all the benefits."

Maggie put her feet up on the ottoman. "George, could you pull off my shoes and get my scuffs out of the closet? These are not my most comfortable pair."

He obliged and shook his head. "Women. I don't understand why they have to have everything a size smaller than they wear."

"Oh, George. They're the right size, they're just made different."

Hawkman raised a hand. "Before I forget, tell me the schedule for meals on Sunday? Do you have the normal three a day routine?"

"Oh, yes." Maggie said. "The dining room is open all day, just as it is during the week." Maggie looked at him questionably. "Why are you interested in the meal schedule?"

"Just curious. What about people who are vegetarians, or allergic to certain foods?"

George stroked his fingers across his chin. "On the menu are special dishes you can order. So it's no problem."

"How is it you get to eat in the dining room, but don't live with Maggie?" Hawkman asked.

"We pay a small extra fee for me to have at least two meals a day."

"Hawkman nodded, then turned toward Maggie. "I'll get out of here so you can prepare for bed. Thanks for a pleasant evening, and I'll talk to you tomorrow."

Maggie rose, tottered a moment, then grabbed her walker. "Oh, I hate almost losing my balance." Once stable, she added. "Have a good evening."

Hawkman headed down the hallway, wondering why Maggie appeared anxious for him to leave. He glanced over his shoulder as he waited for the elevator, and spotted her coming out of her room, pushing the walker at quite a rate of speed.

chapter

THIRTEEN

Hawkman thought about returning to Maggie's apartment, but decided against it, as George could handle her antics. He realized Maggie's freedom to roam the halls and visit her cronies had been squelched by her hovering bodyguards. She probably felt like a caged animal and needed a breather. Also, she needed to reassure her friends that things were okay.

Driving home, he thought about his schedule for tomorrow. He planned to arrive at the office early, then later in the day drop in on Maggie and see if anything new had developed. He still needed to get in touch with Gracie Parker, the old maid sister of George's checker partner, Eddie, and to touch base with Sybil's son.

When he pulled into the driveway, he could see the faint glow of a lamp through the kitchen window. Entering the house, he put his briefcase on the counter and found Jennifer lounging on the couch with a throw over her legs, engrossed in a television program. Miss Marple cuddled beside her, raised her head for a moment, then nestled back in the groove of Jennifer's arm.

"Hi, Hon," Hawkman said.

She put a finger to her lips. "Just a minute, it's almost over and I don't want to miss the ending."

He nodded and opened the refrigerator. His mouth watered at the sight of the potato salad and baked beans she'd saved for their Sunday dinner.

"I could see you drooling all the way in here," Jennifer laughed. She crossed into the kitchen, pulled out the bowls of food and a large package of ham wrapped in foil. "Go ahead, there's plenty for tomorrow too. I gather you didn't get a chance to eat."

"No, and this looks delicious." He took a plate out of the cabinet. "How'd it go today?"

"Real good. Peggy took over a huge chocolate cake, along with a big bean salad Kay had made. The Perlicks were delighted."

"I'm sure it lifted a burden off Carole's shoulders for you gals to volunteer your services," he said, scooping large spoonfuls of food onto his dish.

"It would have worn her out to cook for such a crowd. There are still a dozen or more people there."

He moved around the bar and sat down on a stool. "They have many friends."

"Yes, they do." She plopped down opposite him. "Enough about my day, how'd yours go?"

"Not real productive yet. Still doing background stuff. Once I get it completed, I hope the information will point me in the right direction to solve the problem. If there is one."

"Anything pique your interest yet?"

"I find it sort of disarming all the people passed away in their sleep. I did make a few calls to the relatives of people who'd passed away before the three mentioned Hamptons' friends."

"Dig up anything of interest?"

"One call bothered me, but didn't concern the case." He told her about Faith Lambert who was disliked by everyone, even her family.

Jennifer placed her fingers over her mouth. "Oh, my word. What a horrible story. How could children hate their mother so much?"

***

Sunday morning, Hawkman rolled out of bed and left the house at an early hour. The extra bear claw he'd saved at the office, with a cup of coffee, would make a good breakfast. He drove slowly around Copco Lake, knowing the deer roamed during the dawn hours, and he sure didn't want one to jump out in front of him.

Once on the freeway, he met light traffic, so accelerated to the speed limit, and arrived at the office in record time. He noticed the red light blinking on his answering machine, but first he put on the coffee and removed the pastry from the refrigerator, wrapped it in a paper towel, then zapped it in the microwave for a few seconds. Settling behind his desk with a full mug of steaming brew and the warm delicacy, he punched up the message.

Sybil's son, Jason Patterson, had returned his call and suggested he contact him at his home over the weekend. Hawkman wrote the number the man had recited on the yellow legal pad. He glanced at his watch and figured it was after nine, so probably a good time to call. Washing down the last bite of the bear claw with a gulp of coffee, he punched on the speaker phone and dialed.

"Jason Patterson," a male voice answered.

Hawkman introduced himself again and explained why he'd called. "I'd just like to ask you a few questions."

"Sure, even though I know bad things happen at nursing homes, I researched several, and found no black marks against Morning Glory Haven."

"I've discovered nothing in their background to suggest a problem. My main reason for calling is I wondered if you have any questions in your mind about your mother's sudden demise?"

"Yes and no. Mom had gotten up there in age and had trouble keeping her house clean, along with cooking her meals. My sisters and I were concerned about her using a gas stove. We've heard horror stories of older people catching their garments on fire. We tried to coach Mom into using a microwave for all her cooking as it would be safer. However, she wouldn't have anything to do with these new fangled devices, as she put it. When her friend, Maggie, decided to check into the home, it made it a lot easier on us to talk Mom into going too."

"Getting back to my question. Did your mother have health issues other than old age?"

"Sorry, I got on a tangent there. She was a border line diabetic, but it bothered the family when the doctor told us Mom's heart gave way and she passed in her sleep. We had no idea she had a bad heart."

"Maggie Hampton also said Sybil never mentioned such a condition."

"Oh, Maggie might say anything. She and Mom appeared to be best of friends, but Maggie drove her nuts."

"Really! In what way?"

"She toots her own horn a lot, telling everyone how they've gone from rags to riches. Mom said if she heard the story one more time, she'd pop her one. I got the feeling to hear Mom talk, the woman bragged to the excess."

"I see. Tell me did your mother have a private doctor?"

"She didn't see any specific physician before going into the home, because she seldom got sick, other than an arthritis flare-up now and then. She did go in twice a year and have a blood panel done to keep tabs on the diabetes. We thought her healthy. So her death did come as a shock."

"Was there an autopsy done?"

"No. We didn't suspect foul play. Mother was in her eighties; we just weren't prepared to lose her."

"Thank you for your time. If I have anymore questions, may I feel free to call?"

"Of course, and I'd appreciate a follow-up, if you find anything questionable."

"I'll certainly notify you."

Hawkman hung up and wrote down a few notes, then pulled the phone directory from the desk drawer. It appeared Maggie knew more about George's checkers partner than he did. He flipped open the book to the Parkers and ran his finger down the numerous names and came to a halt on Ed and Grace Parker. It gave an address he recognized as Medford, and he decided it might be a good idea to just drop by. Unplugging the coffee pot, he took his small recorder off the charger, stuck it into his shirt pocket, then picked up the valise, and left the office.

When he arrived at the residence, it surprised him to see cars parked all over the place and people mingling around the yard. It suddenly dawned on Hawkman that he'd come upon a garage sale. He probably wouldn't be able to speak to Grace at this time, but he'd make sure he had the right place. Lucking out, he found a parking place right in front of the house. He wandered around, observing the many things placed on tables, benches and on sheets spread across the lawn. Most of the items seemed to be male oriented. Several wooden checker boards were displayed and Hawkman figured these were Eddie Parker's treasures at one time.

A woman with gray braids wrapped around her head and secured with a large clasp sat on a card table chair near the back. Her braced leg rested on an ottoman. A younger woman accompanied her while several other females floated among the crowd, answering questions, watching customers, and taking money.

Hawkman approached the twosome. "Excuse me, is one of you Grace Parker, the sister of the late Eddie Parker?"

The older woman furrowed her brow. "Are you a bill collector?"

He smiled. "No, I'm Tom Casey, a private investigator."

She threw up her hands. "My word, that's just as bad. Yes, I'm Eddie's sister. I just lost my wonderful brother and am clearing out his stuff. Breaks my heart to do this. So what do you want?"

He explained why he'd been hired by the Hamptons and only wanted to ask a few questions about her brother. "This might not be a good time, since you're busy. I can make it another day."

She gestured toward a vacant stool. "Pull that over. It's as good a time as any."

He carried it over, placed it beside her, and sat down. He pointed to a table containing the checkers boards. "I understand Eddie and George Hampton enjoyed the game."

"Yep, I think they played every night. It thrilled me to know he had a crony to take him on. He loved the challenge and had gained the reputation of the hottest checkers player around. He'd have preferred George come down to his room, because Maggie drove him crazy, but she wanted them right there so she could keep an eye on the two."

Hawkman nodded. "Sounds like you were very fond of your brother."

Tears welled in her eyes. "I loved him dearly and hated being parted when he went into the home. However, he knew I had an arthritic condition," she said, pointing to her leg. "I couldn't take care of him when he came down with gout. All the medications he took didn't agree with his system and there were days he couldn't even walk due to the pain. It would come and go, but when it hit, it knocked him out of whack for days, and was getting worse all the time. It started in his big toe and just traveled to all the joints in his body."

"I'm sorry to hear that. Were you surprised when he passed on?"

Her eyes widened. "Oh, my yes. I didn't suspect gout was life threatening. I guess it was worse than I thought, and affected his heart. Doctor said it just gave out from his pain and he died in his sleep. At least he went peacefully."

"Did he have a private physician?"

"No, he just went to the hospital when he hurt so much he couldn't stand it any longer."

"Did you by any chance have an autopsy done?"

She shook her head. "What good would it do. He was dead."

He stood. "I'd better leave, so I don't chase off any potential buyers. Before I go, could you tell me why Maggie bugged your brother?"

"All I know is he said she blabbed the whole time, and she was so possessive of George, she didn't want him out of her sight."

"Thank you for your time. If I have anymore questions, may I stop by?"

"Sure." She waved a hand toward the merchandise. "Might as well check out some of this stuff. There must be something you can't live without."

chapter

FOURTEEN

Hawkman left Grace's yard sale and drove away. Once he turned a corner, he pulled to the side of the road after his cell phone vibrated against his waist several times. He flipped it open and recognized Kevin's number. Hoping no emergency had occurred, he quickly hit the memory button.

"Hey, what's up?" He listened intently as Kevin related the events of the afternoon.

"Okay, I'll talk to her and clear up the situation. I'm headed over there right now."

Hawkman hung up and drove to Morning Glory Haven. Once inside, he headed straight for Maggie's apartment, and softly knocked. George opened the door.

"Hi, Hawkman. Come on in."

As he stepped inside, his gaze traveled around the apartment. "Where's Maggie?"

"She's out visiting her buddies."

"Why aren't you with her?"

"I can't keep up. My knees just give out."

"I thought you wanted her watched?"

"I do, but she had a fit with your man. He almost quit because she berated him so for following her around."

"His responsibility is to keep an eye on her. You hired my agency for that purpose."

"Yeah, I know. He did his job in spite of her ranting. She got really mad."

"I want to talk to her. Where do you think she is right now?"

He shrugged. "In one of the rooms, I reckon."

Hawkman gritted his teeth. "That doesn't help one bit. I want you to find your wife now and bring her back here."

George harrumphed, stood, didn't move for a moment, then grabbed his cane and hobbled into the hallway. He hadn't been gone five minutes when Hawkman heard the distinct sound of Maggie's voice and a walker scooting down the corridor.

When the two entered the room, Hawkman glared at her. "We need to have a talk, Mrs. Hampton."

She gazed at him with innocent hazel eyes. "My goodness, you look angry."

"Let's just say I'm not happy with you. You're not complying with what we previously set up. Having to put up with your shenanigans makes this job much harder"

She sat down on a chair in the corner and pushed her walking aid to the side. Taking a small mirror from her pocket, she checked her lipstick and hair. "I don't know what you're talking about."

"Don't play games with me. You gave Kevin fits today. He's only doing the job you and your husband have hired us to do. We expect full cooperation."

She narrowed her eyes. "He doesn't have to follow me all over the building."

"Yes, he does." He pointed at George. "He should have been with you at this time. From now on, you tell your friends to come by here so your husband or one of us is present at all times."

"Oh, good grief, I'm a big girl. I don't need a chaperone."

"Unfortunately, at this point in the investigation, you do. You're going to find it very awkward if we have to restrain you completely so we can investigate without worrying about where you are. The more you buck us, the longer it will take. Don't you realize if there is a murderer stalking these halls, he or she knows you've hired a private investigator. You could be the next victim."

Her hand went to her mouth. "Oh, my, I never thought about it in that vein."

"It's time you did. Promise you'll follow my instructions from now on."

She bowed her head. "I'm sorry I've caused this problem."

"Apology accepted. Now I've got work to do. I'll check in with you two later."

Hawkman left the room and took the elevator to the first floor. He doubted he'd find people in their offices today, but thought he'd give it a try. A door stood slightly ajar and the light from inside spilled a long streak across the carpet. He could hear the sound of a printer humming, and the click of fingernails on the keyboard of a computer.

He tapped on the door, forcing it to open a bit more, hoping to get a glimpse of the person before she spotted him. However, the movement caught her eye and she glanced up from her work.

"May I help you?"

"Hello, I'm Tom Casey, the private investigator."

"Oh, yes. Mr. Mackle told me about you. I didn't have a chance to meet you the other night as I was called out of town. I wouldn't normally be here, but needed to catch up on some paperwork. Please come in, and have a seat. What can I do for you?"

Hawkman took the chair in front of her desk and couldn't help but notice her very unusual coiffure. She had very short hair curled tightly on the top of her head, but the sides were straight and split over her ears. Not everyone could wear this style, but it flattered her thin face and long neck. What he could see of her, she appeared to be fairly tall.

"I'm Carmen Sanders, one of the Community Marketing Directors."

"I'm assuming you're familiar with the residents and probably know them by their first names."

She smiled. "Yes, it's part of my job, along with many other duties."

"Have any of the residents seemed hostile or unco-operative?"

"I'm not sure what you mean? We have some who are very quiet and keep to themselves, but I wouldn't classify it as being hostile."

Hawkman shifted his position. "Let me word that differently. Are you aware of anyone who dislikes Maggie Hampton?"

Carmen laughed. "I'd say you worded it quite bluntly." She tapped her pen on the desk and gnawed her lip. "There are a few who don't care for her."

"Why?"

"She's too talkative is one of the complaints. Another is she brags about how she came up from rags to riches. Many of the people in this home have experienced the same lifestyle, but don't rave about it." She pointed a finger in the air. "Don't get me wrong, many people adore Maggie. In fact, more like her than don't. She's full of life and likes to laugh."

"Sounds like quite a mix."

She nodded. "Yes, and everyone loves her husband, George. They figure him as just a good old boy."

Hawkman rose. "Thank you, Ms. Sanders. I really appreciate your time."

"I don't know how much I helped, but happy to assist."

"I've just started the investigation, so I may want to speak with you again."

"No, problem. You can catch me somewhere in the building almost every day."

He left her office and headed back toward Maggie's room. He thought about how Carmen never made eye contact. It made him uncomfortable. She seemed cordial enough, but it always bothered him when people did this. Made him wonder if she'd told the whole truth. He shook his head and could see figuring out if the Hampton's friends died naturally, or were murdered, would be quite a challenge.

He met George and Maggie strolling toward the dining room, told them goodnight and headed out of the building.

chapter

FIFTEEN

The next morning, Hawkman sat at his office desk in Medford, holding the phone to his ear, and drumming his fingers on the desk. He hated being put on hold, but realized Monday happened to be one of the busiest days for doctors. Finally, a female voice came on the line.

"My name is Tom Casey and I'd like to set up an appointment with Dr. Grahm."

He listened a moment, then flopped back in his chair. "No, I'm not a patient and I'm not sick. I just need to talk to him."

Tightening his jaw, he picked up a pencil and tapped it on the yellow tablet in front of him. "I can't wait for a month, I need to speak with him immediately."

He didn't want to reveal the reason, but decided if he didn't scare this little receptionist a bit, he'd have to wait outside the doctor's office and catch him when he left. "Look, I'm a private investigator, checking into the death of a resident of Morning Glory Haven. Dr. Grahm examined this patient and I need to speak with him soon."

The woman sputtered for a moment, then asked if she could call him back.

"Yes." He gave her his cell phone number and hung up.

He wouldn't go this route with Dr. Eva Paulson. Instead, he'd go straight to her office at the hospital, along with Ronald White's oncologist, Dr. Stephen Riley. While in the mood to search out doctors, Hawkman looked up Marion Carter's personal physician, Dr. Phil Hart. He punched in his number and the receptionist answered the phone on the second ring. After explaining who he was, he asked to speak with the doctor. He couldn't believe his luck, punched on the speaker phone, and picked up a pen from the desk.

"Hello, this is Dr. Phil Hart."

"Good morning, Dr. Hart. I'm Tom Casey, private investigator. I promise to take only a minute of your time."

"I can give you a little more time. I had a cancellation, so we've got about fifteen minutes. How can I help you?"

"I understand Marion Carter was a patient of yours?"

"Oh, yes, and what a delightful person. My staff and I enjoyed her visits to the office. She always put everyone in such a positive mood. We truly miss her."

"Did you treat her when she went into Morning Glory Haven?"

"She didn't have any serious problems, but I'd drop by to see her when I could. I know making regular doctor appointments is quite an expense for the elderly on fixed incomes and the home is costly. I'd check her out when I visited, and wouldn't charge."

"She didn't have diabetes?"

"She was borderline, but this happens sometimes in older people. Nothing had changed at the time of her death. Why do you ask?"

"One of the residents figured she'd lost her leg due to the disease."

"Oh, no. She lost it as a child due to a horrible accident with a combine in the fields of her father's farm. She adjusted to only having one leg years ago."

"You said she didn't have any serious conditions. What about her heart?"

"Believe me, I was shocked to discover her heart had failed."

"Were you the doctor who signed the death certificate?"

"Yes, and I might add, there had never been any indication Mrs. Carter had a cardiac problem."

"Did you by any chance recommend the family to have an autopsy?"

"No, I didn't. They were devastated and it would have only caused more grief. At least Marion didn't suffer. I'm sure that's exactly the way she would've wanted her life to end. Peacefully, in her sleep. At least, it calmed her children knowing she went without pain."

"So you're saying, as far as your examinations went, you found nothing wrong with her heart?"

"These questions are worrisome. Are you checking on more than just Marion's death?"

"Yes, but I haven't found anything to warrant suspicion of foul play. However, I do find it odd so many patients have died in their sleep, with no history of heart problems."

"Old age can play tricks on our bodies. What might have been strong one day can turn on you within a few hours."

"This is true. Dr. Hart, I appreciate you taking the time out of your busy schedule to talk with me. May I contact you again if I have more questions?"

"Certainly. If you find anything suspicious in these deaths you're investigating, would you please get back to me? I'd be very interested."

"I certainly will."

Hawkman had just placed the receiver on the cradle when his cell phone rang. The caller I.D. indicated it came from Dr. Grahm's office. When he answered, the receptionist asked if he could come in that evening around six thirty, after Dr. Grahm's last patient.

"I'll be there."

After hanging up, since he had plenty of time, he decided to see if he'd have any luck on seeing Doctors Paulson and Riley.

Driving to the Mercy Hospital, he pondered over the idea that only a couple of the deceased people had a history of heart problems; yet they all died in their sleep from cardiac failure. Sure, people's hearts gave out, but this many deaths with the same diagnosis, in the same place, appeared a bit much to swallow, even for a layman.

He pulled into the hospital lot, parked, and strolled into the large lobby. Glancing around, he didn't see a directory, so ambled up to the information desk. The woman glanced up from her paperwork.

"May I help you?"

"Yes, could you direct me to Dr. Eva Paulson's office?"

She pointed toward the elevators. "Go to the fourth floor. She's at four twenty-one."

Hawkman touched the brim of his hat. "Thank you."

She smiled. "You're welcome."

When Hawkman stepped into the waiting room, only two people occupied chairs. He crossed the room to the receptionist.

Without raising her gaze, she said, "Your name and time, please."

"I'm Tom Casey, private investigator. I don't have an appointment, but need to talk to Dr. Paulson about one of her patients. It's very important."

She jerked up her head. "I'm sorry, but we're not allowed to give out personal information."

"The man has passed away, and my questions are generic. I don't think she'll have a problem."

"I'll have to speak with the doctor first. What was your name again?"

Hawkman handed her a business card. "This will make it easier."

She pointed toward the waiting room. "Have a seat and I'll get back to you shortly."

He sat down and observed the soft shades of pastel paint on the walls. The artificial plants dominating the corners were pleasant to the eye. He noticed the magazines on the tables gave positive messages. Smiling physicians on the front covers with emblazoned titles like, 'It isn't the end of the world' and 'Let us help you gain a strong heart'. Since this was a cardiac specialist's office, he figured they needed a pleasant atmosphere for their patients as they waited for their appointments.

The receptionist reappeared and called his name. He moved to the counter.

"Dr. Paulson would like to know which patient you're interested in."

"Fred Horn."

"Okay, hold on a second. I'll be right back."

Within a few moments, she returned. "The doctor would like to talk to you. She has a break after seeing a couple more patients. Could you wait about thirty minutes?"

"Yes."

She again left his sight and disappeared down a hallway. Hawkman sat down in one of the chairs and picked up a flyer. He watched the last person enter one of the examination rooms. Shortly, the receptionist called his name and motioned for him to follow. She led him down a maze of hallway turns, then finally stopped in front of a closed door and knocked softly.

"Come in."

Opening the door, she said. "Mr. Tom Casey is here."

"Very good, I'll see him now."

The woman left, and Hawkman approached the desk, holding out his hand. "Dr. Paulson, it's a pleasure to meet you."

They shook hands, and she gestured toward a chair. "Please, have a seat. I'm very interested in the reason you're here."

He scrutinized the doctor as he sat down. Her long brown hair cascaded in a French braid down her back. She wore little make-up on a flawless skin, except for just a touch of rose on her cheeks and a pale pink lipstick. Her hazel eyes were nothing out of the ordinary, but her gaze met his without hesitation. Even though, not beautiful, her appearance hit him as very attractive, and her fixed look emitted an air of authority. From what he could see of her frame behind the desk, a white coat hiding her clothing, she seemed slight of build, with small shoulders. Her hands had long fingers and short, unpolished nails, but when he grasped her hand, she had a firm grip. He liked the woman before she even said anything.

"I understand you were Fred Horn's physician?"

"Yes. May I ask why you're so interested in his case?"

Hawkman explained who had hired him and why. "Instead of sticking with those three the Hamptons were concerned with, I thought I'd examine some previous deaths and see if there were any connections. I've discovered most of the families were shocked by their loved ones' sudden death, and they all died in their sleep, just like the three the Hampton's are concerned about. I thought this odd."

She frowned. "Very strange. I'm glad they got suspicious and have hired someone to look into it. I'm not sure what you'll find out, but it's certainly worth the effort." She scooted forward and opened a folder on her desk. "I've pulled his file so I could refresh my memory." She pushed on a pair of glasses that hung around her neck on a gold chain, and glanced through some of the papers. "Fred was a very cheerful and positive person until his wife died. The tests we took indicated he'd experienced some small strokes after the trauma of losing her. I saw him often so I could monitor his heart. But when he went into the home, he couldn't pay their cost, along with the fees from the hospital, so it sort of left me dangling. However, I did drop by on social calls and checked his vital signs while there. Occasionally, I had one of the volunteer associates go by and see him, just to keep a check on his progress. Also wanted to make sure he took his medications regularly. I'm truly sorry Mr. Horn didn't make it."

"Who was the volunteer physician you sent over?"

"Dr. Jeff Grahm."

"Did you talk to the family about his cardiac health?"

"Oh, yes. Susan, his daughter, kept close tabs on her father."

"After his death, did you by any chance advise the family to get an autopsy?"

The doctor leaned back in her chair and sighed. "No, but now I wish I had."

"Why?"

"I just felt there was something fishy about his death."

"In what way?"

"I would have expected another stroke which might have been strong enough to kill him, but there would have been symptoms and help could have been sought. On the other hand, there's the possibility he wasn't taking his medication regularly, even though he insisted he did. The worst scenario I could imagine would be he could have been given the wrong pills from the pharmacy."

"You think that's a possibility?"

"Accidents happen, even in hospitals. So anything is conceivable."

"Could someone have slipped something into his food or drink?"

She smiled. "That's your job to uncover."

Hawkman scratched his sideburn and grinned. "You're right."

A knock sounded on the door.

"Yes," the doctor called.

"Your next patient is here."

"I'll be right there."

Hawkman quickly stood. "I'm sorry to have taken up so much of your time. Thank you for seeing me. If I have more questions, may I contact you again?"

She scribbled something on a piece of paper and handed it to him. "This is my private line at home. Please, feel free to call me. I'd really like to hear more about this case."

"Will do."

He walked down the hallway and took the elevator to the ground floor. Checking his watch, he found he still had time to see Ronald White's oncologist before returning to Dr. Grahm's office. He headed for the information desk.

chapter

SIXTEEN

After getting instructions, Hawkman headed back to the elevator and rode up to the fifth floor. He approached the woman at the front desk and asked if he could speak with Dr. Riley.

"I'm sorry, he won't be back in the office until next week. He's attending a cancer conference. Can I set up an appointment for you?"

"No," Hawkman said. "I just need to ask him some questions. I'll drop by another time." Can't win them all, he thought, as he stepped onto the ground floor.

When he reached his vehicle, he checked the battery in his recorder and noted it had gotten low. He rummaged through the glove compartment where he kept extra car chargers for his equipment. Once he found the right one, he shoved it into the lighter receptacle, then attached it to the small black box. It wouldn't take long to bring it up to full capacity.

He looked at his wristwatch and still had a good forty-five minutes before seeing Dr. Grahm. Since he happened to be parked in the shade, he decided to take a few minutes and jot some notes to refresh his memory on what he'd learned about the deceased patients. He removed the file from his briefcase, and pushed back his seat. After thirty minutes of reading through the folder, he tacked it up, pushed the valise back under the seat and drove toward Dr. Grahm's office. The number of vehicles in the parking area had dwindled down to where Hawkman had his choice of slots.

When he walked into the waiting area, it was empty except for the receptionist, who appeared busy tidying up her desk. She glanced up.

"Hello, Mr. Casey. I'll let Dr. Grahm know you're here when he finishes with the last patient."

"Thank you," Hawkman said, and sat down near the desk. He noticed she kept stealing glimpses at him. Finally she tossed her pen aside.

"Mr. Casey, I'm sorry, but you're not what I'd expect a private investigator to look like."

He laughed. "You mean because I'm not wearing a suit and tie."

"I guess that's it. You remind me more of a cowboy with your Stetson hat, cowboy boots, and jeans."

"I guess we come in all sizes, shapes and dress."

About that time, an older woman came out of one of the examination rooms. Using a cane, she limped to the desk.

"Hello, Mrs. Norris," the receptionist said. "How did things go?"

"As good as can be expected. I'm not getting any younger. What do I owe for this visit?" After they settled the financial part, the woman closed her purse and went out the door.

The receptionist stood. "I'll go tell Dr. Grahm you're here."

He nodded.

Within a few minutes, she and a man in a white coat, stethoscope hanging around his neck, stood at the door leading into the examination rooms and conversed. It gave Hawkman a few moments to scrutinize the doctor and flip on the recorder in his pocket. The man stood about five foot six inches; his receding hair, exposing half of his scalp, had obviously been dyed black with no signs of natural graying one would expect of a man in his sixties. His glasses were round and thick, magnifying the under eye puffiness. The wrinkles around his mouth were definitely turned down, and the fat jowls gave the appearance of a permanent scowl. His ears were probably his nicest feature, as they lay flat against the sides of his head. The white coat and wrinkled tie didn't hide the bulging belly or thick neck. He figured the man could afford to lose about forty or fifty pounds. Hawkman arose as they approached.

"Dr. Grahm, this is Mr. Casey, the private investigator who wanted to meet with you."

The two men shook hands, then Dr. Grahm turned to the woman. "Ms. Carter, there's no sense in you staying, why don't you go home." Then he gestured to Hawkman. "Let's go back to my office."

Following the man down a short hallway, Hawkman noticed the doctor's sagging shoulders. Either the day had worn him out, or he was a discouraged human being.

They turned through an opened door and he pointed at a chair in front of the desk. "Have a seat, Mr. Casey, and tell me what's worrying you. Let's not beat around the bush; something is on your mind or you wouldn't be here."

"I understand you've looked in on other doctor's patients at Morning Glory Haven. What exactly qualifies you to do that?"

"I volunteer my services to help out other busy physicians. They do the same for me."

"You're not a cardiologist or oncologist; you're a medical doctor. How do you take care of people with special needs?"

He frowned. "As I said, I'm an extra. If I see a problem, I immediately notify the doctor who has asked me to check on his patient."

"How many times has this happened?"

He squirmed in his seat and didn't meet Hawkman's gaze. "Seldom."

"I've talked with the relatives of several of the patients who have passed away in the last six months. Most show concern about the untimely deaths and many were unaware their loved ones had heart problems."

The doctor shook his head. "Mr. Casey, the people at Morning Glory are aging. Their hearts can give out anytime."

"Why weren't autopsies performed on these untimely deaths?"

"I have no idea, but my guess is it would have been a waste of time and money."

"Are you aware there were more than the average rate of deaths at the home within six months?"

He narrowed his eyes. "Mr. Casey, I don't have access to Morning Glory's books, and none of the people living there are my patients. There's no way I'd know the death rate in the facility. I don't like this line of questioning."

"Maybe you don't, but we always have to investigate negligence."

He stood, jerked the stethoscope from his neck and took off his white coat. "Don't accuse me of malpractice when you have no evidence. As far as I'm concerned, this meeting is over."

"I might have to talk to you again," Hawkman said, rising.

"I have nothing more to say."

"If I discover these people were murdered, it won't be me you'll be chatting with, it'll be the police."

Grahm's face paled. "Murdered! Are you serious?"

Hawkman turned before walking out of the office and looked him square in the face. "Yes, Dr. Grahm, I'm very serious."

When Hawkman reached the parking lot, he turned off his recorder, then glanced over his shoulder and could see the man's silhouette through the glass front door. "I'm not impressed with you," he said under his breath as he climbed into his vehicle. The personality he'd observed in just the few minutes he'd met with him was sour and grouchy. In addition, he sure didn't like to answer questions.

Driving to Morning Glory Haven, he checked the clock on the dashboard. The dinner hour should be over and he wanted to find out the name of Maggie's physician. He'd really never thought to ask.

He found the hallway fairly sparse of occupants, but could hear the televisions going in almost every room as he passed. Must be some favorite program they all like, he mused as he knocked on Maggie's door.

"Come in," George called.

Hawkman entered the room and found the two with their gazes glued to the set, and then they burst into laughter. He peered at the screen and realized an old Bob Hope rerun special was airing and the Hamptons were enthralled. They both raised a finger to their lips to shush him from speaking. Hawkman took a seat in a vacant chair and waited until the program ended. The Hamptons then turned their attention toward him.

"They sure don't make them like they used to. What a delight to see a good show," Maggie said, wiping tears of laughter from her cheek.

"Nope," George said. "Most of the good actors and comedians are gone. A shame Hollywood didn't raise more to fill their shoes."

"I'm only staying a few minutes," Hawkman said. "I wanted to see how things went today."

"Fine," Maggie said, rolling her eyes. "I let Kevin hang around me all afternoon, and George won't let me out of his sight now, so I have no peace."

Hawkman grinned. "Good. Tell me, do you know a Dr. Grahm?"

Maggie furrowed her brow. "No, I don't recall hearing the name. Should we know him?"

"Not particularly unless your physician had him check on you. I understand he's a volunteer who fills in when the patients' own doctor can't come by."

"We always set up appointments and go to our doctor together."

"What's his name?"

"Dr. Karl Bunker," George said.

"You both use the same one?"

George nodded.

Hawkman jotted down the name. "Is he private practice or affiliated with a hospital?"

"Private," Maggie said. "Do you have one of his business cards, George?"

He pulled a bulky wallet from his back pocket and thumbed through the many cards. "Yep, here's one," he said, handing it to Hawkman.

Glancing at the title, Endocrinologist, he glanced from Maggie to George. "Which one of you has diabetes?"

She pointed at her husband.

chapter

SEVENTEEN

Early Tuesday morning, Hawkman's cell phone rang, jarring him out of a deep sleep. He snatched the instrument off the bedside table and put it to his ear. "Yeah?" He listened, then sat up abruptly, the phone still glued to his ear, grabbed his jeans from the chair next to the wall. "I'll be there within an hour."

Jennifer rolled over. "Who in the heck calls at six in the morning?"

"Maggie." Hawkman dashed into the bathroom, splashed water on his face, brushed his teeth and combed his hair, then headed for the closet. "There's been another death at Morning Glory Haven. Maggie sounded close to hysteria. I want to make sure an autopsy is done on this patient."

"Even if the Hamptons don't know the person?"

After buttoning his shirt, he sat down on the edge of the bed and tugged on his boots. "Maggie knows everyone, except those in the Alzheimer's part of the facility, who are in a completely different building. She said this person lived only a few doors down from her." He reached over and gave Jennifer a peck on the cheek. "Go back to sleep if you can. Sorry about the intrusion."

Jennifer pushed back the covers. "I might just get up and take Pretty Girl out for a hunt. She's really restless. You haven't paid much attention to her lately."

He turned at the doorway and threw her another kiss. "That would be great of you. Thanks, sweetheart."

When he reached the freeway, he knew the Highway Patrol loved this stretch of the road, as they called it 'ticket heaven', so he only pushed the accelerator as fast as he dared. He pulled into Morning Glory's parking lot and spotted the ambulance at the door. Maggie must have found out about the death as soon as it was discovered. He hurried inside, took the stairs instead of the elevator, then jogged down the hallway to Maggie's apartment. She and George stood in the doorway watching the action taking place in the room just a few feet away.

"Maggie rousted me out of bed at six and told me to get my butt down here." George shook his head. "Now, I'm having a time keeping her in the room."

"Do you know any more about the victim?"

"Her name is Gladys Owens, a very kind woman. I don't know anything about her personal history." He pointed to two ladies standing across the hall. "I imagine one of those gals could tell you more."

Hawkman glanced at the two. "I'm sure they could, they're nosier than Maggie." He strolled over to the two women. "Hello, Jessie and Margy, what's going on?"

Jessie put a tissue to her eyes. "Our dear friend has passed away."

"Was she ill?"

"Not that we knew. Occasionally she rolled around in a wheelchair, but most of the time she could make it fine with just her walker."

"Why did she need a wheelchair?"

"Not sure, but arthritis, we think." Margy said. "She didn't talk much about her aches and pains."

Hawkman had his eye on the victim's doorway, when Dr. Grahm backed out, then turned to walk away. Hawkman stepped in front of him. "Hello, Dr. Grahm. I hope you've ordered an autopsy."

The doctor glared at him. "What are you doing here?"

"Remember, I'm investigating the deaths of the residents."

"If you must know, I've requested an autopsy from her personal physician."

"Good. Maybe then we'll get to the bottom of this problem once and for all."

"Would you mind moving out of my way. I've got to go sign some papers."

"My pleasure," Hawkman said, crossing the hall to Maggie's quarters.

The doctor stared at the Hamptons as he passed.

"Who's that guy?" George asked.

"Dr. Jeff Grahm."

"He sure looks grumpy."

"Mark my word, he is." Hawkman stepped into the room and approached Maggie as she plugged in the coffee pot. "What do you know about the woman who just died?"

She pulled a tissue from the box. "Oh, she was such a dear. She called George her darling." Wiping her eyes, she glanced up at Hawkman. "Every time she came near him, she had some sweet something to say. I had to watch him closely, as he'd sneak off and go to visit her when I watched a movie he wasn't interested in, or if I started knitting."

"You sound jealous."

She scoffed. "At my age? I don't think so." Then she winked at him. "Well, maybe a little. After all, he's my man, and most of these old women have lost theirs. If they think hovering over mine is going to get them anywhere, they've got another think coming."

Hawkman brushed a hand across his mouth, suppressing a smile. "Do you know any of Ms. Owens' family?"

"I didn't have a lot in common with her, as we didn't visit much. George might be able to tell you." She blew her nose.

Hawkman knew it would be futile to pump George; he'd already said he didn't know anything personal about the woman. That seemed to be Maggie's specialty. He walked to the door just as George came into the room. "I need to look up some information on the computer. If I don't get back before you leave, tell Kevin to keep a close eye on Maggie."

"Will do."

Hawkman drove to his office and jogged up the stairs. While the computer booted up, he took a soda from the small refrigerator, popped it open and sat down at the desk.

He'd already transcribed the recording from Lisa onto the computer and she'd given the death dates of each of the deceased. He printed out the report, then pulled up a calendar of the year. Checking the dates, he discovered the deaths occurred closer together as time passed. This looked very suspicious. He might be dealing with a serial killer.

Putting the notes aside, he wanted to set up an appointment to see the Hampton's physician. He dug the card George had given him out of his pocket and noticed Dr. Bunker's office happened to be located on a street he passed when heading for Morning Glory Haven from the office. He jotted down the information in his file and figured he'd better talk to George and Maggie, as he certainly wouldn't be able to pry anything out of the doctor about either of their personal health conditions, if he didn't have permission.

He'd stop by Lisa's office when he returned to the home and see if he could find out the relatives of Ms. Owens. Getting this information quickly would be in his favor. Otherwise, depending on what the autopsy revealed, things could become a bit sticky.

chapter

EIGHTEEN

When Hawkman returned to Morning Glory Haven, he went to Lisa Montgomery's office. Her door stood open, so he knocked softly on the jamb.

She glanced up from some paper work. "Come in," she said, her forehead wrinkling into a frown. "I see you've heard the news."

"Yes, and I need to get a bit of information."

"I just talked to Gladys Owens' daughter." Lisa shook her head. "I hate that part of my job. The girl sounded devastated. She wanted to complete the move to her new home and planned to take her mother up for a visit." She bit her lower lip and blinked back tears. "So sad."

Hawkman shifted his stance. "I can't imagine the agony of having to talk with someone whose parent just passed away. It can't be easy."

"No, it isn't." Wiping her eyes with a tissue, she said, "Forgive me. Please have a seat, and tell me what you need."

He sat down and pulled a small note pad from his pocket. "What is Ms. Owens' daughter's name and where does she live?"

Lisa opened the file. "Sidney Wilder, and she just moved to Eugene, Oregon." She stated the address and phone number.

"Any other children?"

"She's the only one listed. Gladys' husband passed away two years ago."

"Is the daughter coming to pick up her mother's things?"

"Not for a few days. Mrs. Owens' physician broke the news to her and explained the body wouldn't be available for at least a week."

"What do you do with the deceased's belongings?"

"We clear the room of all the personal items and place them in a sealed container until the family can pick it up. Then we spend hours sanitizing the area."

"Is anything thrown away?"

"No. We leave that up to the family as we don't know what might be of interest to them. Every scrap of paper is put into the box."

He nodded. "Good. I might need to look through her things."

"I can't give you that kind of permission. You'll have to talk to her daughter."

"I understand." He rose. "Thank you, Ms. Montgomery. You've been more than helpful."

She grimaced. "Mr. Casey, do you suspect foul play?"

"I don't know what to think at this point. I'm hoping the autopsy may give me a lead."

"What happens to the reputation of our wonderful home, if it's found Gladys Owens and some of the others were murdered?"

Hawkman sat back down. "I'd hoped the word wouldn't have traveled that I've been looking into the other deaths. I'd tried to give the impression that Maggie's life had been threatened and we were here as her bodyguards."

"I certainly never told a soul what we talked about. But gossip races through this home, and even the nurses in the other buildings are talking. I'm afraid Maggie's the culprit. She's told everyone why you're here."

He shook his head and threw up his hands. "Guess I should have known she couldn't keep a secret. All we can do is try to keep the lid on as tight as possible. I'll definitely be more closed mouth about what I tell her."

Lisa smiled for the first time since he'd been there. "Good luck."

Hawkman left her office and traveled down the hallway only to meet the Hamptons. Maggie had a purse dangling from her shoulder. "Where are you two going?"

"Maggie wanted to get away from all this trauma, and suggested we go shopping. Such a shame to lose Gladys. I really liked her." George sighed and brushed his chin with his hand. "We've decided to go to the store, then out to have a late lunch."

"Did you inform Kevin you wouldn't be here?"

George snapped his fingers. "Oh, dang it, I knew I'd forgotten something. I better give him a call right now." He turned and headed back toward the elevator.

"Hold on," Hawkman called, removing the cell phone from his belt. "I'll give him a ring. I might not always be here the times you take off. So, please notify one of us of your plans or doctor appointments."

George limped back to them. "Thanks."

After Hawkman informed Kevin he wouldn't be needed today, he walked alongside the couple as they traveled toward the front of the building.

"You should be aware we go shopping about once a week, and pick up a batch of snacks. I also like to run by the house to see Pesky. Then we visit the doctor monthly for our checkups." She flipped a hand in the air. "Furthermore, it's good for me to get away on occasions. Especially like today." She made a face. "This isn't a prison, you know."

"How long will you be gone?" Hawkman asked.

"Not more than a couple of hours, three at the most," George said. "Maggie can't take much longer or she gets too tired."

"Are you seeing your doctor today?"

"No, just shopping and out to eat."

Hawkman pushed open the big swinging door and held it as the Hamptons moved outside. "George, are you going to go home when you return?"

"Naw, I'll stay the rest of the evening."

"I need to talk to you two, so I'll stop by later."

***

George held open the car door for Maggie, then took her walker and slid it onto the back seat. When he settled under the steering wheel and pushed in the key, Maggie let out a disgusted grumble.

"What's the matter?" George asked, backing out of the parking slot.

"I'm getting a little sick of Tom Casey and that Kevin guy. I don't have a private moment."

"It won't last long."

"You and your brainy idea of having me watched every waking hour. It's nerve wracking. Why don't you tell him I don't need a bodyguard?"

"I want them here when I'm not around. If there's a murderer in Morning Glory Haven, I don't want him after you. So be patient."

"My patience is worn thin. He's so damned nosy. Wants to know everything about us and every move I make."

"Private investigators make it their business to inquire into every aspect. That's the way they get clues."

" Are we suspects?"

George rolled his head. "Come on, Maggie, use your brain. It could be someone connected to us. He's just not going to take a chance. Think about it. Sybil died right there in the same apartment you two shared. If someone murdered her, you might be next. That's one reason I wanted you moved into private accommodations."

She reached over and patted his leg. "I guess you're better at looking after me than I am taking care of myself. Thank you, my honey."

"No more of this kind of talk. Let's enjoy our outing. What do you want to do first?"

"Let's drop by the house so I can see Pesky, and I need to get a couple of things from my closet."

"Home it is."

George pulled into the driveway, and helped Maggie out of the car. While she stood clinging to the door, he retrieved her walker from the back seat. They made their way slowly up the sidewalk to the entry. When they entered the house, Pesky yowled and pranced around Maggie until she giggled.

"I do believe she's missed me." She reached down and patted the dog's head. "My sweet girl, I wish I could take you with me."

"You could, you know. For an extra five hundred smackers. Then what would I do? I'd for sure lose my mind without Pesky here."

"Oh, George, I wouldn't take her away from you. She'd go crazy cooped up in my small apartment." She laughed. "I miss her, but not that much."

"Can I help you get what you need from the bedroom?"

"No, give Pesky a treat and I'll tend to my items." She could hear George playing with the dog as she rummaged in the closet and dresser drawers for the things she wanted. After putting them in a small duffle bag, she stood back and observed the clutter. "Oh, my, George, you are messy." She returned to the living room, then moved into the kitchen and shook her head. Dirty dishes were piled in the sink, and the table still had crumbs scattered across the surface. "I'm going to look into getting you a housekeeper."

George frowned. "I don't need one."

She put a hand on her hip. "When did you last make the bed? The covers are all rumpled and half on the floor." She pointed at the sink. "There must be a week's worth of dirty dishes in there. How come you don't put them in the dishwasher? Look at the lint on the carpet. It needs vacuuming."

"Things got ahead of me this week. Thought you said you didn't want any servants in the house."

"I'm talking about one woman once a week, not a hoard of caretakers running around. It would keep the place presentable. You just make sure you're here when she comes."

George shrugged. "I don't know who to get."

"Don't worry, I'll take care of it." She abruptly turned and scooted toward the front door. "Okay, we better get going while I'm still up to it."

They shopped and had a light lunch at one of their favorite restaurants, then headed back to Morning Glory Haven.

"This has been a great day, George. I don't tell you enough how much I appreciate you."

He smiled. "Aah, that's okay. I love you too."

They found Hawkman sitting in the large room as they came in the door.

"Hope you haven't been waiting long," George said, guiding his wife inside.

"No, just got here about ten minutes ago. I went up to your place first, in case I'd missed you. I found Jessie and Margy huddled around your door as if they were picking the lock. I startled them and asked what they were doing."

George scowled. "What'd they say?"

"They said they were listening to see if you were home. When I asked why they didn't just knock, they said Maggie sometimes didn't answer her door. I told them they should take the hint that maybe she didn't want to be disturbed."

George threw back his head and laughed. "Good for you."

Maggie made a face. "I know those two old bags are harmless, but they're regular pests. They're always wanting to borrow something. I told them to go to the store and buy their own stuff."

Hawkman chuckled. "They both hurried away, mumbling to each other."

Once George had settled Maggie on the couch and placed her walker on the side, he turned toward Hawkman. "What did you want to talk to us about?"

Hawkman explained he'd like to speak with Dr. Karl Bunker, but knew he wouldn't be able to get anywhere without their permission. "I'd like you to call him and give your approval, plus write me a permission slip to check your files."

"Why in hell's name do you need to see our health records?" Maggie asked, frowning.

"It's all a part of this type of investigation. Things show up on health records that might help in a murder investigation."

She cocked her head to one side. "Such as?"

"Pharmacists, nurses, and other doctors who might have a connection to Morning Glory Haven."

"Really?" she asked. "Why wouldn't we know about it?"

"Because, it wouldn't be of any significance to your health."

"That sounds strange," she said.

"I might find nothing, but on the other hand, a clue might appear."

She shrugged. "George, you better call Dr. Bunker first thing in the morning. I'll write up a permission slip and we can both sign it."

"Thanks, I appreciate your cooperation," Hawkman said.

chapter

NINETEEN

Wednesday morning, Hawkman went to the office early as he had the surveillance duty from noon until six. He pondered who to talk to next. So far, Kevin's reports had shown nothing to establish any sort of unusual activity around Maggie, other than her being obstinate on occasions.

It would be a few more days before the results of the autopsy came through, so no use fretting about getting hold of Gladys Owens' daughter, Ms. Wilder, until the end of the week.

He picked up the phone and called the Hamptons' physician, Dr. Karl Bunker, and set up an appointment for the next morning just before lunch. Good, he thought, then if we extend a little over the time, it won't matter, unless he has a fetish about eating right at noon.

Placing his notes inside the briefcase, he unplugged the recorder and shoved it into his shirt pocket. He noticed it made a big bulge due to his shoulder holster. Not having a pocket on the other side, he tested the openings on the jeans jacket and discovered they were too shallow. Reluctantly, he placed the small machine in his valise.

He'd grab a sandwich on the way to Morning Glory Haven. Doubting he'd come back to the office, he rinsed out his mug and the coffee pot, picked up his briefcase, then turned out the lights. The cool weather made for a pleasant day as he stepped outside. He brushed a spider off the door, locked up, and headed down the stairs. The aroma of baking pastries circled his head and made his stomach grumble.

After having a bite to eat, he journeyed over to the home and entered the building. Once he embarked from the elevator and turned down the hallway, he heard a familiar loud threatening voice, and hurried toward Maggie's quarters. He found her gripping the walker and barring the entry of her quarters from two women standing on the outside. Her face burned red with rage. He quickly stepped in front of the two females.

"What's going on?" he asked, turning toward Jessie and Margy.

Jessie pointed at Maggie. "She told us she's going to kill us."

"Why?"

"We don't know," they said in unison.

Hawkman then faced Maggie. "Did you say that?"

"Yes. When George and I came back from visiting with a friend down the hall, I found these two trying to get into my apartment."

"What were you looking for?" Hawkman asked the women.

They shrugged. "Just wanted to visit."

"Can't you take a hint? I'm afraid I agree with Maggie; you've gone a bit too far."

"She wouldn't invite us in, even if we asked. Maggie doesn't like us. She's snooty, and won't even give us the time of day if we pass in the hall," Jessie said.

Hawkman shooed the women away. "I think you better get going. I'd suggest you stay away from here."

They scurried down the hallway, and Hawkman glanced at Maggie. "Where's George?"

"I'm here," he said, coming out of the bathroom. "I figured my dear wife could handle those busy bodies."

"Can't you report them to the head people?" Hawkman asked.

He shook his head. "We don't want to cause a problem, nor do we want Maggie to get the reputation as a trouble maker."

"Yes, but if they're trying to pick your lock, they should be reported."

Maggie flopped down on the overstuffed chair. "If they ever make it inside, I'll talk to the authorities."

"Do be careful about threatening people. If something happened to one of those women, you'd be the first the police would question."

"No one heard me."

"I could hear you almost the moment I stepped out of the elevator. If I recognized your voice, anyone near this room would have."

Maggie waved a hand in the air. "I'm not worried. Those two drive us all crazy. It'd be no loss if one of them disappeared."

George jerked his head around. "Don't talk like that. We've lost enough friends."

She made a face. "They are not my friends. I can't stand either of them. No one in this wing likes those two. They're crazy, and should be in a mental institution."

"Settle down Maggie, before your blood pressure goes up." George said, reaching over and stroking her arm. "You shouldn't get so upset."

She pushed his hand away. "I'm fine. Don't preach to me. The next time I catch them near my place, I'll clobber them with my walker."

Hawkman observed George's spouse. He'd never seen her in this state. Margy and Jessie better not come around again, because Maggie sounded like she meant what she said. He'd heard of strange incidents happening in old people's homes, but had never witnessed these problems until he got involved in this case.

"Okay, George, I'm doing the watch today, so you can go home or run your errands."

"Sorry you had to come upon this situation. Hopefully, it will settle down for the rest of the afternoon, and you can enjoy some peace."

"Don't bet on it," Maggie grumbled. "I'll have a dozen people poking their heads in the door, and asking about the commotion."

"It'll keep you busy," Hawkman said, smiling.

George gave Maggie a kiss on the cheek. "Be a good girl, my darling. I'll see you tonight. Is there anything you'd like me to pick up before I return?"

"No, I'm fine."

Once George left, Maggie headed for the bathroom. "Got to freshen up a bit, Mr. Hawkman." She suddenly stopped, jerked her head around and nodded her approval. "You look okay to attend a lecture on aging gracefully."

Hawkman groaned. "Whatever you want to do."

chapter

TWENTY

George returned shortly after six and Hawkman greeted him with a grin. "You missed a great lecture on aging gracefully."

Hampton wrinkled his forehead. "I don't believe a word you say."

"Have a good evening," Hawkman said, chuckling. "I don't think Maggie has anything else planned."

He left the premises and headed toward Copco Lake. It bothered him having no clue at what might be going on at Morning Glory Haven. When he arrived home, Jennifer met him at the door and frowned.

"What's the matter?" he asked.

She ran her fingers across his forehead and down his cheek. "Your worry wrinkles are showing. They don't do your strong, tanned face justice. Even the little dimple in your chin doesn't show. So what's going on?"

"Have you taken up a new hobby of face reading?"

She gave him a hug. "No, but a woman can read her man's expression after so many years. I could tell the minute you walked in the door things weren't right."

He put his arm around her shoulders. "Guess, I better always stay on the straight and narrow, as I wouldn't have a chance telling you any white lies."

She shook her head. "Nope."

"What's cooking? It smells delicious."

"A roast, but it won't be ready for another thirty minutes. I didn't expect you home quite so early. So you've got time to tell me what's going on." She took the valise from his hands and placed it on the counter. "Where do you want to sit?"

"The living room. Let me get a beer, first."

They settled in their matching chairs and their cat, Miss Marple, strolled in and wound her way around Hawkman's boots. "Okay, Miss Prissy, what do you want?"

She jumped upon his lap, banged her head against his chin a couple of times, then settled on his thighs.

"I wish she'd find another way of expressing love. Sure glad you don't do that."

Jennifer laughed. "That's our kitty."

He flipped up his eye-patch and rubbed his eyes. "This is the most clueless case I've ever encountered. In fact, I'm not sure any murders have been committed. I'm eager to hear the results on Mrs. Owens' autopsy."

"How long do you think it'll take?"

"Probably won't hear anything until next week, and those reports will just be the preliminaries. I don't know how deep of an examination they'll do. I'm lucky Dr. Grahm even told me he'd put in a request to Ms. Owens' physician."

"So you didn't hit it off with him very well?"

Hawkman looked at the ceiling. "Not at all. He showed his disgust at the first meeting we had. I have a gut feeling he isn't a competent doctor, and he knew I'd already figured it out. I think he's covering his butt."

"What do you think he's done?"

"Probably nothing. He's just a fill in, which tells me he's probably getting a salary for his services, even though he says he volunteers. What's hard for me to swallow is believing all those people died of heart failure and none of the relatives were aware of any cardiac problems. Mighty fishy, if you ask me."

"You think this doctor is afraid of getting sued?"

"I'm sure it's entered his mind that I might suggest to the family of any of the deceased patients he'd seen, to throw a malpractice charge against him."

Jennifer slid to the front of the chair, concern written across her face. "That's a pretty strong statement."

He exhaled loudly. "He knows I'm an investigator, and he gave the impression he's not comfortable with any type of law officer."

"I don't imagine any physician would be, under the circumstances. Are you any closer to figuring out what's happening?"

Stretching his arms above his head, he let his hands drop to the armrest with a loud slap, sending Miss Marple fleeing from his lap. "No, and it's really bugging me."

"What's on your schedule for tomorrow?"

"I have an appointment with George and Maggie's doctor."

She furrowed her brows. "Why do you want to see their doctor?"

"I need to know about their medical conditions. It still puzzles me why Maggie is at Morning Glory Haven and not at her own home with round the clock nurses to take care of her needs. Money is no problem."

"Have you talked to George about it?"

"He gives me a song and dance story about Maggie not wanting strangers in the house. She supposedly doesn't like young women combing through her stuff. However, she told me this afternoon she's going to hire a cleaning woman, as George doesn't keep the house like she thinks it should be. A bunch of nonsense if you ask me, but he's fallen for it hard."

Jennifer shrugged and rose. "Let's eat."

Hawkman watched her cross the room and into the kitchen. He moved to the bar and slid onto one of the stools. "I figured you'd have a comment."

She took the roast out of the oven and placed the hot pan on a cold burner on top of the stove. Her mouth was set in a straight line as she took a couple of plates from the cabinet. The solemn expression indicated to Hawkman she had some deep thoughts on the subject.

"Okay, sweetheart, what's going through that beautiful head of yours."

She wrinkled her nose. "Well, I'm not sure I agree with you on the idea that Maggie not wanting strangers in the house is nonsense."

"Give me your explanation; maybe you'll change my mind."

Jennifer dished up their meals and handed Hawkman his, then scooted his silverware toward him. She sat down on the opposite side of the kitchen bar with her dinner and placed a large napkin on her lap. He sat patiently until she settled.

"Anytime you're ready," he said.

She sighed. "If I put myself into Maggie's shoes, I can understand why she wouldn't want a group of people running around her house. She probably has some expensive items in her home and the thought of having one of them stolen would prey on her brain. Having to watch every move of paid help could be quite taxing, or she might feel she'd have to hide everything before they showed up. There'd probably be a big turnover in the servants or nurses and the whole thing could become a real pain in the neck, as she'd be in constant worry. Hired workers can sometimes be more trouble than they're worth, especially day in and day out." Jennifer took a bite, then looked into husband's face. "Having a housekeeper once a week would not present such problems. Those are my comments on the subject."

He nodded. "Very good ones, too. I hadn't looked at it from a woman's point of view."

She smiled. "See how much you need me?"

Laughing, he reached across the kitchen bar and patted her hand. "I couldn't live without you."

***

The next morning, Hawkman checked the charge on his recorder, placed it in his pocket, then left for Medford around nine. The appointment with the Hamptons' doctor wasn't until eleven, but he wanted to give himself plenty of time. Even though he felt familiar with that area of town, he didn't know the exact location of Dr. Bunker's office.

When he reached the complex of medical buildings, he had to circle the parking lot several times before he finally spotted a car pulling out. He debated about taking in the briefcase, but decided against it. After removing the Hamptons' permission slip, he slid it back under the passenger's seat.

When he entered the office, the young receptionist glanced up, then immediately averted her gaze to the surface of the desk. Hawkman smiled to himself. He must remember to ask Jennifer why the eye-patch seemed to intimidate all females.

Approaching the young woman, he noticed her posture shifted and she appeared uneasy. "My name's Tom Casey and I have an appointment with Dr. Bunker."

She quickly pulled her book toward her without ever making eye contact. "Please, have a seat, Mr. Casey. You're the next patient."

Hawkman made his way to a vacant chair, and had no more sat down when a woman came out of a hallway which must have led to the examination rooms. The receptionist got to her feet and disappeared down the aisle, then returned within a few minutes and called his name.

"Follow me, Mr. Casey." She stopped in front of a door with 'Dr. Karl Bunker' stenciled across the wood. "He'll see you in his office." Knocking lightly, she then turned the knob and poked her head inside. "Mr. Casey is here."

"Thank you, Amanda, have him come in."

She gestured for Hawkman to enter, then left.

A distinguished looking man, probably in his early fifties, with graying brown hair stood. Hawkman guessed him to be approximately six feet tall and from the looks of his well muscled shoulders, he more than likely worked out. When the doctor smiled, Hawkman figured all the women in the office swooned. His white coat with the stethoscope still looped around his neck, gave the appearance of a super model advertising the latest lab attire.

"Hello, Mr. Casey," he said extending his hand. "It's a pleasure meeting you in person. George and Maggie have spoken highly of you."

"Thanks. I'm assuming one of the Hamptons called and explained why I wanted to speak with you, and gave their permission. I also have written authorization."

"Yes, have a seat. I would like to have the consent for my files."

Hawkman handed him the sheet with the Hamptons' signatures.

The doctor sat down and dragged two very large folders toward him from the corner of the desk. "I pulled their medical files so we could discuss them. Before we get started, I'm very curious why you're interested in their files since they're the ones who hired you to investigate the deaths of some of their friends."

"My profession is similar to yours. I need background checks. You need to know a person's symptoms and medications before ever examining him or her. I need to know who's hired me and why."

He nodded, a grin curling the corners of his mouth. "Which one would you like to start with?"

chapter

TWENTY-ONE

Hawkman pointed at the files. "The one on top will be fine."

Dr. Bunker lifted the folder and placed it in front of him. "This is George's. Where would you like to begin?"

Hawkman removed his recorder from his shirt pocket and flipped it on. "Hope you don't mind if I use this; it's more efficient than my notes."

He looked a little surprised, but nodded. "Sure, no problem. I use one myself."

He put the small black box on the edge of the desk. "I know Mr. Hampton has several medical problems. One being diabetes. What are the others?"

The doctor let out a sigh. "I really think he should be at Morning Glory Haven with Maggie. His health has gone downhill for the past two years. I worry about him being at home alone."

"Why?"

"George is a type two diabetic, but he's not good about keeping track of his blood sugar. He should be taking insulin based upon the readings. I'm afraid he doesn't pay much attention, and could go into a coma. He's very careless. Always ordering more insulin because he's lost a dose by misplacing his pen or dropping it and breaking off the needle. Without Maggie at home with him, he appears very reckless. So what I did was order an extra batch so she has it at her apartment. That way, when George is there, she can take his blood count and administer the insulin, or at least make sure he gets what he needs."

Hawkman leaned forward. "I read up on the disease. Why can't he use an insulin pump?"

"Good question. I've even mentioned it to George, but he doesn't want to fool with it. He said he knows how to use the pen, but these new fangled gadgets with all the digital numbers blow him away. He doesn't trust the technology and is afraid it might pump more into his body than he needs, sending him into shock."

"I can see George thinking along those lines. Is the diabetes the reason he's never gotten his knees fixed?"

"Yes, he's afraid. Not only of surgery, but the therapy afterwards might be more than he can bear. After hearing stories from his cronies, he wants nothing to do with such an operation. George always adds the comment afterwards, that being diabetic puts him at risk. I figure it will take him the agony of not being able to get out of bed and walk, to force him to reconsider. I'm more concerned about heart disease and strokes which are more prevalent among diabetics, along with keeping his weight under control. He needs to lose a few pounds."

"I'm sure you've elaborated on these things."

"Lectured him numerous times, but to no avail."

"Sounds like you've at least tried to keep the bases covered."

He laughed. "I try. Not sure how successful it's working, but lately, George has done better."

"What other ailments does he have?"

"So far, so good. He has a little skin irritation, but with creams and lotions we've been able to keep it under control. His kidneys are in good condition, and his other organs seem to be functioning normally right now." Bunker raised his hands and let them drop to the desk. "It's only a matter of time."

"I can understand your frustration." Hawkman motioned toward the other file. "Let's go to Maggie."

He closed George's and pulled the other one forward. "She's a bit more complex."

"How's that?"

Dr. Bunker grinned. "Are you married?"

"Yes."

"Then surely you understand how complicated women can be."

"Definitely," Hawkman chuckled. "I thought you meant Maggie's medical condition was a challenge."

"That too." Frowning, the doctor fingered through some papers. "Her arthritis is really bad, and when she broke her hip several years ago, it never healed properly. Then she came down with pneumonia, which really knocked her immune system for a loop. I thought we were going to lose her. Regardless of all the trauma her body has been through, her heart seems strong and her other organs are working fine. She's very stubborn and a fighter"

"And mighty feisty," Hawkman added.

"Yes, sometimes to her detriment."

"What do you mean?"

"I had Maggie set up for therapy, but she never went, telling me she could walk just fine with the walker. I tried to explain she could probably give it up if she did the exercises. She goes her merry way, content with the pain pills and sleep aids."

"How do you find Maggie's attitude?"

"It varies. Sometimes she's hostile and negative, but mostly I find her fairly happy. However, she does have George wrapped around her little finger. He'll do anything she wants, which isn't always the best for either of them. Like her insisting to go live at Morning Glory Haven."

"You didn't think it necessary?"

"Not really." He shrugged. "Maggie has never gotten used to the fact she and George have plenty of money. They worked very hard to get where they are now. She developed a few strange quirks, and became very possessive of her belongings, such as her spouse, and their home. She doesn't want to pay any stranger to invade her private life."

Hawkman leaned forward, putting his elbows on his thighs. "You think those feelings are strong enough for her to uproot from her own place and go live in a costly home? Doesn't make any sense."

"No, it doesn't. At first, I thought she really thought about George's health and how he wouldn't be able to take care of her needs." He waved a hand in the air. "I might add, he wouldn't have been able to take care of her properly. However, as time went by, I discovered Maggie loves to be in control. When she and George had a big business, she hired and fired. Once they sold and retired, she lost that power. She knows many of the residents at the home want to be close to her and they try to worm their way into her circle of friends. The thought of being able to keep some at bay makes her feel more in charge again."

"I've seen her in action. I pity the ones who've tried to get her attention, and failed." Hawkman stood when he noticed the doctor checking his watch. "I've kept you long enough. Is there anything we might have left out about these two?"

"No, I think we've covered their lives. If you have more questions, don't hesitate to give me a call, or stop by." He rose and held out his hand. "It's been a pleasure."

Picking up the recorder off the edge of the desk, Hawkman punched the off button and dropped it into his pocket. "Thanks for all the information. Have a good lunch."

Leaving the medical center, Hawkman tried to sift through what Bunker had told him, but decided to wait until he could listen to the recording before making any judgments.

When he reached his office, he noticed the answering machine blinking. He poked it with his finger and his attention immediately piqued when he heard Dr. Jeff Grahm's voice.

"Mr. Casey, I wanted to inform you the preliminary test on Gladys Owens are in. There were some discrepancies and the lab is sending the body to a forensic laboratory for microscopic, chemical-toxicological and biochemical analyses of tissue and body fluid samples. It might take up to two weeks before any results are sent back, depending on how busy they are. I will let you know when they've arrived."

Hawkman leaned back in his chair. Sounds suspicious, he thought, twirling a pen between his fingers.

chapter

TWENTY-
TWO

Hawkman figured evidence of poison or drugs had been found in Mrs. Owens' body, and they needed the experts to decipher what kind. It's possible the woman could have overdosed on her own medication. It's been recorded patients have saved enough pills to commit suicide.

He didn't feel a murderer broke into the apartment. There would've been signs of struggle, not only on the body, but within the room. So whoever killed Mrs. Owens was someone she knew. The question of how they induced poison into her body, if that's what happened, baffled him. Could the killer be a resident taking out some sort of crazy vengeance on innocent souls? He'd be anxious to see the autopsy report.

While listening to Dr. Bunker's interview off the recorder, he paced the floor mulling over what he'd learned so far, which didn't appear to be much. Flopping down in the chair, he swiveled around to face the desk, took off his cowboy hat and hung it on hook he'd installed on the wall nearby. Opening the Hamptons' file, he read through all his notes again, then scratched his head as he studied the scribbling, knowing he must be missing something. Soon he slammed the folder shut and grumbled, "Not a clue."

Frustrated, he snatched his hat, shoved it on his head, threw the file into the briefcase and left the office.

***

Friday morning, Hawkman strolled out on the deck to visit his falcon and decided he had time to clean the cage before heading into town. Miss Marple, her tail slowly waving back and forth, sat on the inside ledge of the picture window, scrutinizing his every move. When Pretty Girl squawked, the cat jumped to the floor in terror and dashed across the living room carpet.

"Brave little tiger we own," he laughed.

When he stepped out of the enclosure carrying the water and food tray, his pet let out a loud protest. "I know, you want to hunt, but I don't have time today. Maybe this weekend. However, I have a great treat for you inside."

Hawkman went to the freezer and pulled out a whole frozen dove he'd saved from one of his hunts. He defrosted it in the microwave while filling the water tray.

"She's definitely going to like that," Jennifer said, glancing up from her computer as he walked by with the morsel resting on the falcon's food tray. "Maybe it will keep her happy for another day or two."

"I hope so. I feel bad about not taking her out to hunt. Just haven't had time since I took on this case."

"Maybe I can take her out again in the next few days."

"Thanks, hon, I'd appreciate it."

He returned from the deck with a pleasant expression. "Pretty Girl attacked the dove like she'd caught it herself." He glanced up at the kitchen wall clock. "I've got to get out of here. I want to talk to Kevin, and I have no idea what Maggie has planned for him today." He laughed. "Remind me to tell you about all the things she drags us to." He dashed back to his home office, grabbed his briefcase, threw Jennifer a kiss and headed out the door.

Driving toward Medford, he wondered if he'd get any information out of Kevin he didn't already know, but figured two heads were better than one. A few ideas rumbled through his mind, but he felt them premature and didn't want to act on anything until he heard more about the autopsy. There might be a problem for Dr. Grahm to tell him the results, since he wasn't Gladys Owens' personal physician.

Hawkman arrived at Morning Glory Haven and made his way to Maggie's apartment. He could hear the low volume of the television and knocked on the door. Kevin let him in.

"Boy, you're decked out," Hawkman exclaimed stepping back and giving him the once over. "All dressed in slacks and sports coat. I don't think I've ever seen you in anything but a uniform or jeans."

Kevin wagged his head back and forth. "Yeah, Maggie told me I had to dress a little better, so when we go to events people won't think her escort is a bum."

Hawkman looked around the room. "Where is she?"

Kevin thumbed toward the closed door of the bedroom. "Getting ready so we can attend a piano concert down in the big recreation room."

"The entertainment in this place appears first class."

"Yeah, I really haven't minded attending these events with Maggie. I have to admit it's a change from watching television." He shook his head. "However, she's one strange woman. I don't see how George puts up with her day in and day out.

"Oh, yeah. Tell me about it."

Kevin shot a glance toward the bedroom and lowered his voice. "Her mood can change from hot to cold in the blink of an eye. One minute she's as sweet as pie and the next she's ranting and raving. It's like treading on egg shells. You never know what will set her off. Glad I only have six hours every other day to put up with her behavior."

"Other than Maggie's temper tantrums, have you noticed anything unusual going on?"

He raised a finger. "One thing sort of nags at me."

"What's that?"

"One of the employees, a Carmen Sanders, I believe she said her title is 'Marketing Manager'. She wanders these halls an awful lot."

"It's part of her job to mingle with the residents."

Kevin frowned. "I don't see much mingling, more like invasion."

Hawkman gave him a questioning glance. "What do you mean?"

"I saw her go into one of the rooms, using her master key."

"There could be an explanation."

"For instance?" Kevin asked.

"Someone could have asked her to retrieve a coat or jacket. She could also be checking on a sick resident and used her key so the person wouldn't have to get out of bed to answer the door."

"You've got a point. They're very organized around here, and seem genuinely concerned about their patrons. I have to admit, this is a unique place."

Maggie came out of the bedroom dressed in a blue silk pants suit, silver shoes and to top off the attire, a matching blue pill box hat resting on the back of her head.

Hawkman let out a whistle. "My goodness, you look spiffy."

"Thank you, Mr. Hawkman. Doesn't our Mr. Kevin look handsome?"

"Yes, you two make a charming couple. Does George mind you being escorted by this strange man?"

"Are you kidding?" she smirked. "He's so relieved he doesn't have to go. Social events are not my hubby's thing." She motioned for Kevin. "Come on, we've got to get going or we won't get a good seat."

Hawkman accompanied them down to the main floor, where he zigzagged through the crowd and departed out the front door. He drove toward his office with Maggie on his mind. There'd been several negative remarks about her, and he came to the conclusion she was definitely headstrong. If the truth be known, he imagined few people really got along with her. It made him wonder what she might be capable of doing. However, the people who'd passed on were supposedly dear friends of the Hamptons. He couldn't imagine her murdering them. But one really never knows.

When he reached the office, he immediately sat down at his desk and jotted down a few pertinent points, closed the file and decided to wrap it up for the day. A cold breeze snapped at his ears as he stepped outside. He hooked up his collar and jogged down the stairs where he met Clyde the baker coming around the corner of the building, bundled in a heavy coat.

"Good evening, Mr. Casey. I think winter is upon us," he said, hurrying to his vehicle.

"I believe you're right. The northerner the meteorologist warned us about has hit," Hawkman said, as he hastened to the SUV. A gust of icy wind slammed into him before he could get the door closed and vibrated the whole 4x4. He quickly inserted the key, turned on the heater, and headed home.

When he arrived, he immediately went to Pretty Girl's cage, lowered the wooden window and buckled down the tarp so she'd be protected from the cold weather. Jennifer had pulled on a sweatshirt and had the fireplace going. Miss Marple lay curled up on one side of the hearth.

"I think old man winter has arrived," she said, as he stepped inside.

"Yeah, with a vengeance."

***

Saturday morning, Hawkman crawled out of bed and shivered. He immediately flipped on the furnace and glanced out the kitchen window. A light layer of snow feathered the ground and flakes were slowly drifting from the heavens. The overcast appeared heavy, which would make for a dreary day.

He dressed, had breakfast with Jennifer, then slid into his sheepskin jacket and left for Medford to do his turn of chaperoning Maggie. The roads weren't icy yet, but if rain mixed with the snow, it wouldn't take long. Very treacherous driving under those circumstances, because even the four-wheel drive wouldn't do much good on slick pavement.

Driving more cautiously than usual, he made it into Medford without incident and drove to Morning Glory Haven. When he walked down the halls, he noticed there weren't many walking the frigid corridor, and those who were had bundled in sweaters and heavy coats. When he approached Maggie's apartment, George stood outside the door with a cup of coffee.

"What are you doing out here in this breezy hallway?" Hawkman asked.

"Waiting for Maggie to get over her tirade."

"What's her problem today?"

"She's fussing at me about not keeping track of my blood sugar. No big deal, I'm used to her nagging." George turned and opened the door. "Come on in, I'll let her know you're here."

They stepped into the living room and Maggie sat on the couch with her arms folded across her chest. "Hello, Mr. Hawkman. I'm actually glad to see you. George, go and run your errands. Don't forget to get the list of items I gave you."

He gave her a peck on the cheek, winked at Hawkman and limped into the hallway.

As the door slid shut, Hawkman felt the cell phone vibrate against his waist. He pulled it from the pouch on his belt and noted the call came from Jennifer. Quickly answering, he laughed. "Okay, I'll put it on my grocery list." After returning the phone, he slapped his shirt pocket and realized he'd forgotten to carry a pen. He reached down on the small coffee table, snatched up the one lying there and started to write on the paper pad. When he punched the top, instead of the end of an ink end protruding, a needle emerged, and dripped liquid over the paper. "What the hell is this?"

chapter

TWENTY-THREE

Maggie jerked her head toward Hawkman, then held out her hand. "Oh, for crying out loud, give me that. George must have left it on the table. I don't know what I'm going to do with my absent minded husband."

Hawkman turned the instrument in his hand as he studied it. "What is this?"

She dropped her uplifted arm to her lap. "It's an insulin pen. Haven't you seen them before?"

"No, but I see the needle, and this one seems full of liquid. So this is what your doctor kept referring to when he talked about George's diabetes. I never got the chance to ask him." Hawkman handed it to her. "I don't think it's a good idea to leave it out in the open."

"Of course it isn't. I'll put it away. I filled the vial with George's dosage and told him to stick it in his pocket before he left. We were watching a program on the television and he was so engrossed, he must have completely forgotten about it."

"I could probably catch him before he gets to his car."

She flipped her hand in the air. "He's got a supply at home and can take care of himself. For crying out loud, he's a grown man and should do a better job of keeping tabs on his medications. I get so frustrated because he's always losing these pens. It surprises me Dr. Bunker keeps filling the prescription."

"Maybe you should change places with him," Hawkman said. "Or better yet, you both live in Morning Glory Haven."

Her mouth dropped open. "Are you kidding me? George would go nuts."

He shrugged. "Just a suggestion."

"Who'd take care of our property and Pesky?"

"Sell it, and bring your dog here."

She threw back her shoulders, and glared at Hawkman. "I'd never give up my home or confine my precious pet to such close living quarters. She loves to run outside and play."

"Do you intend to move back to your real home soon?"

Her face fell, and she clutched her hands in her lap. "Not unless I improve. Right now my condition is staying much the same, and there's no way George can take care of me, the house, and Pesky. It would just be too much. At least I can go visit, even spend the night, if I so desire. However, I don't dare leave here overnight."

Hawkman frowned. "Why?"

"Some things have gone missing. Unfortunately, I can't prove it."

"What items?"

She lifted a finger in the air. "A pair of earrings, a necklace, a porcelain coffee cup, stuff that doesn't really amount to anything, but it's mine."

Both glanced toward the door when it opened.

"Hey, what's the big conference about?" George asked, as he strolled back into the room.

Hawkman stepped back. "You forget something?"

"Thought you might need a break from my other half," George chuckled. Then he turned to Maggie. "My sweetheart. I thought if you were up to it, we'd go for a ride and out to lunch?"

"Wonderful idea. I need a breath of fresh air. Give me a few minutes, and I'll be right with you."

He helped her up so she could get a good grasp on her walker. Once she'd scooted into the bedroom and closed the door, George spoke to Hawkman, "What was the big confab about when I walked in?"

"Maggie said you forgot your insulin pen. She also told me about some items missing from her room."

George frowned. "Oh dear, yes, I completely forgot the pen and she'd fixed it all up for me too. As far as the little items she thinks have been stolen, could be anywhere in this apartment. I'm not the only one who misplaces stuff."

"You seem to be feeling good and in fine spirits, even after forgetting your medication," Hawkman commented.

George automatically put his hand to his chest. "I didn't have a pocket in this shirt, and put the pen on the table. It's no big deal. I have plenty of insulin at the house. Maggie just makes it easier, as she fixes the dosage and I don't have to worry about it."

"You like the pens?"

"Yeah, they're not as conspicuous as a syringe."

"Understood." Hawkman said. "If you're leaving for the afternoon, I might as well get out of your way and let you handle your feisty spouse."

Hawkman left relieved he didn't have to stay with Maggie. He headed out of the building to the parking lot, and drove to the grocery store to pick up the items on Jennifer's list.

***

Sunday morning, Hawkman decided to stay home, and take Pretty Girl for a hunt. He bundled up, as the wind blew in cold gusts and whistled around the corners of the house, shaking the window panes. The falcon wouldn't mind the frigid weather with the excitement of a hunt on her mind.

Loading the portable perch into his SUV, he slipped on the leather glove, then walked around the house and fetched her from the cage. She flapped her wings, almost knocking off his hat.

"Hey, girl, take it easy. I know you're excited. We'll get there shortly."

He tethered her to the perch, then drove across the bridge and made a left on Ager Beswick Road. Bucking the wind and a smattering of moisture hitting the windshield, he decided to stop at an open field instead of driving all the way to Richard's place.

Pulling to the side on a wide spot in the road, he got out and went around to the passenger side of the vehicle. He released Pretty Girl's leg, then carried her on his protected arm to the edge of the field, and let her go. The beauty of her flight never ceased to amaze him, as she soared high in the sky. The wind only showed her strength as she circled, never faltering. Soon, she straightened out and headed toward the river, then dove into a grove of trees where she disappeared.

Hawkman pulled up the collar of his sheepherder's coat and thrust his hands into the fur-lined pockets. "Think I'll wait in the 4X4," he mumbled

Once inside, protected from the freezing wind, he took his binoculars from the glove compartment and searched the landscape for his beloved pet. She hadn't been gone long, but he always worried on each hunt she'd take off and leave him forever. Several minutes passed when out of the clump of trees two birds rose into the air. His heart sunk; this is what he'd feared could happen. A male falcon pursuing his beautiful female.

Hawkman quickly jumped out of the vehicle and headed for the center of the field. His lips cold, it took him a few seconds to whistle the familiar tune Pretty Girl would recognize. He watched the two playing in the currents above him. Scared the wind carried his sound away, he let forth the signal as loud as he could. It appeared she was ignoring him, but he didn't give up. About the time he thought he'd lost his falcon, one of the birds broke away from the circled flight and headed down in a dive. He stretched out his leather clad arm and prayed she wasn't teasing.

Holding his breath as she flew above him, he called her name over and over. Then she set her wings and made a perfect landing on the glove.

"You beautiful falcon. I thought I'd lost you to a handsome guy."

She let out a squawk and settled on his arm as he headed back to the 4X4. He cooed to her all the way home, so thankful he still had his wonderful pet.

When Hawkman arrived at the house, he placed Pretty Girl in her cage, then went inside and told Jennifer what had happened.

"You had a close call. Maybe you shouldn't use that area anymore for her hunting. There may be a group of hawks and falcons congregating by the river."

"Think you're right. I won't risk it again."

chapter

TWENTY-FOUR

Monday morning, when Hawkman reached the office, he flipped on the answering machine to hear Dr. Grahm's voice requesting a meeting, and asked him to call to set up a time.

Hawkman quickly placed the small sack with the bear claw pastry on the desk, sat down and punched in the number recited on the message. When a female answered, he recognized the voice of Dr. Grahm's receptionist. He identified himself, then listened to her instructions.

"Yes, I can be there at eleven thirty."

After hanging up, he put on the coffee pot, then stared out the window overlooking the parking lot. He figured Dr. Grahm had received more of the autopsy reports on Gladys Owens.

In deep thought, Hawkman meandered over to the counter, poured himself a cup of the hot brew and returned to the desk. He wondered if the good doctor would confide the results, or just take great pleasure informing him her death was due to natural causes. Considering this man's type of personality, he could picture the satisfied expression on his face to report such news. If the report showed a suspicious cause, which Hawkman felt in his gut, would Grahm tell him?

These thoughts plagued Hawkman's mind as he feasted on the pastry, and again, read through the notes he'd filed in the Morning Glory folder. He felt he'd surely missed something, but nothing jumped out at him. After underlining several items to pursue, he closed the folder and booted up the computer. He Googled 'insulin pens', and ran across several interesting descriptions and pictures of the small instrument and could see how they could be a very popular item among diabetics. They could inject their insulin without feeling people were scrutinizing them when they plunged a syringe into their body.

Hawkman bookmarked the sites, thinking he'd ask George if he or Maggie knew how to use a computer, and pass the urls over. Then he chuckled to himself and shook his head, "You're dreaming," he mumbled. "George doesn't even like to calculate his own medication, he doesn't have a cell phone, so why in heaven's name would you think he could use a complicated machine."

He checked his watch and shut down the computer. After turning off the coffee urn, he slipped the file into his briefcase, the recorder into his shirt pocket and left the office for the meeting with Dr. Grahm.

When he walked into the empty waiting room, the receptionist acknowledged him.

"Hello, Mr. Casey. Dr. Grahm is with his last patient before the lunch hour, so you shouldn't have to wait long."

Hawkman gave a small salute and took a seat. Within a few minutes, a short, thin man, assisted by a cane, limped into view, and stopped at the receptionist's desk. His hands trembled as he pulled his wallet from his back pocket.

"Hello, Mr. Taylor. I understand you're doing real well on your new medication."

Despite the hearing aids hooked on each ear, he cupped a hand over one. "Whatcha say?"

She repeated her statement and told him the fee.

"Yeah, I feel much better. Thanks to the doc." He paid in cash, waited for the receipt, then hobbled out the door.

She wrote in her journal, then stood. "Follow me, Mr. Casey."

Hawkman rose, flipped on the recorder and trailed her down the hallway to the same door she'd led him to at the last meeting.

She knocked softly, then poked her head inside. "Mr. Casey's here."

"Good, have him come in."

When Hawkman entered, the door closed softly and the doctor motioned at the chair in front of his desk. "Have a seat."

Hawkman noted the man looked extremely tired; deep, creased worry lines crossed his forehead, and dark circles had formed under his eyes.

He let out a loud sigh, then spoke. "I could get into a lot of trouble for confiding in you about this report. Mrs. Owens' physician is on vacation for a month and I do have the authority to take care of any serious business at hand. I felt this important."

"I'm game. If you didn't give it to me, I'm sure I could get permission from her daughter to receive a copy."

"The report came early this morning, and it's disturbing. They're also doing more tests." He opened the file in front of him and rattled off medical terms.

Hawkman interrupted. "Doctor, hold it. Could you give me this information in lay terms? I haven't the vaguest idea what you're talking about."

Grahm ran a hand across his face. "Sorry, my fault. These items are so familiar to me, I don't even think about it." He leaned back in his chair. "Mrs. Owens died of an insulin overdose."

Hawkman came forward in his seat. "Was she diabetic?"

"Yes."

"Wouldn't there be some pre-warning before the person died?"

"Not necessarily. If she'd been sedated and someone wasn't available at the time it happened to observe a problem, the person would usually die."

"Why is there more testing being done, if they know why she succumbed?"

"They're trying to determine the type of insulin, the brand, and what other drugs are present in her body."

"Have you called the police?"

He shook his head. "Not yet. I needed to talk to you first. This could have been an accident. It does happen. I wondered if you'd come up with other incidents at Morning Glory Haven like this one?"

"This is the first autopsy that's been conducted. So I have no idea about the other deaths except from what the doctor reports indicated. I still question why autopsies weren't done."

Grahm bowed his head, then glanced up at Hawkman. "You have to understand; this is an old folk's home. These people have all kinds of medical problems and really aren't expected to live much longer after being put in there." He threw up his hands in frustration. "When the sickly die, I can honestly tell you, in most cases their hearts simply give out. However, after Mrs. Owens' death, I thought something askew, because after reviewing her file, I discovered she didn't have any real bad health issues that would cause her sudden demise, except for the diabetes."

"What would you look for that would make you request one?"

"There is the possibility an older person might ingest a poison without even knowing what he's doing. If a person dies of toxic poisoning, there are signs, such as facial contortions or limbs drawn up, and usually they could call for help before death. With insulin overdose the patient may not be aware they need help, especially if they've taken a sleep aid."

"Dr. Grahm, I'm not sure how the police will look at this situation. I'd just advise you to have a lawyer handy. I appreciate your confiding in me, and I'll certainly come to your defense. Right now I think you'd better contact the police, and let them know what has been discovered. It's possible Ms. Owens was murdered."

His shoulders slumped and his mouth turned down in a grim line. "I had a feeling you'd give such advice. I've already contacted an attorney and will call the authorities before the afternoon is over. I'm sure you'll know when they've been notified, as uniformed men will invade Morning Glory Haven."

Hawkman left a shattered doctor and headed for Morning Glory Haven. He wanted to warn them of the upcoming confusion, so they could handle the situation in a calm manner. The case now took on a new look as his mind kept traveling back to this morning, when he found the full insulin pen in Maggie's room.

chapter

TWENTY-FIVE

Hawkman stopped on the side of the road before reaching the home and called Kevin. He explained what he'd just learned and warned him to be very vigilant on guarding Maggie, and double check anyone loitering around her apartment. Kevin understood the graveness of the problem and assured him he'd be on high alert. After hanging up, Hawkman exhaled loudly.

He stared out the windshield as he rang his friend, Detective Williams of the Medford Police Force. After warning him of what might be coming down the pike, he pulled back onto the pavement and continued toward Morning Glory Haven.

Hawkman worried mostly about the time span during which George supposedly kept an eye on his wife. He knew Maggie had her husband tied around her little finger and could get away with murder. "Ugh," he murmured, as he drove into the parking lot.

When he entered the building, it appeared more quiet and subdued than normal.

He wondered if the news had already reached the staff. Riding the elevator, he stepped out on the second floor, and turned toward Maggie's quarters. Margy and Jessie hurried past him coming from the opposite direction and he suspected they'd been harassing Mrs. Hampton again.

When he knocked on the door and received no answer, he roamed up and down the hallway searching for any sign of her or Kevin, but to no avail. "Where the heck are they?" he hissed. Then it dawned on him. There could be a program going on in the entertainment hall. He hurried back to the main floor and down the corridor leading to the center.

The door stood open to the area where he'd joined George and Maggie for bingo. He poked his head inside, and spotted Kevin in a chair against the wall, his head bobbing up and down as he caught a snooze. Maggie sat at the table in front of him concentrating on an array of artificial flowers as she worked them into a small vase. A woman stood in the middle of the circle of tables talking about colors and how to compliment your bouquet.

Hawkman quietly made his way down the side until he arrived beside Kevin and gently poked him on the shoulder. Almost jumping out of his seat, Kevin jerked around and stammered. "Yeah, time to go?"

Hawkman shushed him and pointed to the door.

Kevin brushed his hand across his mouth. "Sorry," he said sheepishly as Maggie glared at him.

The two men exited into the hallway.

"Thanks for rescuing me," Kevin said. "Some of these programs are not my choice of entertainment."

"I'm concerned we might have a real problem on our hands," Hawkman said, stopping before they got out of sight of the craft room.

"From what you told me on the phone, it could be a horrible situation."

"Possible murder. The police will be here soon, and they'll want to question all the residents and staff; but I have my suspicions they'll concentrate on the diabetics. They're going to want to know what kind of insulin George uses and no telling what else. I just wanted you to be prepared when you see the uniformed guys entering the home."

"Does the director know about this turn of events?"

"I'm not sure if Mr. Mackle's been notified, but I'm heading for his office right now."

Kevin looked at the floor and shook his head. "You want me to tell Maggie? You know they're going to ask about the other deaths."

Hawkman shrugged. "If you want, or I can tell them both when George comes back this evening. I don't think there's any reason to scare Maggie about getting questions on the other deaths. Only if they classify Owens' death as murder, will there be a deeper investigation and then the bodies might have to be exhumed."

As he leaned against the wall, Kevin's expression turned grim. "Any of these people could be suspect."

"True, and anyone who has access to insulin."

He shot a look at Hawkman. "You mean Maggie, too?"

"Yes."

Running a hand through his thinning hair, Kevin let out a sigh. "Maggie's not going to take this news lightly, and George is going to wish he'd never consented for his wife to live here."

"I agree with you on both accounts. You better get back to the craft room. I've got to catch Mr. Mackle before he leaves. I'll see you upstairs shortly."

Kevin headed back to retrieve Maggie. At the doorway, he, turned and watched his boss striding toward the row of offices.

Hawkman stopped in front of the closed door marked 'Director' and knocked. A young woman he hadn't seen before poked out her head. "Yes, may I help you?"

"Is Mr. Mackle in?"

"Yes, do you have an appointment?"

"No, but would you ask him if he has time to speak with Tom Casey."

"Okay, I'll check." She closed the door, but within a few seconds was back holding it open. "Please come in."

The office was larger than the others he'd been in. A partition separated the receptionist's desk from the main room where a large oak desk took up much of the floor. A computer and other business paraphernalia cluttered the surface. Four leather chairs were situated around it in an orderly fashion. Mr. Mackle stood staring out the window, his thick gray hair shining under the light. His suit jacket hung over the back of the desk chair, and his white dress shirt sleeves were rolled up as if he'd been working manual labor. He turned abruptly.

"Ms. Lindsay, why don't you take a fifteen minute break. I need to speak with Mr. Casey in private."

"Okay." She grabbed a small handbag off her desk and exited.

"Have a seat, Mr. Casey. Unfortunately, I know why you're here. I received a call from Dr. Grahm about thirty minutes ago. This is a very serious situation. Many jobs are at stake, not to mention the reputation of this institution."

"I realize your dilemma. This could have been an accident, but if a murder was committed and the culprit is outside the realm of the staff, the home will regain its credibility in no time."

Mackle flopped down in the chair behind the desk. "I realize what you're saying is true, but during the length of an investigation, how many of my residents will leave or be yanked out by relatives fearing for their loved ones' lives? News like this travels like wildfire and I won't be able to fill those apartments until people know it's safe. The home will lose so much financially, it could force us into bankruptcy. Also, I'm fearful of lawsuits. We could be inundated with them from former relatives whose loved ones have passed away at Morning Glory Haven." He dropped his head into his hands. "It's a nightmare, Mr. Casey. A horrible, horrible, nightmare."

"I'm sure your insurance will cover many things, plus I'm assuming you have lawyers to protect the establishment."

Mr. Mackle, leaned back in his chair and exhaled. "Yes, of course. I'll be in touch with them first thing. Right now I'm just trying absorb what's happened."

"The police will be here soon. Have you informed your staff?"

"No. I should do that immediately." He rose from the chair. "They'll be scared spit-less when the uniforms start coming through the door."

"I'd advise it, and you might want to have the residents stay in their rooms instead of roaming the halls. This way it would be easier to keep track of everyone."

"Mr. Casey, you must excuse me so I can get things in order before all chaos breaks loose."

"I understand," Hawkman said, as he headed for the door. "If you need any help, I'm available."

"Thank you."

chapter

TWENTY-SIX

As Hawkman stepped out of the office, the group of seniors had just exited the craft workshop. He stood back and watched as they paraded down the hallway toward their quarters. Each clutched a vase or flat dish holding their creations. When Maggie and Kevin filed by, he fell into the line and followed.

Once they arrived at her apartment, she pushed her walker to the side and flopped down on the small sofa in the sitting area. "Okay, what's going on? Kevin wouldn't tell me a thing about why you called him outside."

"I didn't think it appropriate to give you bad news in a public place," Kevin said, placing the artificial flower bouquet on the coffee table. "Now that Mr. Casey is here, he can explain the situation."

Her gaze lit on Hawkman. "Well?"

After he told her about Dr. Grahm receiving the results of the autopsy and what it revealed, her hands flew to her ashen face. "Oh, my, this is morbid news. Who in the world could have done such a deed?"

Hawkman raised his hands. "Hold on. I'm not saying it was murder, it could well have been an accident. I just wanted you to know the police will probably be here shortly and everyone will be questioned. Especially those who have access to insulin."

"What if some stranger killed her?"

"Now, Maggie, you're jumping to conclusions. We don't know anything yet. But the police will come. They'll question all the employees and residents extensively, then make a decision if they feel foul play is involved."

Maggie shook her head. "What about the other poor souls who died earlier?"

"I have no idea whether they'll exhume the bodies or not. It'll depend on the conclusion of the lab tests on Mrs. Owens."

George walked in at the tail end of the conversation, and his eyes grew wide as Hawkman clued him in on what had occurred. He sat down beside Maggie and took her hand. "I want to get you out of here and take you home. We'll manage somehow."

She pulled away, and looked him in the eye. "I have round the clock protection. Why should I go home and end up yelling at you to come help me all the time?"

He looked at her with pleading eyes. "I'd do it."

"That's not the point, George. We don't have to make each other miserable. I don't want to hear anymore about me going home until I can care for myself."

Hawkman pulled up a chair so he faced the Hamptons. "You two can discuss this at another time. Right now I need to talk to you about what's getting ready to come down the pike."

Maggie frowned. "How does this involve us?"

"George is diabetic and insulin is available. I need you to keep track of all the pens, how much insulin he's taken, and what's left. There's a possibility some may have gotten stolen. The times you thought George lost his, it might have ended up in a murderer's hands."

She hugged herself. "Oh, my word. I can't believe someone would steal insulin. Sleeping or pain pills I can see, as people get addicted to those." An expression of fear flashed across her face. "Is it possible we could be suspects?"

Hawkman nodded. "Yes."

She grabbed George's arm. "We could go to jail."

"Let's not go to extremes here," Hawkman said, leaning forward. "I want you to listen and do what I tell you. For the next few days, as hard as it may seem, I don't want you leaving your apartment. I'm hoping Mr. Mackle will give those instructions to all the residents. Every item in here will probably be searched by the police or an investigation crew. Don't try to hide anything, because they'll find it, and it will make you look guilty."

Suddenly, their heads all jerked toward the commotion in the hallway. Hawkman quickly crossed to the door, where he saw a couple of the staff members, followed by two police officers herding a group of residents down the hall. The seniors' voices had become excited with fear as they scuffed down the corridor.

"Things are going to be okay," one of the management kept reassuring them. "We'll stay with you if you like."

Hawkman turned to the Hamptons. "The police are here. I'm going to go talk to the detective. I'll be back shortly. Stay calm."

"I'm leaving too," Kevin said, as he followed Hawkman. The two men stepped out of the elevator and strolled toward the front of the building.

"I'll see you tomorrow," Kevin said as he exited.

Hawkman waved, then continued the search for his friend, Detective Williams. When he passed the entry to the dining room, he saw several of the kitchen crew huddled in clusters of two or three. He knew they were scared and worried. His gaze traveled over the group of officers and plain clothes-men guarding the entry. He spotted one he knew, and approached him.

"Hi, Matt."

"Mr. Casey, what are you doing here?"

"Long story. Is Detective Williams with you?"

"Yes." He pointed toward the row of offices.

"Thanks." He headed for Mackle's, where the door stood ajar.

The young receptionist he'd seen earlier in the day stood against the wall biting her fingernails, a frightened look on her face. Her eyes grew wide when she saw him, and she edged farther down the hall.

Hawkman stopped outside the door for a second, until he heard and recognized Williams' voice. Then he stepped inside.

The detective twisted around and held out his hand. "Hello, Casey, looks like we have a complicated case developing."

Mackle looked at one, then the other, his brows furrowed. "You know each other?"

"Oh, yeah. We've worked on and solved many cases together. You couldn't have a better man on your side," Williams said.

He then continued his conversation with Mackle. "You say the apartment has been cleaned and wiped down with a disinfectant?"

"Yes, we always go in and do that after a person passes on. We have to get it ready for the next occupant. Little did we realize we had anything but a natural death on our hands."

"What did you do with Mrs. Owens' belongings?"

"We still have those, as the daughter lives in another town and the doctor informed her of the autopsy, explaining it would be several days before she could pick up her mother's body. So she asked us to store the items."

"I'd like my lab group to go through them. Do you have the daughter's phone number? It would be good to get her permission; then I wouldn't have to go through a judge."

Mackle nodded. "Understood. I'm sure my Business Manager has the information; she's been instructed to co-operate with the police."

"We're interviewing your employees as we speak and will do this throughout the next twenty-four hours so we can reach each one. We'll be around for several days and would like you to follow any schedules you've set up, and keep things as normal as possible. The only thing we might ask is to have the residents remain in their apartments, so we can find them when we're ready to talk to each individual."

"That might be a little hard to do, but we'll do the best we can," Mackle said.

"I'll check in with you on a regular basis."

The detective and Hawkman left the office and stood in the hallway.

"Any idea what's going on here?" Williams asked.

"Not yet. I'll let you know when I get a handle on it."

Williams put a fist on his hip as he surveyed the area. "Sad to see the reputation of such an exquisite place go down due to a murder investigation. It will plummet for a while."

"Yes, I know and I'm hoping none of the staff are involved," Hawkman said. "That will help it rebound."

The detective nodded. "I'm at loss why autopsies weren't ordered on the last few deaths. I'm glad you stepped in and insisted on this one."

"Yeah, me too. I'm going to stop by the patient coordinator's office and get a list of all the diabetics in this wing of the home. It might give us some clues. Whoever did this has access to insulin."

"Good idea. Make a copy for me."

"Will do."

The two men separated, Hawkman went to Lisa Montgomery's office and Williams left to check the progress of the investigation.

Once Hawkman finished persuading Ms. Montgomery to bend the rules and give him a list of the diabetics, he folded his copy of names and slipped them into his pocket, then dropped off the other to Detective Williams. He then went up the elevator and headed down the hallway where he spotted Maggie and George coming out of the room across the hall.

chapter

TWENTY-SEVEN

Hawkman stood at Maggie's doorway, with his arms crossed, as she and George made their way across the corridor. "I can see you two don't follow orders very well."

She glared at him. "Mr. Casey, these people are scared to death. I decided to go over and let them in on the scuttlebutt about what's going on."

He stepped aside so they could enter the room. "You should leave that to the authorities. We're not even sure there's been any foul play. If you used the word murder, you've probably scared them worse."

"People should know the truth. They handle situations better."

Hawkman pointed a finger at her nose. "Okay, you've done your good deed. Now I want you to stay in your room, take stock of the insulin and write it down. Do you keep it in the refrigerator?"

She shook her head. "No, only if it's been opened. They've improved it so much, I can keep the extra in my dresser drawer."

"I'll be back in about an hour and I expect a list." He diverted his attention to George. "Do you bring insulin here for Maggie to store?"

"Yeah, sometimes."

"Do you know what you have at home?"

"Not off the top of my head."

"Tonight take inventory, just so you know what you have."

He nodded. "Will do."

Hawkman stepped out of the apartment and continued down to the first floor in hopes of finding Detective Williams free. Noticing the entry area had cleared except for a couple of guards at the door, he asked the officers if the detective had left.

They gestured toward the craft room. "He's set up headquarters in a small room down that hallway."

Hawkman gave a wave. "Thanks." He crossed the room and moved down the corridor. When he entered the opened door, he found Williams sitting at a small table talking to a couple of police detectives. He glanced up when Hawkman entered.

"Come on in and put in your two cents worth."

Hawkman scooted up an empty chair and sat down. "So what's your first line of attack on this problem?"

Williams hooked a thumb toward the two men sitting next to him. "These guys are getting ready to split up the list of diabetics and ask a few pertinent questions. Then Dr. Grahm will be here in an hour. He volunteered to come in and assist as much as he could."

Hawkman raised his brows. "That's interesting."

"Really, why?"

Not wanting to sound negative, Hawkman skimmed the surface of his meeting with Grahm. "I think he's petrified at being in this predicament. He'll more than likely be very cooperative."

Williams leaned back and looped his arm over the nearby chair. "You think he's guilty of anything?"

"I doubt it. He's just in deeper than he ever thought a so called volunteer job would get him."

The detective came forward and put his hands on the table. "Give it to me upfront. I know you've got some idea of what's going on. Clue me in."

Hawkman raised his cowboy hat and ran a hand through his hair, then pushed it back on his head. "I wish I had an inkling, but right now I don't have the vaguest idea who's doing these people in."

Williams raised his brows. "People? I thought there was just one."

"I think more have died under suspicious circumstances, but there's no proof unless you want to exhume some bodies." He gave him the rundown on the deaths of the last six months.

The detective hit the table with his fist. "Damn, sounds like we've got a serial killer on our hands."

"Could be. I figure one or two of those deaths were natural. However, I think the others were murder, and the killer is right under our noses."

"Why do you think so?"

"The victims were all diabetic. They gave themselves their insulin shots. I could understand a mistake or two, but not with all of them. It appears someone was fooling with their dosages."

"What about the staff?"

"I've chatted with each of the employees at one time or the other. None of them aroused my suspicions. However, I haven't done an in depth investigation on any of them yet. One could very well be skilled at killing people."

"What about the outside contractors?"

"All the people who work here are in-house employees. The only one contracted is the yard maintenance and none of them come inside."

Williams shook his head. "What the hell would be the motive for getting rid of old people?"

"Some weird cases have occurred throughout history, but many boil down to putting people out of their misery. Doesn't make sense in this scenario because some of these just had bad arthritic conditions or were at a phase in their lives where they didn't want the responsibility of a home and yard anymore. Oh, sure, each one had some sort of medical problem, but not to the point of dying the next day, if you know what I mean." Hawkman took a deep breath.

"Unfortunately, all the people who have passed away are somehow connected to my clients."

Williams tilted his head and stared at him. "You're joshing, aren't you?"

"I wish." He then related the story of how George had hired him. "So it really doesn't surprise me, as they thought something didn't smell right. I went back a few months in the books with the patient coordinator and we discovered several deaths had occurred within a six month period. I can't put a finger on a motive."

"Did the victims have something in common besides being diabetic?"

"They knew each other. Maybe not as close friends, but acquaintances."

The detective ran his hands over his face. "I can see right now, we've got a complicated mess on our hands."

chapter

TWENTY-
EIGHT

"I worry about getting any reliable information from these people." Hawkman raised a hand and wiggled it in front of him. "Many don't have good eyesight and half the time they don't remember from one minute to the next. It's not going to be an easy task."

"What about the ones who are delinquent in their bills?" Williams asked.

"I've checked it out. Everyone is paid up, even the ones who passed away had their payments up to date. Mackle is worried many residents will move out after they hear about the murder investigation, and he won't be able to fill the apartments, causing a financial burden on the facility. So mark him off your list. He'd have no reason to kill off a paying customer."

"What's in these other wings of the building?"

"One holds the assisted living group and the other one is Alzheimer patients. The Alzheimer section is completely locked off from the other two groups. There's no way they can even get into either section without being discovered immediately."

Williams slapped a hand on the table. "You have any suggestions on where the hell we should begin?"

"I'm hoping Mackle can get it through the residents' heads to stay in their rooms after dinner, so you can find them. Why don't you station a couple of men in each hallway, so if someone leaves they can keep an eye on their apartment and make sure no stranger enters the place. Try to keep the daytime events going so the people don't get too nervous."

"Can you hang around awhile and show us the ropes, since you're more familiar with the territory?"

"Sure."

Williams rose. "Let's go talk to my men and get a routine scheduled."

The two headed toward the entry where the police officers had gathered.

***

Maggie finished jotting down the insulin supplies she had stored in the dresser drawer, and pushed her way into the living room where George had the television on. She waved the paper. "Okay, I've got it all written out for our dear Mr. Casey."

He twisted around in the chair. "Good girl."

"George, turn off that boob tube. We need to talk."

He frowned. "What about?"

She hobbled toward the couch and flopped down. The paper still in her hand, she held it up. "About all of this."

He turned off the television and tossed the remote on the coffee table. "Yeah, what's the problem. Hawkman said the police would want a list."

"Well, it's not just about the inventory of the medications. I'm sick of the whole thing. I'm tired of being followed around, told I can't leave my quarters and scolded like a kid. I want you to let Mr. Casey go."

George's mouth dropped open. "Why? He's protecting you. I can't take the chance of you getting hurt, especially now."

She shook a finger at him. "I'm a grown woman. I don't need to be hovered over, and it's very irritating. Half my friends are afraid to come visit me because of all the attention this whole mess is getting. They don't like being stopped at the door by a guard."

George held up his hands in protest. "Get off your high horse. He's only doing what I pay him to do, and it won't last forever."

"That's another item we need to talk about." She stared at him, her eyes narrowed into slits. "He's costing us a small fortune and we can get the same thing free from the police."

"Maggie, you don't seem to understand. Mr. Casey is concerned only about you. The police are spreading themselves thin over the whole place and you won't get the personal attention."

She let out a loud sigh. "Exactly. No one will be breathing down my collar."

"You still won't be able to leave and roam around. They've already put out the order that all residents are to stay in their apartments after dinner."

"Well, they'll have a hard time enforcing it."

"Maggie," he spat, "they're trying to find a murderer. Don't you want to cooperate?"

"I think this whole fiasco is a farce."

"How can you say such a thing? Gladys died because of an insulin overdose. Someone gave her a fatal shot."

Maggie pointed a crooked finger. "How do we know it's true?"

"The autopsy proved it."

"If you hadn't hired Tom Casey to begin with, Morning Glory Haven would never be in this mess. He has stirred up a bumble bee's nest and see where it's got us." She raised her arms in frustration. "The whole place is in an uproar."

"Someone would have gotten suspicious eventually."

"Who would have disputed a doctor's diagnosis? No one was the wiser until that smart ass detective you hired came into the picture."

"You were also worried about the other deaths."

She harrumphed. "I had no idea you'd go out and hire a private investigator agency. Little did I realize what a pain in the butt it would be having a crew of men monitoring my every move. They've even gotten you so involved, I can't be out of your sight for a minute."

"The reasoning all makes perfect sense to me. Why can't you see it?"

She sighed, kicked off her shoes and rested her feet on the couch. "Just get rid of Casey and his helper."

"I'll have to think about it."

"If you don't, I'll fire him."

George rose from his chair, his cheeks flaming red. He grabbed his cane resting at the side and jammed it hard against the floor. "Woman, you make me so mad, I want to spit fire. Trying to do the right thing for you is like chewing nails."

She raised a hand and flitted her fingers in the air. "You'll get over it."

George limped toward the door, banging the walking stick against the entry tile on each step.

"Where are you going?"

He turned and scowled. "I'm going to go find Mr. Casey and fire him."

With a smirk, Maggie stood, slipped her feet into her shoes and grabbed the walker. "I'm going to dinner. You can join me if you wish."

"I'm not hungry. Enjoy your meal." He lumbered out of the room and down the hallway.

chapter

TWENTY-
NINE

George stepped out of the elevator, then hobbled down the corridor, hardly noticing the nods or greetings of residents heading toward the dining room. He had no idea if Tom Casey still lingered in the building, but he'd do a search to make Maggie happy. Stopping for a moment to rest his knees, he glanced around the large room and immediately recognized the tall, lanky figure with the cowboy hat perched on his head standing near the front door. He and another man appeared to be in a deep conversation. Out of breath, George decided to wait and sat down on one of the plush sofas in the living room area.

The Marketing Director, Carmen Sanders, happened by at the moment. "Are you all right, Mr. Hampton?"

He nodded. "I'm fine. Just waiting for Mr. Casey."

She smiled and headed down one of the corridors.

Soon, Hawkman glanced in his direction, and motioned for the other man to follow. George stood for a moment as he shook his bones into shape, then using his cane for support, limped toward the private investigator.

"Hello, George. Have you met Detective Williams?"

After they shook hands, George addressed Hawkman. "I wonder if I could speak to you a moment in private?"

Detective Williams backed away. "I'll be in the facility headquarters if you need me."

Hawkman waved and turned back to Hampton. "You want to go back to Maggie's room?"

George shook his head. "No, let's go outside."

"It's nippy out there. You think your sweater will keep you warm enough?"

"I'll be fine. This won't take but a minute."

Hawkman noticed Maggie scooting by with her walker, but she didn't even glance in their direction. He held the door open, and they stepped out into a gusty breeze. "Let's stay within the alcove." Hawkman said. It will protect us from that cold wind."

George leaned against the wall, clutched his walking stick with both hands, and scowled. "I want you to know I'm not happy about what I'm about to say."

Hawkman frowned. "Is there a problem?"

"Yes, Maggie wants me to fire you."

Surprised, Hawkman stepped back and stared at George. "Why?" Then he raised a hand. "Don't tell me, I bet I know. She's sick of being followed."

"Yep," George nodded, "and she argues I shouldn't have to pay you for protection, when the police will give it to us free."

"Does she realize she won't get the same individual attention from the force as from me?"

"I tried to talk some sense into her, but she waved it off. She's my spouse, and this is all very frustrating for her. I can't have my better half upset, so guess I'm going to have to let you go."

"I'm sorry she feels that way."

"Let me know what I owe you and I'll write out a check."

"I haven't done the paperwork on the case yet. I'll send you a bill if your advance didn't cover all the hours we've put in. Or I'll reimburse you for anything left."

George rubbed his arms. "Thank you, for all you've done."

Hawkman reached over and opened the door. "You better get in out of this cold. Tell Maggie her freedom begins now. I'll get in touch with Kevin and tell him of your decision."

George hobbled inside, glanced toward the dining hall, took a deep breath, and limped toward the eatery.

***

Hawkman headed out into the parking lot where he'd get a better signal with his cell phone. Holding onto his hat, he braved the gusts of wind and sought shelter behind his 4X4. He dialed Kevin and told him the news. He grumbled a little about not having the easy job anymore, but assured him he wouldn't miss it.

Hurrying back into the building, Hawkman made his way to the detectives' headquarters where he found Williams bent over some paperwork at his makeshift desk. "Good grief, does the paper trail follow you, even when you're out on an active case?"

Williams glanced up. "It follows me to bed at night." He placed the pen on top of the stack and leaned back in the chair. "So what did Hampton want?"

"He fired me. Said no need to pay for what the police would do for him free."

The detective threw back his head and guffawed. When he regained his composure, he leaned forward. "Sorry about that my friend, but it just struck my funny bone."

Hawkman grinned. "It hit my wallet."

"I bet it did. Are you going to abandon the case completely?"

"Not if you don't mind me hanging around. I'm in this pretty deep and would like to see what else I can find out."

"Glad to have you, but unfortunately can't put you on the payroll."

"No problem." A shadow caught Hawkman's eye, and he glanced at the door, then lowered his voice. "The doctor's here. I'll leave you two and stroll the halls for a bit."

Dr. Grahm slowly moved inside the doorway. "Hello, Mr. Casey. I hope I'm not interrupting."

"Not at all. I'm just leaving."

Hawkman stepped out into the stream of residents leaving the dining hall. He crossed through the group where he didn't have to worry about being slowed by someone pushing a walker or using a cane. Not seeing Maggie, he assumed George had joined her and they were going to be a bit late getting out. He'd like to have one last chat with her before deleting the case from his books.

He stood in the corridor awaiting the Hamptons return when he noted Margy and Jessie coming back from dinner. As they moved past him, he wondered if the women were related. They had the same gestures and even resembled each other in their facial features. He'd stop by Lisa's office one of these days and ask her.

"What are you doing hanging around my door?"

Hawkman jerked around to find Maggie standing in the arms of her walker, her face contorted in a frown.

"Waiting for you."

"I thought George let you go?"

"He did. I just came by to tell you Kevin won't be bothering you anymore. I called and relieved him of his duties."

"Thank goodness. I'll have an evening of peace. I can hardly wait to tell my friends, so they'll feel comfortable in coming around again."

"Remember Maggie, everyone is confined to their rooms after dinner."

She waved a hand. "That's a bunch of baloney. Do they suspect any of us old cronies are killers?"

"Very possible, so I wouldn't cause any problems. The police are not patient and might haul you off to spend the night in a jail cell."

She tossed her head, hitched the walker around, and headed into her room.

"Oh, by the way, where's George?"

"I sent him home. He drives me as batty as you and your helper."

chapter

THIRTY

Hawkman shook his head as Maggie disappeared into her room. He strolled to the elevator, and as he stepped onto the main floor, the smell of food made his stomach growl. He decided to go grab a sandwich and return later. First, he checked the bulletin board, and observed no event had been scheduled for today, so that would help keep the traffic down. Making his way toward the front door, he noticed the large room stood empty of residents who usually lingered and chatted after dinner. He figured they'd gone directly to their rooms.

When he went outside, the wind had died down considerably. At least he wouldn't have to hold onto his hat, or end up chasing it across the parking lot. He drove to a fast food place, ordered a hamburger, fries, and soda to go. Deciding to eat on the premises, he found a vacant slot at the front of the building and parked.

As he headed back to Morning Glory Haven, he tried to evaluate what he'd learned so far. It made him a little on edge to know Maggie had insulin in her room, and he wouldn't be there to protect her. He realized the murderer could be diabetic, and have plenty of insulin on hand to carry out a horrible deed. If he or she wasn't diabetic, they'd have to get the insulin from another source. George seemed to lose his pens or mess up a dose fairly often, and Hawkman doubted Maggie kept track of the amount on hand except when it got low. How many people had she complained to about her husband's carelessness?

If the guilty party had heard her rants, and observed her behavior, the person would know how often she left the room. Now, with George her only guardian, it wouldn't take long for the perp to discover things were back to normal. The minute the Hamptons disappeared down the hallway, it would only take a minute to pick the lock on Maggie's quarters, and take the insulin without ever getting caught.

Hawkman decided to talk to Detective Williams about checking the amount of insulin the diabetics had stored in their apartments against a next day count, minus what they'd used; then they'd know if any had disappeared. It would also help in knowing who had insulin available. It might help in tracking down the culprit. He was willing to try anything, as he didn't want another unnecessary death to occur. These people deserved every day of life they could muster.

When he reached Morning Glory Haven, he immediately went to find Williams, only to find the door locked. Searching through the first floor, he came across an officer guarding the corridor and asked where the detective had gone.

"He was called out on an emergency and should be back shortly," he said.

"Are the residents cooperating?"

"So far, except for the Hampton woman on the second floor. She doesn't want to stay in her quarters."

Hawkman suppressed a grin. "Figures. Where does she want to go?"

"I walked with her up and down the hallway as she knocked on almost every door and said goodnight."

"Sounds mighty calm so far. By the way, do you know if Detective Williams got a list of the diabetics?"

"Yes, he got them on all floors and we've talked with each person. They all keep extra insulin in their rooms. We recorded the amounts and the detective has the information in his files."

"Good. How about Maggie Hampton?"

He nodded.

Since Williams had already gotten the information, he didn't need to bother Maggie again. She didn't appear in the best of moods, and he didn't particularly care about hearing her tirade again. He headed toward the front door and since the lab had found sleep inducing chemicals in Mrs. Owens' body, he wondered if she'd taken an extra dose on her own? He needed to talk to her daughter. Tomorrow he'd speak to Ms. Montgomery and ask if Sidney Wilder had come to pick up her mother's things yet.

His thoughts were interrupted when he spotted Detective Williams hurrying toward the makeshift headquarters. He motioned for Hawkman to follow. After turning on the lights, Williams flopped down in the chair at the table and opened the file he had in his hands.

"I received the full autopsy report on Gladys Owens. We now have the brand of insulin administered. The problem is, it's very popular and every pharmacy in town carries it, plus the mail-in places where it would be almost impossible to check, unless we found a receipt."

"Did the report tell what kind of sleeping aid they found? Hawkman asked.

"Yes, a prescription drug called Halcion. Very strong medication. I'm going to check with her physician and see if it was prescribed."

"She must have had trouble getting a good night's rest."

Williams nodded. "Sure sounds like it."

"Have you scheduled a follow up on the insulin each person has in his or her personal stash?"

"Yes, we'll compare it with the record we have each day, minus new prescriptions and the amount used."

"Good. Of course, until we have another death, which I hate to think about, we might not find our scoundrel."

"Unless we can catch the perp in the act."

Hawkman rose. "I'm going to call it a night and head out of here. I'll see you in the morning."

Williams raked his fingers across the stubble on his chin. "Soon as the fresh crew checks in, I hope to take off, get a shower and a few winks of sleep myself."

"See ya tomorrow."

Hawkman left the building, climbed into his SUV and journeyed home.

***

Tuesday morning, Hawkman arrived at his office before the donut baker had the ovens fired up. He made a pot of coffee and sat down at his desk to go over the Hamptons' financial statement. After writing out the hours Kevin had documented and his part of the fee, he discovered George would owe about five hundred extra dollars over the initial payment. He leaned back in his chair and wondered if Maggie had figured this out herself, and decided they'd paid him enough. Grinning at the thought, he wrote out a check for Kevin, addressed an envelope, and planned to mail it on his way to Morning Glory Haven. He tucked the invoice for George into his pocket and had just unplugged the coffee urn when the phone rang.

Punching on the speaker, he gave his usual greeting.

"Hawkman, Detective Williams. I'm glad you're at the office. I need your help in trying to talk some sense into your ex-client."

"The Hamptons?"

"Yeah, the Mrs., she's a spitfire and won't cooperate with my officers."

"Okay, I'll be right over, but not sure I can do any good. Is George there yet?"

"No, and I can't reach him on the phone. Tried several times, but no answer."

Hawkman frowned. "That's odd. He's usually there by now. I think I'll run by his place and check on him."

"You think there might be a problem?"

"He's diabetic and not good about checking his blood sugar. His doctor told me he worried about him. I better make sure he's okay. Has Maggie tried to reach him?"

"Yeah, but she doesn't seem too concerned. Says he might be in the shower or running an errand."

"I'll be there after I run by his place."

Hawkman hurried out of the office and drove to the Hamptons' home. When he pulled up in front, he noticed the white Cadillac sitting in the driveway and not tucked in the garage. "Looks like he's been out this morning," he mumbled, heading for the entry.

He heard Pesky barking as the doorbell chimed. It sounded as if she was running back and forth for George to hurry.

"Stay," he heard Hampton say, as he opened the door.

When he saw Hawkman, his face clouded. "Something wrong?"

Pesky darted by George and ran around Hawkman's legs. He reached down and petted the beast to calm her. "I don't know. Got a call from Detective Williams a few minutes ago. He said you hadn't shown up and he couldn't reach you, so thought I'd drop by."

George stepped back. "Come in. I ran to the pharmacy to pick up some insulin; I was running low. What's the problem? Is Maggie okay?"

"As far as I know she's fine physically, but giving the police a hard time, not sure what about. I'm headed over there now."

George threw his hands in the air. "I don't know what I'm going to do with that woman. I'd like to bring her home so I could keep an eye on her. All the attention she gets over there makes me unhappy. I'm afraid someone's going to hurt her."

"Since you're okay, I'm going to head over to Morning Glory Haven and find out what's going on." Hawkman turned to leave, then swiveled around, and pulled the sheet of paper from his pocket. "Oh, before I forget, here's the invoice for my services. You owe five hundred. Thanks for hiring me."

"I'll get a check to you. Sorry it was a short haul. I'd been happy to keep you on until this whole mess was solved."

"I understand."

"Tell Maggie I'll be there shortly."

Hawkman left Hampton holding Pesky by the collar and trying to get her back into the house. As he pulled away from the curb, he glanced in the side mirror, and noticed George must have finally succeeded in getting his pet inside, as he'd shut the front door. His mind went back to their conversation. What did he mean about all the attention Maggie got at the home? Hawkman wasn't sure what to make of it, but shook it off as one of George's offhanded remarks.

chapter

THIRTY-ONE

Hawkman arrived at Morning Glory and went straight to Maggie's room without stopping to check with Detective Williams. Stepping out of the elevator he almost ran into Carmen Sanders. She let out a yelp as he grabbed her shoulder so she wouldn't fall.

"Forgive me, I had so much on my mind I wasn't paying attention," Hawkman said.

Straightening herself, she forced a smile. "No problem. It's been a bit hectic around here. I don't think any of us are in our right minds at the moment."

"How are the residents taking the rumor of a possible murder in the facility?"

She shook her head and gazed at the floor. "Not good, I'm afraid. Many are talking about moving out, even though I've told them Mrs. Owens death could have been an accident caused by her own hand."

"I'm sure they fear for themselves."

Nodding, she stepped past him and moved into the elevator. "Have a good day."

He watched the door slide shut and heard the hum of the pulleys as the machine carried her to the ground floor. Moving down the hallway to Maggie's apartment, he knocked.

"Come in," she said.

Not knowing what reaction he'd meet with when Maggie saw him, he turned the knob and pushed the door open slowly. She sat on the couch near the window, and he could hear the clicking of her knitting needles. A woman who could go from one mood to the next in a blink of an eye, Maggie looked very serene at the moment.

When she glanced up, her facial features turned sour. "Damn, I just dropped a stitch. What are you doing here?"

Hawkman stepped inside. "A couple of things. First, George told me to tell you he'd be here shortly."

"You didn't have to come up here to tell me. I just talked to him on the phone. Our life was quiet and calm until you entered the picture. Now everything is turned upside down."

"Really? I don't understand your statement. George hired me, I didn't go to him."

She threw her knitting in the basket. "Okay, what's the other thing?"

"Detective Williams asked me to talk to you about your behavior. He said you were giving his officers trouble."

"Oh, my, what a bunch of baloney. I got hungry last night and went to the dining room before it closed, got a bite to eat, then stopped and worked on a jig saw puzzle." She slapped her hands on her thighs. "I didn't want to come back to my apartment and told them so."

"Don't you think a little cooperation with the police might help? They won't be here long and want to keep everyone safe. You make it hard when they can't keep track of your whereabouts."

"Why do they care about an old crippled woman using a walker? Do they think I'm a killer?"

"They don't know."

She pointed a finger. "You tell them."

"I don't know either, Maggie."

Her mouth dropped open, then she frowned. "What do you mean, you don't know?"

About that time, George entered the room, glanced at the two, tossed the sack he carried in his hand onto the coffee table, then flopped down on the couch, leaning his cane against the arm. "I can tell by the looks on both your faces, things are not peaches and cream."

"Your dear private investigator just called me a murderer."

George straightened and threw a disarming look at Hawkman. "Why?"

Hawkman scowled. "I told her, I didn't know if she was one."

"What the hell brought this on?"

He quickly related their conversation. "Maggie is determined to cause problems. If she continues in this vein, it wouldn't surprise me if Detective Williams didn't haul her down to the jailhouse and let her spend a couple of days behind bars."

"He wouldn't do that," Maggie said with disgust.

"If you're hindering an investigation, he certainly could. I'm just warning you." He glanced at George. "It's up to you to keep her under control. I'm just passing along the message."

Hawkman put his hand on the door knob. "I won't be bothering you anymore, so please heed my words."

He left the apartment and went in search of the detective and found him in the makeshift headquarters reading through a stack of papers.

Williams glanced up. "Pull up a chair. Did you talk any sense into the Hampton woman?"

"All I can say, is I tried. I told her you might take her to jail for a day or two if she didn't straighten up."

The detective smirked. "I doubt she believed you, but let's hope she thinks about it." Williams then pulled out a sheet of paper from the stack, and handed it to Hawkman. "Thought you might be interested in this last report from the lab on Mrs. Owens' tests."

After reading it, he frowned. "This sounds like the woman committed suicide."

"I'm not buying it. I spoke with Mrs. Owens' doctor this morning and he has no record of prescribing Halcion. He said she never complained about having trouble sleeping. I also spoke with her daughter. She swears her mother never had suicidal tendencies, was a happy person, loved

Morning Glory Haven and was excited about her upcoming visit to their new home. Owens' friends have said much the same thing."

"Then it sounds like someone drugged her, but how?"

"This stuff dissolves in alcohol, and Ms. Owens liked her toddy at night. They found residue of Halcion in her glass."

Hawkman rubbed his chin. "Sounds like someone stopped by for a drink."

Williams pointed his pencil. "She didn't have a roommate, so it could have been anyone. Since she let them inside, she obviously knew the person."

Hawkman leaned forward, resting his arms on his thighs. "It means all her friends are under suspicion."

Williams nodded.

Scratching his head, Hawkman made a face. "Did any of the residents see anyone coming or going from her room that evening?"

"No one."

The detective leaned back in his chair. "Tell me again why Mrs. Hampton keeps extra insulin in her room?"

Hawkman explained about George and his neglect of his own health. "Why are you interested in them?"

"What do you know about George personally, besides his health history? Do you know what kind of business he had before he retired?"

"Now that you've asked," Hawkman shrugged. "No, I don't know, other than he must have done quite well."

"I did a little checking. He had a machine shop, and on the side, he worked as a locksmith. A very skilled one from what I understand. The man could get into these apartments with little effort."

Hawkman stiffened. "You're not suggesting George is a killer?"

"His wife played a major role in their business. She knew how to run the machines and make keys. She even went with him when a home had several locks to change. Her skills were as good as his."

"Why would they hire me to investigate?"

"They also fired you. Probably because you were keeping too close an eye on the misses. I'd say it's a clever scheme. The ploy kept the heat off them, until they thought you were getting too near the truth."

"That's really hard for me to buy," Hawkman said, shaking his head.

"Maybe, but give it some thought. It's hard for me to believe a successful businessman can't keep track of his insulin."

"What's their motive?"

"Who knows. There have been stranger cases."

chapter

THIRTY-TWO

Hawkman left the detective's makeshift office and wandered into the big recreation room. Williams had planted a devastating seed into his head. It made sense, but he didn't like it. He thought about returning to Maggie's apartment, gave it a second thought, and decided it wasn't the right time to approach the Hamptons about this problem. The police would converge on them soon enough, and he knew Maggie wouldn't stand for it. All hell would probably break loose in the next few days. The whole scenario worried him.

He pulled a toothpick from his pocket and chewed on it. A cigarette would taste mighty good right now. He leaned against the wall and observed what the people were doing. Several were playing card games, some men were concentrating on their checkers, and a few others were relaxing with an open book on the comfortable chairs in the library area. Everything looked so peaceful. No one seemed uptight about what was going on.

Out of the corner of his eye, a movement caught his attention. He turned his head and recognized the Marketing Director, Carmen Sanders, coming down the hallway with a sweater draped over her arm. Hawkman pushed away from the wall and touched his hat. "Hello, Ms. Sanders, you seem in a hurry."

"One of our ladies always forgets to take her sweater when she goes to the dining room, and asked me to get it."

"Do they give you their key to do these chores?" he asked.

"Sometimes, otherwise, I use my master key. Excuse me, I need to deliver this to her before she has one of the waitresses call me." She turned abruptly, and headed toward the dining area.

Hawkman watched as she disappeared around the corner and wondered how many master keys floated around the place. It could put a few more people under scrutiny. He decided to talk to Williams about such a possibility.

He poked his head into the room, only to find a couple of officers conferring in a serious tone with the detective. Figuring this wasn't an appropriate time to disturb him, he backed out of the room and decided to try Mr. Mackle's office.

When Hawkman approached the receptionist, she glanced up and sucked in her breath.

"Hello, Mr. Casey. Can I help you?"

"I'd like to speak with Mr. Mackle. I only need a couple minutes."

"I'll see if he's available." She left her desk, knocked softly on the closed door between the two offices, then stepped inside. Returning within a few seconds, she gestured for Hawkman to enter.

"He'll see you now."

Mr. Mackle stood and held out his hand. "Hello, Mr. Casey. I hope you don't have bad news."

"Neither bad nor good. I need to know how many master keys are floating around."

He frowned. "Only my top staff are issued them. We have to be able to get into the flats in case there's an emergency. It would be foolish to only have one set in my office, which could cause a delay in getting help."

"I understand. How many are out there?"

"Six."

"Who has them?"

"I have one, plus an extra in my safe. The others were given to, Lisa Montgomery, Perry Foster, Don Jackson, and Carmen Sanders."

"Do they carry them or are they left in their offices?"

"Preferably, they secure them on their main key rings. I've instructed my employees not to leave the keys in an unlocked office. That would be asking for trouble."

"Have you ever had a resident complain about an invasion of their rooms?"

Mackle shook his head. "Never."

"I won't keep you any longer. Thank you for being candid with me. I appreciate it."

"No problem. The sooner we can get the police out of here, the happier I'll be."

"How are the people doing?"

"My staff are nervous wrecks. A few of the residents have complained about having to retreat to their rooms after dinner. I've assured them all, things will be back to normal very soon. One advantage in dealing with the older population, they do adjust well. However, I don't want to lose any tenants, and their patience will only hold out so long before they feel their freedoms are being trampled on. I can't blame them, they want to be able to take care of themselves as long as possible. This investigation is hampering their independence."

"Hopefully, things will be resolved quickly."

Hawkman left Mackle's office and went back to see if Williams was free. When he entered the makeshift office, he saw him reading what looked like a report. The detective glanced up, put it down, and leaned back in his chair.

"I'm going to go question the Hamptons in a few minutes. I hope the Mister is there too. You want to come?"

"George should be at her apartment by now. I think I better stay out of it. Maggie's not happy with me, and it would just hamper your interrogation."

"Have you stumbled onto anything that might help us out?"

"I spoke with Mr. Mackle about master keys. It appears several employees carry them, and have access to the apartments."

"Did you find out their names?"

"Yes, but haven't had a chance to examine their resumes."

"I'm going to have to pull my men out of here tomorrow, as we've got a big drug sting coming up in the next few days. Hope you'll stay around and keep a handle on things."

"If word gets out about the Hamptons firing me, I don't think the facility would be comfortable with me hanging about."

Williams tapped his temple with his forefinger. "I'm sure you owe me one. What about if I ask you to keep on investigating without pay?"

Hawkman suppressed a grin. "Do you remember the favor you did for me?"

"Not right off the top of my head, but I'm sure there's one."

"Sounds good to me. I'd like to nose around here for a while, as my gut tells me there's something going on."

"I'll speak with Mr. Mackle and tell him I've hired you. I'll give him the word to cooperate fully."

"You think he'll buy it?"

He pulled out his badge and flipped open the leather holder. "This works wonders."

"You're right."

About that moment, one of the officers walked into the room. "Did you call for me, sir?"

Williams stood. "Yes, I want you to accompany me while a question one of the residents."

Hawkman stepped back. "If you don't mind, I'll wander around until you're through. I'd like to hear the results of this interview."

Williams furrowed his brows. "Are you trying to tell me something I don't already know?"

Hawkman grinned as he watched the two men head for the elevator. "Good luck."

Meandering over to the library section, he spotted a newspaper and decided to catch up on the news. He sat down in one of the luxurious leather chairs facing the living room, so he wouldn't miss the detective when he returned from questioning Maggie. Engrossed in an article, he jerked his head around when someone tapped him on the shoulder.

"Sorry, Mr. Casey, I didn't mean to disturb you."

"Hello, Mr. Jackson. No problem, I'm just waiting for Detective Williams. Where have you been? The only Marketing Director I've seen around here lately has been Ms. Sanders."

"She did double time for me when I caught a virus and had to stay home. I just returned to work today, and Mr. Mackle informed me about all that's been going on. What a shock."

Hawkman folded up the paper. "Do you have a minute?"

Don sat down in the chair next to him. "Sure."

"Do you carry a master key to all the apartments."

"Yes. If there's an emergency, I need to get into the room immediately."

"I understand where that would be a necessity. Do you ever enter the private quarters at any other times."

"On occasions one of the residents might ask me to retrieve something for them, you know, like a sweater or coat. One time a woman asked me to get her purse. She'd walked off without it and it had her key inside. Sometimes they lock themselves out, so it comes in handy."

"I can definitely see why. Tell me about Ms. Sanders. She seems a bit distant."

"She's different, but gets along very well with the residents." Don stood. "I could visit for hours, but guess I better get busy with my duties."

"Thanks for your time. I appreciate it."

Hawkman watched Jackson take off down the hallway. About that time, the elevator door slid open. Williams and his officer stepped out on the main floor. He could tell by the frown on the detective's face, things had not gone well.

chapter

THIRTY-THREE

Detective Williams excused his officer, then motioned for Hawkman. "We need to talk."

The two men entered the makeshift office. Williams flopped down in the chair and ran his hands across his face. "I'm still trying to figure out how the hell you worked with those two people, especially, Maggie?"

"Did she give you a hard time again?"

"When I started questioning her about the insulin, she yelled at me and told me to get out."

"Were you able to settle her down?"

"Not until I told her I'd take her to headquarters, throw her in jail, then search her apartment, if she didn't cooperate."

"Have you come to a conclusion about the couple?"

Williams nodded. "The Hamptons are number one on my suspects list. Especially, the woman."

Hawkman stiffened. "Really! Why?"

"Her attitude. A very cocky and obstinate person. She told me if it hadn't been for you being so nosey, none of this would be happening. No one would have found out Gladys Owens died of an overdose, if you hadn't suggested an autopsy."

Hawkman shook his head. "That's all circumstantial evidence. She's very aggressive when you push her buttons. I don't think she'd kill anyone."

Williams stared at Hawkman. "That's where we differ."

"I'm not doubting your reasoning. It's just hard for me to believe."

"I can see where you'd never expect those two to plan a scheme. You were to close to the situation. He hired you on the premise of finding a killer. Naturally, you wouldn't look in their direction."

"You've definitely got a point. Who else do you have on your list?"

"No one right now. I'm hoping while I'm directing the outside sting operation you'll be able to get some information on the staff. With luck, this project won't take too long and I'll be able to get back with you in less than a week."

"After you get Mackle's approval, I'll start probing."

"I'm heading there now. Maybe I can catch him before he leaves for the day."

"I'll wait here to get your report."

"Okay, I should be back in a few."

Detective Williams scurried down the hallway and made a beeline for Mackle's office. It didn't take fifteen minutes before he returned. He gave Hawkman the okay sign. "We're set, he'll cooperate with you fully and have his staff do the same. I'm taking my men out tonight. So feel free to start first thing in the morning."

Hawkman stood. "I'll be here early."

***

When Hawkman arrived home, Jennifer bombarded him with questions about the Hamptons. "At least Detective Williams wants you to remain on the case. Do you really think George or Maggie are capable of murder?"

"I wish I could answer your question. At first, I certainly didn't have them on my list, but Williams is convinced they've played me for a fool. After I thought about it, I'm not sure what to think."

Jennifer frowned. "If they're guilty of foul play, they used you, but not as a fool. You're not a dummy."

He smiled. "Thank you, my sweet wife. Now, I've got to get some sleep. I have much work to do tomorrow."

Wednesday morning, Hawkman scooted out of bed, so as not to awaken Jennifer, dressed and grabbed a yogurt out of the refrigerator to eat on the way to Medford. He had his briefcase stored under the passenger seat, so he didn't need to stop at the office, so he drove straight to Morning Glory Haven.

As he strolled through the large recreation room, carrying the valise, he noticed the place had a lighter atmosphere as the residents sat at the tables with their cups of coffee, talking and laughing. The minute they saw him, the chatter ceased and he felt their stares follow him across the room. He hurried through and went to Mr. Mackle's office where he was immediately admitted.

"Hello, Mr. Casey," Mackle said. "Detective Williams talked to me about you taking over the investigation for a few days until he and his officers returned. How can I help you?"

"I'm sure you were hoping this would be over by now, but we still haven't come to any conclusions and need more information. It appears you've informed the residents the police have left."

"Yes, I conferred with the detective and he said I could relax the rules until they got back."

"Excellent, because my job is to go through the files of your staff and it won't involve any of the patrons."

"Good, they'll be able to enjoy a few days without the feeling of being watched. How can I help?"

"I'd like all the resumes and application forms from each of the staff when they applied for their jobs. I'd like to start with your top members and work down the list. Who should I talk to about obtaining these records?"

"My manager, Peter Foster. I'll accompany you to his office."

The two men stepped into the hallway and walked down the corridor. Mr. Mackle instructed Foster to cooperate fully with Hawkman. He then left the two men to work out the specifics.

"Good seeing you again, Mr. Casey."

"Same here," Hawkman said, as they shook hands.

"How would you like to do this?"

"I'm sure you don't want the originals removed, and you certainly don't want me taking up a corner of your office for several days. I'll pick out what I need from each file and make copies.

"Sounds fine. Whose would you like to see first?"

"I'd like to start with Mr. Mackle."

Perry raised his brows. "I'm sorry, but we don't have his file in this office. It would be with the owner, since he's the one who hires the executive directors for the homes."

"Okay, let's begin with yours, and go down the line."

He moved to the filing cabinet in the far corner, removed several folders, and carried them to the desk. "This should keep you busy. Hand me the papers you want copied and I'll tend to that task." Perry opened a drawer and gave Hawkman a couple of empty folders. "You can put your copies in these."

"Thanks."

They worked closely as Hawkman went through each folder and meticulously chose what he wanted. Perry copied the papers, placed the originals back in the files and handed Hawkman the duplicates.

"We've gone through what I'd call the top staff. Do you want to start on the secondary employees?"

Hawkman raised his hand. "Not right now. These will keep me busy. However, I don't see a file for Carmen Sanders."

Foster shuffled through the stack of folders on his desk. "You're right." Going back to the filing cabinet, he got down on his haunches and sorted through the rest, then stood with his fist on his hips. That's odd, I haven't needed any of these files for at least a year. Let me check with Ms. Montgomery." He crossed over to the phone, picked it up and dialed. After several seconds, he hung up. "She's not available right now. I'll check with her later and find out if she's got it, or knows where it went."

After placing the folders into his briefcase, Hawkman stood. "I'll stop by this afternoon or tomorrow, and see if you've found it. Thank you for your patience and taking the time to work with me on collecting this data. I really appreciate it."

Perry smiled. "No problem. I hope you find everything in order and no shadows cast on our small group."

"I hope so too."

Hawkman left the home and went to his office. While his computer booted up, he put on the coffee pot and settled in for some serious investigating.

chapter

THIRTY-FOUR

Hawkman removed his hat, hung it on the nail nearby, pulled the two folders of copies from his briefcase, and leaned back in his chair. The first group of papers he picked from the file were Perry Foster's. He read through the resume and discovered Foster had been with another company for years before moving in as Manager of Morning Glory Haven. A letter of recommendation was attached and indicated he'd been a highly successful manager. Unfortunately, the former company had folded.

Foster had served four years in the military, graduated from college, married, and had three children. He played an active role in the community and his church. The man had worked steadily for many years, and appeared to be a level headed guy. Hawkman saw no black marks that would indicate any sort of problems.

He took a new file from his desk, marked it 'read' with a black marker, and placed Foster's papers inside, then pulled the next set toward him. These belonged to Lisa Montgomery. He noted she'd held down several jobs, and had never been married. She had a college education with a major in business management. Her former employments were in the same field, but it appeared she'd searched for a better salary, as she had the full responsibility of her elderly mother, who shared the home. Several letters of recommendations from former employers were attached, along with a letter from her pastor. She'd also taken several classes in her field at the local college.

Hawkman saw nothing suspicious in her records. He slid the papers into the read file, and poured himself a cup of coffee. Before sitting back down, he walked over to the window and stared out over the parking lot. His mind drifted to his dealings with George and Maggie. He didn't agree with Detective Williams, but he'd been wrong before. He shook his head and ventured back to the desk.

The next set of papers belonged to Don Jackson, the marketing director who'd showed him around Morning Glory Haven, and whom he'd just seen again. He had graduated from high school, and college, then gone into the service, where he served eight years, spending the majority of the time in a Special Service Unit in Iraq. Hawkman read on quite impressed with the accomplishments of this young man. His talents included top marksmanship with several different types of weapons, along with speaking three different languages fluently.

Hawkman wondered why this young man in his late thirties, with such a great background, would settle on being a Marketing Director in an old folks home? It certainly didn't pay as much as he could be making. He realized jobs were scarce in this economy and it might just be a stopover gap in Jackson's life, until he could find something better. He was still single, so he only had to take care of his own needs. Maybe he just needed easy employment so he could enjoy some downtime after the service. Surely, he didn't hold a grudge against the elderly, especially, after seeing what they'd gone through in a war-torn country. There were several reference letters in the young man's favor, ranging from a ranking officer, to the pastor of a small local church.

Hawkman put Jackson's papers into the read file. So far, he'd only gained a small insight into the people involved at Morning Glory Haven, no suspects. He'd noticed there were no updates on any of the files so far. Obviously, people were working out and doing well. Perry Foster had told him there were very decent perks at the facility for all the employees. Something that most companies were no longer offering.

Standing and stretching his tall frame, Hawkman dumped the cold coffee down the sink in the half-bath, then poured a fresh cup and sat back down at the desk. He went through the rest of the top employees involved with the Independent Living part of the organization, which consisted of two chefs, the kitchen manager, head of the cleaning staff, and the top handy man. There were still many employees to check, but he'd decided to research a few at a time and see what he could come up with. So far, he lacked the file on Carmen Sanders.

Placing the resumes into his briefcase, he'd just about decided to call it a day when he heard a loud banging which sounded vaguely familiar. He went to the door and looked down the stairwell. There stood George Hampton, with his cane in the air.

"What's going on?" Hawkman called.

"I need to talk to you. Could you come down here for a moment?"

"Sure. Want a cup of coffee?"

"Not this time, I'm going home and have a stiff drink."

Hawkman loped down the stairs and joined George at the bottom. "So what's on your mind?"

George held out his hand with a check in it. "For one thing here's the extra money I owe you."

"Thank you."

"Now I want to start all over and hire you back,"

Hawkman stared at the man. "Did I hear you right? You want to hire me again?"

A breeze caught the old man's thinning hair and blew it into his face. He took a swat at the strands with his gnarled fingers and shoved them out of his eyes. "Yep, Maggie wants you back."

"What in the world changed her mind?"

"She doesn't like the detective. Says he's mean and she likes you a lot better. At least when you scolded her, you didn't threaten to send her to jail like he did."

Hawkman grinned. "Williams has a duty to do and he doesn't show favorites. He's a good man and does a fine job."

George leaned on his cane. "She feels like he suspects us as the murderers. To tell the truth, it scares us both."

"Why do you think he's suspicious of you two?"

"Because Maggie keeps my insulin in her room. The police don't seem to think it's necessary, since I'm the diabetic, not Maggie."

Hawkman shrugged. "He also knows you were a locksmith and Maggie had the skill too, as she helped you out on occasions. So you could pick one of those locks in the home without leaving a scratch. So he came to a reasonable conclusion. Wouldn't you say?"

Hampton pointed his cane. "Do you think we're guilty of killing our friends?"

"I don't know. Are you?"

George's face turned red and he slammed his cane against the bannister. "You're no better than the police. I take it back. I don't want to hire you again."

"I'm being the devil's advocate and trying to show you how the detective came to his decision. He hasn't finished his investigation, but right now you two are the prime suspects. It makes sense."

"It don't to me." George turned his back to Hawkman. "I'll have to think about this whole mess."

"Detective Williams has asked me to stay on the case. He won't be around for a few days and I'm taking over. So I really can't help you out right now. However, I'll do my best on trying to prove your innocence, if it's warranted."

George turned and glared at him. "What do you mean, if it's warranted? I've never killed anyone, neither has Maggie. We're not that kind of people."

"Seldom does a murderer ever admit it."

chapter

THIRTY-FIVE

Hawkman watched George as he stormed toward his car at an awkward gait. He kicked at a pebble on the sidewalk, then turned and went upstairs. In his heart, he knew those two people wouldn't hurt anyone intentionally. Their behavior had sent Detective Williams into a tantrum and he could understand why. If you didn't know the Hamptons, the actions and verbal outrages they displayed made them look guiltier than hell. It would be up to him to prove their innocence. He rinsed his cup and coffee pot, picked up his briefcase, locked the door, then left for home. It'd been a long day.

When he arrived at Copco Lake, Jennifer greeted him with a big kiss, while Ms. Marple twined around his ankles.

"Glad you're home before midnight. I'm dying to hear the latest on the case."

Placing his valise on the counter, he opened the refrigerator and removed a beer. "Want me to fix you a drink?"

"Not yet, after I eat." She reached around him and lifted out a platter holding two big marinated steaks.

"Wow! Those look delicious."

"I figured if you didn't make it home in time tonight, I could let them set until tomorrow."

"While I'm getting things ready, tell me what you've done all day."

"Not a whole lot. George asked me to work for him again."

Jennifer twisted her head around. "You're kidding. What brought that on?"

"Maggie didn't like the way Detective Williams talked to her. He accused her and George, in so many words, of being murderers."

She put her hands on her hips. "That doesn't sound like Williams."

"Maggie knows how to push people's buttons, and she found the detective's. It sent him off on a tirade."

"Boy, she must have punched him hard, as he's usually very patient."

"He's got a lot on his mind, plus he's short of men and funds. Some of them have to work double shifts, and he doesn't like to push them to the point of danger. I think that's why he wanted me to help. I could cover Morning Glory Haven while he went out on the drug sting."

"You're not taking any pay. At least Hampton wanted to hire you."

"I owed Williams."

Jennifer threw back her head and laughed. "Right."

Hawkman grinned. "You won't let me get by with anything."

"Nope," she said, with a mischievous smile.

***

Thursday morning, Hawkman left Copco Lake and drove straight to Morning Glory Haven. He hoisted the briefcase from the passenger seat and carried it inside. When he turned down the hallway toward Ms. Montgomery's office, Julie, the receptionist at the front desk, called out to him.

"Mr. Casey, you won't find anyone in their offices right now. They're in a staff meeting."

He turned on his heel. "How long do they usually last?"

She shrugged. "All depends on what's on the agenda. Sometimes they get out within thirty minutes, other times they're in there all morning." She checked her watch. "It looks like a long session today as they've already been in there over an hour."

"I knew I should have called ahead of time. I'll drop by after lunch."

"You'll have better luck then."

"Thanks," he said, moving toward the entry.

Just as he grabbed the handle of the front door, he heard someone calling his name. He swiveled around and saw Maggie pushing her walker from the dining room area, waving a hand.

"Mr. Casey, wait a minute."

He met her half way and she pointed to the couch in one of the sitting areas.

"Let's chat a minute," she said, plopping down on the sofa.

Hawkman took the overstuffed chair across from her and placed his briefcase on the coffee table. "Okay, what do you want to talk about."

She had a very demure expression, and folded her hands in her lap. "George called me last night after talking to you. He said you were now investigating for the police and he'd decided he didn't want you working for him again after all. I disagreed with him completely, and want you to let us hire you back."

"You didn't like the way I did things, so why the change of mind?"

She looked up at him with tears in her eyes. "Because I'm scared the detective is going to put George and me in jail. We need your help."

"If you haven't done anything wrong, he's not going to do that."

She kept wringing her hands. "He thinks I have no business storing George's insulin in my room." Her teary eyes immediately turned fiery. "It's none of his business what sort of things George and I have worked out. It's in our best interest."

"Did you explain the situation."

Throwing her hands up in exasperation, she clamored, "No, he didn't give me a chance. He just kept threatening us."

"Right now, Maggie, I can't take George's money while I'm helping out the police. When the detective returns, I'll bring him to your apartment and you can explain to him why you have the insulin in your room. If you still want me to pick up where I left off, then we'll talk about it again."

She nodded. "Okay. How long will it be before he's back?"

"Next week."

Heaving herself off the couch, she grabbed her walker. "Maybe you'll find the killer beforehand."

"If there is one."

"I hope, regardless or not, you can end this problem before it ruins me."

"I'll do the best I can."

Hawkman watched Maggie, her shoulders slumped, scoot toward the elevator. She didn't appear as the vibrant woman of a few days ago. He exhaled loudly, picked up his valise and exited the building. Driving to his office, he couldn't get the Hamptons off his mind. They were going through a rough time, and he didn't like seeing what it was doing to them.

He detoured to the bakery before climbing the stairs to the office. A cup of coffee and a bear claw would satisfy his appetite for several hours. He booted up the computer and went to the special search site which he was registered to use due to his employment in the Agency. He threw up Robert Mackle's name first and it came up with no problem. The man's record appeared impeccable. Hawkman could see why this investigation made Mackle nervous. A black mark on his record could keep him from getting other employment in his field.

Next he typed in Carmen Sanders. It stopped him in his tracks as he read with interest the history of this woman. He printed out the background that started in high school and ended the day she took the job at Morning Glory Haven. Leaning back in his chair, he stared at the sheets in his hand. Marking several passages in red, he rubbed a hand across his chin. This case was starting to take on a completely new look. It really made him curious to see her file.

He placed the paper aside and returned to the computer. He hadn't looked up Lisa Montgomery yet, so he typed in her name. It appeared to be quite a common handle, so he had to scroll several pages and read many introductions before coming across her history. He printed out what he found. As questions formed in his mind, he glanced at the clock on his computer. Taking a couple of folders from his desk drawer, he marked them with Carmen's and Lisa's names. Sliding the separate papers into each one, he placed the files into his briefcase, left the office, and headed back to Morning Glory Haven.

chapter

THIRTY-SIX

Briefcase in hand, Hawkman crossed the large recreation room in long strides, then turned down the hallway toward the head offices. When he reached Foster's, he knocked, then stepped inside when he heard the instructions to come in.

Immediately upon seeing Hawkman, Foster slapped his forehead. "Oh, my gosh, I completely forgot to touch base with Ms. Montgomery on Ms. Sanders' file. Have a seat and I'll go check right now."

When he entered Lisa's cubicle, she glanced up, removed the reading glasses perched on her nose, and placed them on the desk.

"Hi. What can I do for you?"

"Do you have a few minutes? I need to discuss an important matter."

"Certainly." She gestured toward the chair in front of her desk. "Have a seat."

"Mr. Casey is doing some serious investigation, and we discovered yesterday the application file of Carmen Sanders is missing. Do you have it or know where it went?"

She frowned and rose from her desk. "Gee, I haven't had to look at those files for a long time. Let me check." After rummaging through her cabinet, she turned. "I certainly don't have it here." She tapped her chin. "You know I might have left it at my house, as I remember now, I needed some information for Mr. Mackle and took several folders home over a weekend. I'll run and check. I know right where it might be, if it's there."

"Great, I'd appreciate it." He stood and went back to his office.

***

Lisa waited until Perry shut the door, then opened the top drawer of her desk and withdrew the portable intercom. She punched the number and the small screen flashed 'no response'. Knowing this meant the machine was turned off, she checked the duty roster and noted Carmen wasn't scheduled to come in until one in the afternoon. She flipped through the Rolodex, picked up the phone and dialed. This time she heard the answering machine.

"Carmen, if you're there, please pick up. This is Lisa at work." She chewed on her lower lip for several seconds before dropping the receiver on the cradle. "Damn!" she hissed. She then tried Carmen's cell phone and it kept giving her a bad signal alert.

Getting out of her chair, she paced the office floor. This could become a big mess if that private investigator digs any deeper. She left the office, carrying her purse, and stopped at the receptionist's desk. "I'll be gone about a half hour." Lisa went out to the parking lot, climbed into her car and drove off.

***

Hawkman had checked with Perry Foster and knew Carmen Sanders wouldn't be on duty until later, so he went to his vehicle, deciding to catch her when she came into work. It appeared the employees tended to park all in one area, and he found an empty slot. He saw Lisa Montgomery go to her car, and figured she was going to search for Carmen Sanders' file; Perry said she could have it at home. Since he had time, he decided to follow her and see where she lived. The woman had no idea what type of vehicle he drove, so he didn't worry about her spotting him if he stayed at a distance, and better yet, if he removed his cowboy hat. He knew it changed his whole appearance, so he placed it on the passenger seat.

Lisa definitely had a destination in mind as Hawkman tailed her. When she stopped in front of an address, he had the idea it wasn't her home because she parked in the street and not in the driveway. He pulled behind a parked van a block away. Taking his binoculars from the glove compartment, he watched her hurry to the front door. She rang the bell, stood for several seconds, then removed a pad of paper and pen from her purse. After writing something, she peered into the mailbox hanging beside the front door, then dropped the piece of paper inside, and hastened back to her car.

Hawkman now became more interested in what Lisa wrote than following her. He waited until she turned the corner before he parked in front of the house. He strolled up the front sidewalk and knocked. Knowing his height would shield the mailbox from the street's view, he lifted out the paper and quickly read the content. 'URGENT! I need to speak to you immediately. Do NOT talk to Mr. Casey before seeing me. Lisa.' He dropped the note back inside, and stepped off the small porch. Why would she leave such a message? It might be best to wait right here and catch Ms. Sanders before she had a chance to read her mail.

Hawkman stayed in his vehicle and watched Carmen's house until twenty minutes before she was due at work. He doubted now she'd come home, but would go straight to Morning Glory Haven. Turning the key, he drove away.

Driving back to the facility, he had second thoughts about hitting Carmen immediately about the note. He didn't want to turn her off completely and decided it might be best for him to question her about what he'd found on the internet and how she qualified for the job. Laying a little ground work might be best.

When he arrived at the home, he parked in the same slot as before, and noticed Lisa Montgomery had returned. Not knowing the make of Ms. Sanders' car, he decided to go inside and check her office. If she hadn't shown up, he'd wait in the lobby. She'd have to pass through there first.

Pushing on his hat, Hawkman grabbed the briefcase, hopped out of the SUV and went to the front door. The recreation room had several people reading the paper, talking and playing cards or checkers. This time they didn't pay much attention to him, which made him feel less conspicuous. He went to Carmen's office, and tried the door, only to find it locked. He detoured back to the main waiting room, and stopped at the receptionist's desk.

"Hi, Julie. Could you tell me if Carmen Sanders is in?"

She glanced at the roster. "No, she hasn't signed in yet, but is due any minute."

"Thank you. I'll wait." He drifted over to the large couch, but before he could sit down, Ms. Sanders came hurrying through the entry. Waiting for her to check in, he then stepped in front of her. "Ms. Sanders, I need to talk with you. It's of utmost importance."

Her expression turned solemn. "What about?"

"I'd rather talk in private. Could we go to your office?"

"I guess, but I don't have much time. I've been running late all morning and must get to my duties."

"It will only take a few minutes."

He followed her down the corridor and into her small cubicle. She instantly went to her desk, removed the portable intercom, turned it on, picked up a clipboard and stood, glaring at him. "Well, what is it you want to see me about?"

"How'd you get this job?"

She furrowed her forehead. "Pardon?"

"From what I've read about you, you're not qualified. How'd you land this position?"

"Why is that important? That was three years ago. I thought you were investigating a murder."

"I research anyone I hold as a suspect."

Her mouth dropped open. "You think I'm a murderer?"

"I'm suspicious of everyone who works here. Now please answer my question."

She dropped into her desk chair, gripped a pencil until her fingers turned white. "Mr. Casey, I've well proven myself. I'm not only very good at my job, I love working here. I'd never do anything to jeopardize it."

"I don't doubt your good intentions. I just need information. Who helped you get this employment?"

"I hope it was on my own merit."

Hawkman reached down, opened his briefcase and handed her a sheet of paper. "I found this about you on the internet. I see nothing indicating you're qualified."

Carmen read the content, and handed it back to him. "Mr. Casey, I had a rough time growing up and am not too proud of my past. Those years are all behind me now." She stood and picked up her clipboard and intercom. "If you'll excuse me, I really must get to my duties."

"Someone had to pull some strings for you to get this job. Who?"

"If you must know, Mr. Mackle is my uncle. He's my deceased mother's brother."

"Is it true you were married at one time?"

"Years ago, but I had it annulled. I was too young and had just graduated high school."

Hawkman slid the papers back into the case and rose. "I'm sorry to have kept you so long. I'd like to talk with you again."

She nodded.

He strolled down the corridor slightly behind Carmen until she stepped into the elevator and the doors closed. Curious about where the truth lay, he glanced back at the offices and wondered if he should approach Mr. Mackle. He probably hired her so she wouldn't have to live on the streets after her mother died. Something didn't smell right, and he wanted to get to the bottom of it.

His mind spun with different ideas, and he decided to see if Maggie and George would still talk to him. They might be able to clear up a few things. He stepped into the elevator and rode up to the second floor. The noise of the television sounded through the door as he knocked.

"Come in," George called.

Cautiously, Hawkman stuck his head inside. "Can I talk to you two for a few minutes?"

"Sure. Come on in," George said. "We don't hold no grudges."

Hawkman smiled. "Good, because I need your help."

Immediately, Maggie put her knitting into a small bag on the floor, then waved her hand at her husband. "George, turn off the television. Mr. Casey needs our attention."

Hawkman sat down on the overstuffed chair, placed his briefcase on the floor, put his elbows on his thighs and folded his hands. "Tell me anything you know about Carmen Sanders."

George shrugged. "I know who she is, but seldom talk to her."

The two men turned their gazes toward Maggie.

"Ms. Sanders is a very kind and caring young woman. There are times after her shift she stops by and has a toddy with the residents."

"In their rooms or at the bar?" Hawkman asked.

"Both. She's come by here and chatted with me on occasions, brought her own glass and liqueur." She screwed up her mouth and made a funny face. "I don't like sweetened booze, but that's okay. I have my own bottle and make my own drink. We'll chat for several minutes before she takes her leave to go down the hallway to the next place. She's very cheerful and sometimes very comical. Her jokes are very amusing."

"The few times I've spoken with her, she seems very reserved, not outgoing at all," Hawkman said.

Maggie threw up her hands. "No wonder, you're a private investigator and probably grilled her with questions the whole time you conversed."

He nodded. "You've got a point."

"She's a fine person and appears to love her job. Very thoughtful, always asking if we need anything and if there are any problems."

"What do you know about Lisa Montgomery?"

Maggie tapped her chin. "Not much. Only talked with her a couple of times. Once when I registered to live here and another time when there was an emergency down the hall. She's part of the top brass and works most of the time in her office doing book work."

"What kind of guy is Don Jackson?"

"Now, that's a fine young chap," George piped in. "He tends to mingle with people in the recreation and dining room. Always a smile on his face and very friendly."

"George is right. Don tends to meet with people in groups. He doesn't make the rounds to the apartments."

She pointed at George. "That's why he knows him better than Carmen."

"Does Ms. Sanders always come by after George has left?" Hawkman asked.

"Yes, it's usually after her shift, between nine-thirty and ten or after. She knocks and ask if I'm off to bed or would like to visit." Maggie laughed. "I'm always up to talking." She leaned forward and wiggled a finger. "I have a feeling she's very lonely and we here at the home are her only social life."

"What makes you think that?"

"One night she told me about her mother. They lived together and after she passed away, she had no one. She even made the comment about how lonely she felt walking into an empty house."

"Did she tell you how her mother died?"

"Stroke, but even though she lived a while afterwards, her diabetes made it very difficult for her to completely recover. She had tears in her eyes telling me how she watched her mother take that last breath."

chapter

THIRTY-SEVEN

Hawkman left Maggie's apartment, confused about the conflicting information he'd received on Carmen Sanders and Lisa Montgomery. He needed to dig deeper.

Stepping out of the elevator, he stopped at the receptionist's desk.

"Is Mr. Mackle in?"

"No, he's gone to a conference and won't return until Monday."

"Who's in charge?"

"Mr. Foster."

"Thanks," he said, moving down the corridor.

Lisa Montgomery started to step out of her office, but stopped abruptly when she saw Hawkman, and immediately, went back inside, closing the door behind her. He wondered if she'd found out he'd talked with Carmen Sanders.

Hawkman continued down the hallway and knocked on Foster's door. Perry's distinct voice instructed him to come in.

"Hello, again," Perry said, glancing up. "Take a seat. I finally got Carmen Sanders' file." He handed it to Hawkman. "I just copied the whole thing because there isn't much there."

"Thanks. Could I take another look at Lisa Montgomery's folder?"

"Sure."

Foster went to the last drawer of the cabinet and removed it. "Here you go," he said.

"Who else has access to your office besides you?"

"Ms. Montgomery and Mr. Mackle are free to come in and check the files.

"Do you lock your office when you leave?"

"Only in the evening, when I go home, but during the day it's usually open. I don't have anything in here I'd really worry about, except the files. Why do you ask?"

"I'm a private investigator and ask crazy questions.

Perry chuckled. "Makes sense."

Hawkman glanced through Lisa Montgomery's file and found it intact. "I'd also like to see the one on Don Jackson again." Perry brought it forth and Hawkman thumbed through it. Satisfied he'd gotten everything of importance, he returned it to him. "Thank you. I hope I won't have to bug you again."

"No problem. Glad Ms. Montgomery found the Sanders' file."

"Me, too." He slid it into his briefcase and stood. "Oh, I wanted to verify something. I understand the outside doors are locked at ten at night. For a person to get in, he needs someone from the inside to admit him. Is that right?"

"Yes, a resident has to let you in. The employees all have passes."

"I think the system makes for good security. There isn't much this facility hasn't done to increase its attractiveness."

"Thank you. We're very proud of it."

"Thanks for your help."

"You're welcome. By the way, may I ask a personal question?"

"Sure."

He pointed at Hawkman's chest. "Do you always carry a weapon?"

"Yes, how'd you know?"

Foster smiled. "My brother's in the secret service and I've noticed the familiar bulge in your jacket each time I've seen you."

"You're very observant. Most people wouldn't notice. Don't worry, it won't be drawn unless absolutely necessary."

He left, glanced at Lisa Montgomery's door as he passed, then decided to go up to the Hamptons and ask one more question before going to his office. He knocked and Maggie answered.

"Sorry to bother you, but need to talk to you about one more thing."

"Come on in," she said, leaving the door open." Not using her walker, she wobbled over to the couch, turned her magazine over, then flopped down.

"Where's George?" he asked, sitting on the over-stuffed chair.

"He needed to run to town before the hardware store closed, to pick up a faucet for the kitchen sink at home. The plumber told George if he'd get the supplies, he'd only charge him half."

"Sounds like a deal."

"What'd you need?"

"How late do you stay up?"

"Usually until about eleven, sometimes midnight. Why?"

"Since they lock the place up at ten, if I needed to come and spy on someone, could you come down and let me in?"

"Of course, just call me. If I don't answer, leave a message. Sometimes I roam the halls late, but am usually back in my room within fifteen minutes. It makes me sleep better, even with a sleeping pill, to walk around before bedtime." She grinned. "Also, they leave pastries out on one of the serving tables in the dining room, in case people get hungry."

"Very tempting. When you're out there, do you ever see others coming and going from their apartments?"

"Yes, but we all look like shadows in the night, be-cause they dim the lights in the corridors about the same time they close the doors." She laughed. "We look like a group of ghosts floating around in a spooky hallway."

Hawkman rose, and took his valise. "You look all dressed up and ready for dinner, so I'll get out of here."

"We'll go when George returns. Shopping makes him so hungry."

He opened the door and touched his hat. "Thanks for your time, Maggie. I'll probably see you tomorrow."

Wanting to get back to his office so he could go through Carmen Sander's folder, he hurried to the elevator and out the front door. He parked in the alley behind his office and jogged up the stairs. Placing the briefcase on the desk, he opened the window a crack, as the room smelled musty. He booted up the computer, then put on the coffee pot. Hanging his hat on the nail, he ran his hand through his hair and sat down in the swivel chair. He opened the valise and pulled out the copied files.

As he studied the papers, it appeared Ms. Sanders had told the truth. She was the niece of Mr. Mackle and he had hired her on his own. He made the statement in a letter to Perry Foster: he'd give Carmen six months to prove herself. If she didn't work out, they'd find someone else. Hawkman didn't find any application form.

He turned to the computer, clicked into the secure search area, and typed in his password. When the form came up, he decided to look up Don Jackson. Another common handle and he had to eliminate several before finding the right one. He raised his brows as he read the information.

chapter

THIRTY-EIGHT

Hawkman printed out the information he'd found on Don Jackson. He sat back and thumped his pencil on the desk. Mr. Mackle must have a big heart. Some of the people's reputations are questionable. However, they'd all been employed there for three or more years, obviously doing good work. He saw no complaints recorded in their files. Picking up one of the sheets on Carmen Sanders, he noted Mackle had put her date of birth on the recommendation to hire her. The woman was thirty-one years old.

The note left on Carmen's door by Ms. Montgomery still baffled him. Why would she leave such a warning? He'd have a talk with both these women and discover what they thought about each other. Could turn out very interesting, if they told the truth.

He decided to wrap it up for the day, but first jotted down Ms. Montgomery's address from the information in her folder. Seeing where a person lives sometimes exposes a bit about their character. He'd drive by her place on the way home. He packed the files into his briefcase, unplugged the coffee pot, turned out the lights and left. A cool breeze smacked him in the face as he jogged down the stairs, which made him shiver. Unlocking his vehicle, he quickly climbed inside. "Winter is upon us," he mumbled, slamming the door.

Familiar with the area where Lisa lived, he didn't have to enter the street into the GPS. The setting sun's bright rays glanced off his windshield, almost blinding him when he turned westward. Happy to locate the main drag to Ms. Montgomery's home, he turned away from the shafts of light and continued slowly, not exactly sure where her street criss-crossed. He soon spotted it and pulled the piece of paper from his pocket to check the numbers. The neighborhood appeared quiet, the homes neat and tidy. He finally found the address and as he drove by Montgomery's house, the electric garage door slid down over two cars parked in the garage. An older woman came out the front door, walked across the lawn, picked up the newspaper, flipped off the rubber band and shook it on her way back into the house.

He picked up speed as he parted the area and turned onto the ramp for the freeway.

When he arrived home, Jennifer asked him a million questions about what all he'd learned so far. He told her about Carmen Sanders' file, and Lisa Montgomery's note.

"That's really strange," she said, her eyes wide. "Sounds like the Montgomery woman might be blackmailing Carmen."

"I agree, but what about?"

Jennifer shrugged. "Who knows? You're going to have to find out. She's got something on her. Why leave such a note, if she didn't?"

Hawkman lay in bed staring at the ceiling. Sleep didn't want to come and he envied his pretty wife as her breathing had settled into soft whispers at least two hours ago. He knew he had to get up early in the morning, as he wanted to talk with Ms. Montgomery first thing, then hoped he could corner Carmen Sanders before the Friday night plans of a fall festival kicked into play. They'd be too busy to talk to him then. He finally fell asleep and awoke with a jerk as Miss Marple jumped onto his chest and knocked his chin with her head.

"What the heck do you want, you little pest?"

Jennifer rolled over. "Oh, shoot, I forgot to put any dry food out for her last night. Bet her dish is empty."

"I'll take care of it, I have to get going anyway. Go back to sleep if you can."

"Thanks, hon," she said, as she rolled over onto her side.

Hawkman grabbed his clothes in one hand and carried the kitten, balanced against his chest, with the other. He managed to close the bedroom door, so the cat couldn't sneak back in and disturb Jennifer. Sure enough, Miss Marple's dish stood empty. He quickly filled it, gave her fresh water, then went to the middle bathroom where he showered, shaved, and dressed.

When he got ready to leave the house, he smiled, as Miss Marple had climbed into his chair, her tail flicking back and forth, as she watched the falcon out the window. Pretty Girl gave her quite a show, flapping her wings and walking about on her perch.

"You're dreaming, little one. That bird would make mincemeat out of you," he chuckled, as he closed the door.

Driving toward Medford, he thought about how he'd approach Ms. Montgomery concerning her dealings with Carmen Sanders. Something appeared fishy, but he doubted he'd find it out much today; still he'd give it a try. He pulled into the parking lot, found a vacant slot, picked up his briefcase, and exited the vehicle. On his way inside, he flipped on the recorder in his pocket. When he reached her office, he found the door ajar and poked his head inside. Lisa sat at her desk, concentrating on an open ledger. When he cleared his throat, she jerked up her head.

"Excuse me, Mr. Casey. I didn't hear you knock."

"Actually, I didn't, your door was open, so I just came in."

"What can I do for you?"

He noticed a tone of impatience in her voice. "I'd like to talk to you about Don Jackson and Carmen Sanders."

She took off her reading glasses, dropped her pencil on the desk, and leaned back in the chair. "What do you want to know?"

"Do you and Mr. Foster interview the clients for jobs?"

"Normally, yes. If Perry and I agree the person's a good pick, we give Mr. Mackle our preferences; then he takes it from there. He reviews their applications, our reports, and makes the final decision."

"How did Don Jackson qualify?"

"What do you mean?"

"I've done some research and he was fired from his last job for sexual harassment. Didn't you think having him around here might cause a problem."

Lisa leaned forward and put her elbows on the desk. "Mr. Casey, he's a good looking man and from what I read of the report, a young woman trumped up a charge against him because she couldn't get his attention. These things happen all the time, and it's a shame for it to have to go on a person's record. He told us all about it when we interviewed him."

"You believed him?"

"Yes."

"What if I told you, it wasn't the only time he'd been hit with such a suit."

She frowned. "There was only the one charge on his record."

"Time might have protected him."

"How many are there?"

"Three counting the one you know about."

"Oh, my." She sat back and rubbed her forehead. "We've had no problems so far."

"I'm glad to hear it. He might never mouth off again. Hopefully, he's learned his lesson and doesn't want to lose this job."

"You've really hit me with baffling news. I guess we should search deeper when we're hiring a person."

"How long have you known Ms. Sanders?"

"For years. Our mothers were the best of friends. Even though I'm a few years older than Carmen, when our mothers would get together, we'd be forced to put up with each other."

"That arrangement obviously didn't suit you."

She shrugged. "I would have preferred being with friends my own age."

"Did you keep in touch with Carmen as you grew older?"

"No, I quit going over to the Sanders home when I got old enough to stay alone."

"Did your mother ever mention Carmen?"

"She thought Mrs. Sanders let her get by with murder. When Carmen hit the teenage years, she got into drugs, then got married right out of high school. However, it didn't last long and Carmen had the marriage annulled. She went into rehab; then when her father died she had a nervous breakdown and spent over five years in and out of a psychiatric ward."

"You seem to know a lot about her."

"Mother kept me updated when I'd come home from college."

"So Carmen never had any formal education other than high school?"

Lisa shook her head. "No. Once her mother had a stroke, Carmen took care of her night and day. When her mother passed away, she had no means of support as it took all the money they had to take care of the medical needs and their upkeep. She grew up quite a bit during that time."

"How did she qualify for this job?"

Lisa squirmed in her chair and exhaled. "I have no idea. Mr. Mackle hired her. You'll have to talk to him about the details. I must say, she's worked out beautifully, and all the residents love her. I really don't understand why you're making such an issue out of how these people got hired."

Hawkman stared at her. "Because I'm investigating a murder, and I need to know their backgrounds. Same as with you. I've researched your resume and you definitely qualify for the job."

"Thank you."

"You said your mother also had a stroke. Is she still alive?"

"Oh, yes. She's fully recovered, drives and does her own thing."

"What does she think about Carmen working here?"

"She thinks it's great."

"You told me the residents love Carmen. What's your opinion?"

"Mr. Casey, my personal judgment isn't important. The girl works here and is doing a good job. That's what counts."

"Why did you have her file at your house?"

She let out a bored breath. "Mr. Mackle needed some statistics, so I took several folders home. Somehow, Carmen's slipped out of the stack and fell behind my desk. I didn't leave it at my house on purpose."

"Did your mother read the file?"

She raised her brows. "What an odd question. I really doubt it, but I don't think you have any right to bring my mother into your investigation. She has nothing to do with Morning Glory Haven."

"I'm trying to hit all bases, because there's something going on that doesn't fit the picture. Believe me, I'm going to find out what it is." He picked up the briefcase and headed toward the door, then turned. "I'll be talking to you again."

chapter

THIRTY-NINE

Hawkman plopped down on the large couch in the lounge area opposite the recreation room. He pulled Lisa's file from his briefcase, and glanced down through the application. Her tone during the interview appeared impatient through the whole session. She definitely had animosity toward Ms. Sanders. He'd sure like to know the reason; it might answer the question of why she left such a note in Carmen's mailbox.

A movement caught Hawkman's eye and he turned to see Don Jackson talking to one of the residents. While watching the two converse, he noticed when Jackson reached into his back pocket for something, what looked like a diabetic pump hung from the belt of his trousers. When he removed his hand, the tail of his coat caught on the instrument. He stepped away from the person and Hawkman called out.

"Mr. Jackson."

"Hello, Mr. Casey. Didn't see you."

He pointed to the small machine. "You diabetic?"

He twisted around, and flipped the tail of his coat. "Yeah, and the darn thing gets hung up on my clothes all the time. However, it's a life saver, otherwise I'd be jabbing myself constantly."

"You have a minute?" Hawkman asked.

"Just a quickie, I've got a doctor's appointment, and when Ms. Sanders arrives, I've got to take off. What do you need?"

"Do you like your job?"

"Yeah, a lot."

"You have a girlfriend?"

"Can't afford one right now."

"I'd like to talk to you about the harassment charges on your record."

Don's smile disappeared and he turned pale. "Mr. Casey, please keep those to yourself. My life has turned around and I've learned a big lesson. I need this employment."

"Keep your nose clean, and you'll keep it. We'll talk when you have more time."

Jackson crossed the room toward the corridor, ran a hand along the side of his head and disappeared around the corner toward his office.

Soon, Carmen Sanders entered the wing, and headed down the hallway. Hawkman waited until Don came down the corridor and hurried out the door before he rose and went to Ms. Sanders office. He knocked and heard her say 'come in'. When he opened the door, her face fell. She dropped the mail she held in her hand onto the desk and took a deep breath.

"Oh, it's you."

"Sorry, I'm not who you'd like to see, but I've got to talk to you."

"I have nothing else to tell you."

"You know you haven't leveled with me, so I'm going to keep asking questions until you do. Otherwise, the police will be back next week with their own version, and I don't think you want them harassing you."

"I don't know what you mean."

Hawkman sat down in front of her desk. "I'm sure Mr. Jackson took care of most of the duties before he had to leave, so why don't you relax and let's talk."

She eased down into her desk chair, but remained rigid. "What more do you want to know?"

"What's the beef between you and Lisa Montgomery?"

She stared at him. "What are you talking about?"

"Something's going on between you two. I followed her to your house and read the note she left in your mailbox."

Immediately she jumped up, her eyes wide. "How dare you. That's a federal offense to read other people's mail."

"It didn't have a stamp on it. If you want to get technical about it, she shouldn't have put it in your box, as that is a federal offense also. Especially, a threatening note. Have you talked to her since she left it?"

"Yes."

"Why didn't she want you to talk to me?"

"She doesn't want me to say anything that might get her into trouble."

"What's she afraid of?"

"Losing her job."

"How could you influence the security of her employment?"

"Because Mr. Mackle is my uncle, and she thinks I might say something to him that could jeopardize it."

"So you're saying she's blackmailing you?"

A flash of fear crossed her face, as she dropped back into her seat. "Yes."

"What has she got against you?"

"Lots of stuff, so she thinks. Lisa and her mother are evil. My mother warned me about them years ago."

"Tell me more."

Carmen took a deep breath. "For one, you can't imagine how happy Lisa was when she heard Mrs. Owens had died of an overdose of insulin. It gave her something else to add to her list against me."

"What does that have to do with you?"

"I'm sure you've discovered in your investigation, I'm diabetic and so was my mom. When she had the stroke, things got very complicated because of her diabetes. She had to take medications, plus insulin. I had to run to the pharmacy to pick up some of her medicine and thought she was asleep. When I returned she was in insulin shock. She'd gone to the refrigerator, taken out two syringes, one of mine and one of hers, and injected them both. I called emergency, but she was already dead. It was horrible to watch one you loved so much, die in such a way. To this day Lisa Montgomery accuses me of murdering my mother."

Hawkman saw the pain and tears reflected in her face. "Were you charged."

"Of course not. The doctor knew my mother was horribly depressed about her condition, and she'd asked him more than once to end her life. Lisa still thinks I gave my mother an overdose."

"Does your uncle know about the threats from Ms. Montgomery?"

Carmen shook her head. "No. I'd never burden him with her pettiness. Besides, he doesn't need to know about all my problems. He's lost his wife, a sister and a son in the war, all in the last five years. Enough heartache and worry for one man in such a short time. To top it off, he fretted about me not having a job when mom died. He took a big chance on hiring me since I had no prior experience of anything. He's a wonderful man and I'm not about to let him down."

"If you were cleared of any charges, why does she continue to torment you?"

"I wish I knew. I've tried to figure it out. She's never cared for me or my mother. I think she might have been jealous over the attention her mother gave to mine. However, I can't be sure."

"You said her mother was evil too. What made you say that?"

"When my mother was healthy, she used to get real exasperated with May for trying to tell her how to raise me. She accused mom of letting me run wild, which I have to say she did, but it wasn't any of May's business. My dad didn't like her at all and wondered what mom saw in the woman.

He always said May had an ulterior motive for befriending mom, as they had nothing in common."

"Did it ever surface?"

"I don't know. Being too young to really understand much of the women's behavior toward one another, I can only tell you what I overheard my folks say."

"Did your mother and Lisa's have their strokes close together?"

"Mom had hers first, then May had one about six weeks later."

"Did May ever come to visit your mother?"

"Not one time, nor did she ever call to ask about her."

"Ms. Sanders, I appreciate how candid you've been with me."

"Mr. Casey, it's really strange, but I feel like a huge burden has been lifted off my shoulders. I really didn't want to talk to you about this stuff, but there's something about your kindness that draws out the inner thoughts of a person."

"Thank you." He rose and picked up his valise. "I'm going to get out of here so you can get to work." Snapping his fingers, he said. "Oh, by the way. Do you work the weekends?"

"Mr. Jackson and I trade off every other one. He'll be working this Saturday and Sunday.

Before he could leave Carmen's office, the door swung open. He grabbed the edge before it hit him in the face as Lisa Montgomery charged into the room.

She glared at Hawkman, then jerked around and faced Carmen. "I need to talk to you immediately. Please come to my office."

He noticed Carmen had thrown back her shoulders, and an invisible armor coated her countenance as she trailed Lisa into the corridor.

chapter

FORTY

Hawkman left the building and climbed into his 4X4. He sat for a moment pondering over what Carmen had told him. Did she tell the truth, or had she given her mother an overdose of insulin three years ago? He could find out real quick if any charges had been filed. Since the court house had closed for the weekend, he'd need to check with Detective Williams. Accelerating, he left Morning Glory Haven and drove to the police station. Not sure he'd find the detective in his office with the drug case pending, he decided to try.

He parked in the visitor's section and jogged up the stairs to the front door. When he entered the building, he came upon a hubbub of activity. Catching a few telltale words, he figured the sting had gone down successfully. This was not the time to talk to Williams about an old case. The man would be busy with this mess over the weekend. He twisted on his heel and exited. He'd bide his time until Monday.

Hawkman drove back to Morning Glory Haven, and hoped to find Maggie in her room after dinner. Glancing around the recreation room, he didn't spot the Hamptons, so he rode the elevator to the second floor and knocked on her door.

"Come in," the familiar voice called.

He found Maggie in a house robe, sitting on the couch by the window, sipping on a drink with a dinner tray on a small table beside her.

"How come you're not eating at the dining hall?"

"Hello, Mr. Casey. I've been under the weather today; my arthritis is really acting up. Didn't feel like even getting dressed, much less walking anywhere. I called the chef and he had my meal sent up."

"I'm sorry to hear you're not feeling good. Can I do anything for you?" he asked, sitting down on the opposite sofa.

"No, George has run to get one of my prescriptions refilled before the pharmacy closes. What do you need?"

"I don't want to bother you if you're not up to it."

"It's okay, as long as you don't want me to dance a jig."

Hawkman smiled. "At least you've still got your sense of humor."

"Have to, or I'd cry."

"I wondered if you've ever met Lisa Montgomery's mother?"

"Oh, yes. Her name is May. She helps out when they have special events."

"Is she hired to do these things?"

"I don't know. She does show up at many of the regular doings. I've seen her at bingo several times. There's a certain group of people she's real friendly toward."

"Makes sense, with her daughter working here. She's probably encouraged people to check out this place. Have you had any personal contact with the woman?"

"No, I don't think she likes me."

"Why?"

"I tried to visit with her one day when she sat next to me at a piano recital. She brushed me off like I was a bug on her sleeve."

"Probably your imagination."

"She did it more than once. So I avoid her."

"So you're saying she's snooty?"

Maggie laughed. "Great word, describes her exactly."

"Does her daughter accompany her to these events?"

"Oh, I'm sure she's around, but doesn't have the freedom to socialize like her mother does. She's all business, and works behind the scenes."

"Did you know May had a stroke several years ago?"

"I've heard talk, but it must have been before I arrived. You certainly wouldn't know it looking at her today."

George opened the door and hobbled inside. "Ah, ha, caught you. Can't leave my good looking woman alone for any time before some guy's knocking at her door."

Maggie giggled. "Cut it out, you dirty old man."

Hawkman grinned. "I'd hoped to get out of here before you returned."

"How's the investigation going?" George asked,

"I'm working on it, but right now it seems stalled."

George shook his head. "Sorry to hear such news. I'd hoped it would have come to a head by now."

"I still have questions that need to be answered. I don't even know if you can help me."

"Shoot, we can try," George said, flopping into the overstuffed chair and leaning his cane against the side.

"How does the emergency alarm system work, say, if someone falls in the middle of the night and pushes the button? Who calls the paramedics?"

"Oh, I can answer," Maggie said. "When they lock up at night, the alarm system automatically goes straight to the 911 service."

"So there's no one on duty downstairs after ten at night?"

"No, not in our section."

"How do the paramedics get in?"

"They must have a special password, because one night an older man down the hall, got up after midnight to go to the bathroom, slipped on some water on the floor and couldn't get up. He managed to punch the button or pull the cord, there are two ways you can activate it. Anyway, the emergency crew came right up."

"Makes sense. So who's here until ten?"

"Usually Jackson or Sanders," George said. "I've seen them roaming the halls when I leave at night."

"Do you by any chance know if they work split shifts, or do they come in later?"

George shrugged. "I have no idea. You'll have to ask the person. It's hard to remember the times I've spotted them about the place."

Hawkman rose. "I'll get out of here so Maggie can rest." Holding onto the door knob he turned to George. "You take care of the little lady. Can't have her sick."

"She'll be fine by tomorrow. Not much can keep my gal down."

He left the Hamptons and went down to the first floor lounge where he flopped down on the large couch facing a huge fireplace. He looked out over the recreation room and noted the population had thinned considerably. A few stragglers in a hot checker game and a couple tables of bridge were still going strong. He checked his watch and noted the time to be eight thirty. Picking up a newspaper someone had left on the sofa, he read the first page; then a sound of laughter echoed from the bridge table and the couples stood. He heard them talking about their next time. They soon left and the only ones remaining were two men, seriously contemplating their checker moves.

By nine thirty, the room had cleared. A cleaning woman made her way into the area with a vacuum and dust cloth. It didn't take her long before she had the room back in order, then she made her way into the lounge. Hawkman took his paper, went into the far corner of the recreation center where a television and small couch stood. When the lights in the hallway dimmed, he noted the other lights went off, and a clicking noise sounded as the front door threw on the night lock, then a small light above the door came on. He reached over, tried the switch on the lamp and it turned on. The overhead and door locks must be set on timers, he thought. Quite a technical operation.

The employees filed out of the dining room, and all left through the front door. Soon, George came down the elevator and headed across the room.

When he spotted Hawkman, he stopped. "You still here?"

"Just observing. I noted It doesn't matter if you leave the building from inside, but you can't come in. Is that right?"

"Yep. I always make sure I've got everything when I leave Maggie, as I'd hate to have her come down here and let me back in."

"How would you notify her? You don't have a cell."

"There's an in-house phone right outside the front door. I'd call her from there."

Hawkman shook his head. "Boy, this place thinks of everything."

George waved. "I'm getting tired, so I'm heading out."

Must be hard for him coming here every day, he thought, as he watched the old fellow limp out the door with the aid of his cane.

Hawkman had just about given up on seeing who had the shift until ten tonight, when the elevator door opened and Lisa Montgomery stepped out. An older woman accompanied her and they were chatting as they headed for the front door. He moved in front of them and Lisa jumped, putting her hand to her throat.

"Good Lord, you scared me to death. I certainly didn't expect to see you here tonight." She gestured toward the other woman. "This is my mother, May Montgomery. Mom this is Tom Casey, the private investigator I've told you about."

He touched the brim of his hat. "My pleasure, Mrs. Montgomery."

"Call me May," she said, extending her hand.

Hawkman looked at Lisa. "Do you take this shift often?"

"Occasionally, I'll let Don or Carmen off. Mom joins me and we visit with the residents on a relaxed basis."

"Seems like a nice gesture."

"Mom has talked several of her colleagues into living here, so we feel it's the right thing to do." She put a hand on her hip. "By the way, what are you doing here at this hour?"

"Investigating a murder."

Lisa gave her mother a gentle push toward the door. "It's getting late. We've got to get home."

Just as Hawkman bid them goodnight and turned to pick up the newspaper from the couch, a shadowy figure left through the door leading into the garden between the two buildings. He raced forward, but it clicked shut before he had a chance to get sight of the person. As he looked through the glass, he noted the walkway between the buildings was shrouded in darkness. The only thing he could see from the faint light coming from the assisted living structure was the slowly closing door.

chapter

FORTY-ONE

Early the next morning, Hawkman received a frantic phone call from Maggie. He jumped out of bed, grabbed some clothes from the closet, and dressed.

Jennifer rolled over and watched him as he sat on the edge of the bed yanking on his boots. "Uh, oh. What's happened?"

"Another person has died at Morning Glory Haven."

"Natural or otherwise?"

"Don't know yet. I'll call you.'

He hurried out the door and jumped into the 4X4. Driving to Medford as fast as allowed, he arrived at the home. Several police cars were parked in front, along with the coroner's wagon. Hawkman hoofed it inside and found an officer who told him the action was on the second floor. Taking the stairs, Hawkman found the apartment, glanced inside and saw Detective Williams.

Hawkman stayed in the hallway and watched as they hoisted the covered body onto the gurney. The lab men immediately went to work on searching for evidence. Williams finally stepped into the corridor.

"What's the verdict?" Hawkman asked.

"Not sure yet, but appears suspicious. We won't know anything until they do an autopsy."

"Do you think there's been foul play?"

He pointed toward a man standing with a clipboard in his hand. "He's her doctor and last week he gave her a thorough checkup. Everything looked fine."

"Was she a diabetic?"

"Yes."

"When you get through here, I want to talk to you."

"Okay, I'll meet you downstairs in about fifteen minutes."

Hawkman left the area and took the stairs down to the first floor. He strolled toward the office area and noted the doors were all locked. Mackle might return a day early with this occurrence. As he headed toward the recreation room, Perry Foster charged through the entry. His suit looked like he'd slept in it, and his expression was harried.

When he saw Hawkman, he stopped in his tracks. "Dear Lord, I can't believe this has happened again."

"It could be a natural death."

"Not with Hazel. She's been in the prime of health as long as she's been here, full of energy and has regular medical examinations."

"Have you contacted Mr. Mackle?"

"Yes, he's coming home when he can get a flight. He's worried sick."

"Where's the rest of the staff?"

"I haven't had time to contact them. I'll do that shortly. We're going to need all hands aboard today and tomorrow. Keep your fingers crossed we don't lose any of our tenants." He ran a hand through his tousled hair. "I better get up to Hazel's apartment. I'm sure the police are crawling all over the place."

Hawkman nodded. "I doubt they'll let you inside."

"I need to talk to the man in charge." Foster took off in a dash toward the elevator and disappeared behind the sliding doors.

Hawkman strolled outside into the garden area. A tall wrought iron fence enclosed the area, with an opened gate leading to the next building. The shadowy figure he saw leaving last night could have been an employee from the assisted living facility.

He walked back into the living room area and spotted Detective Williams and Perry Foster standing in the corridor conversing. Hawkman waited for the two men to finish. When Foster veered off toward his office, he stepped forward. "Where do you want to talk?"

"Let's head for the room I used before. I doubt anything will be going on at this early hour."

The residents had started meandering toward the dining room, speaking in whispers and pointing at Hawkman and Williams.

"News must travel mighty fast here," the detective said, as he nodded at the people. "Let's get the hell out of their way. I don't need any questions right now."

They quickly exited out of the hallway and into the bingo room. Sitting down at one of the tables, Williams placed his clipboard on the surface, rubbed his chin with his hand, and exhaled.

"How's the sting operation going?"

"Better than expected. Now, I need to focus on this case. I hope you've uncovered something, I definitely need help."

"First tell me, who reported this woman's death?"

"One of the other residents. She said they always go to an early breakfast on Saturday mornings, then go shopping at the mall. When she couldn't rouse her by knocking on the door this morning, she got worried. No one answered the call at the desk, so she went into her own apartment and pushed the emergency button, which brought the paramedics. We were immediately called, due to the pending case. The rest is obvious."

"Did she notice anyone lingering around her friend's room?"

"No. Now, what were you going to tell me?"

"I hung around here last night until this place closed up and a couple of things happened that might be worth looking into."

"Shoot."

"'I' heard a rumor that Carmen Sanders might have murdered her mother. I'd like to see if there's a record of any charges filed against her.

Williams frowned. "How long ago?"

"Three or so years."

"Off the top of my head, I don't recall any. Must not have amounted to anything. Remind me to check next week."

Hawkman nodded.

"Anything else?"

"Yes, Lisa Montgomery and her mother, May, were here last night until after ten. I chatted with them for a few minutes on their way out, and they told me they were visiting friends her mom had encouraged to live here. Lisa gave her mother the rush act, so I didn't get any information about the resident's name. They'd no more than left when someone slipped through the door heading out to the garden. I heard the click of the lock and tried to get to the entry in time to see who it was, but the only thing I caught was a shadowy figure entering the other building. I didn't follow because once these doors are hatched down, you can go out, but you can't get back in, unless you have the password. Supposedly, only the top employers have it. So whoever left here, and went into the other building, knew it."

Williams leaned back in his chair with a solemn expression. "Sounds like the staff might be involved."

"Someone could have stolen or leaked the code."

"Wonder if they change it often?"

"I can ask Perry Foster. He'll know."

"Let's go check."

As they headed for the man's office, several of the employees came in and went to their stations. Some appeared nervous, while others acted as if nothing had happened.

The manager's door stood open, so Hawkman stepped inside. Perry had the phone pressed to his ear. When he glanced up, he waved for the two men to come inside and motioned toward the chairs in front of his desk.

Soon he hung up and stared at the two men. "Is there any news?"

"Not yet," Williams said. "We won't know the cause of death for a few days."

Perry ran his hands over his face. "This isn't good."

"We need to know how often the codes are changed for the outside doors?"

"Once a month."

"What type of code is it?" the detective asked.

Perry produced a small piece of plastic that looked like a credit card. "I have a machine that will put on a new code. The staff members turn them in on the first of the month, then I redo each one and give them back."

"Is there any way someone could get hold of the machine, other than you?" Hawkman asked.

"No, I keep it in the safe. Mr. Mackle and I are the only ones authorized to use it."

"What about the people who work in the other sections?"

"I take care of the whole facility. It's their responsibility to get them to me before the code is changed on the doors. I check off each person, and notify the ones I haven't seen.

"How do you remind them?"

"Through e-mail."

Hawkman leaned forward. "Mr. Foster, I want an honest answer. What is your opinion of Lisa Montgomery?"

"Uh." Perry appeared lost for words for a moment. 'She's a good worker."

"I didn't ask how she worked. Do you trust her?"

"You really put me on a spot."

"This doesn't go any farther than the detective and me."

He looked toward the ceiling, closed his eyes, snapped them open, then looked Hawkman straight in the face. "No."

chapter

FORTY-TWO

Hawkman and Detective Williams strolled down the hallway toward the bingo room.

"You didn't seem very shocked over Foster's answer about not trusting Ms. Montgomery," Williams said.

"No, because after talking with other people, I've found her personality is not pleasing to several. Whether she's capable of murder is another question."

"Give me an example."

"If Carmen Sanders is telling the truth, Montgomery is blackmailing her in a very devious manner. Part of it involves the death of Sanders' mother."

"Anything we can get a handle on?"

Hawkman shook his head. "No."

"Now I can see why you wanted to check on any charges filed against the Sanders woman." The detective suddenly stopped and removed his cell phone from his belt. "Excuse me, I've got a call."

Hawkman stepped out of hearing distance and spotted Lisa Montgomery scurrying toward Perry Foster's office. When Williams hung up, he exhaled loudly. "I'm leaving you to interview some of these people. I've got to get back to the station. I thought this sting had wound down, but my boys have found another place. So we're hitting it tonight. I hope I can be back on this case by Monday. Do you want me to leave a man with you?"

"No. You'll need all your men for a dangerous operation. I can handle this and report to you if I need help."

"Make a citizen's arrest if you have to."

"Will do."

The detective rounded up the officers he'd brought, and they left the premises. When Lisa came out of Foster's office and went into her own, Hawkman crossed the hallway, opened her door and stepped inside.

She narrowed her eyes. "I see you've quit bothering to knock."

Deciding not to sit down, he looked into her face. "Under the circumstances, you're right. Did you know the woman who passed away?"

"Yes."

"Is she one of the people your mother encouraged to move into Morning Glory Haven?"

"No."

"Did you visit this woman last night?"

"No."

"Did you see anyone enter or leave her room?"

"No, but we weren't near her apartment. She lived on the opposite end of where mother and I were."

"Why do you dislike Ms. Sanders so much?"

She frowned. "Excuse me?"

"You heard me. You've threatened her. Why?"

"I don't know what you're talking about."

"Then why did you leave the note in her mailbox not to talk to me? What are you afraid she might say?"

"You're crazy, or she is, if she told you such a story."

"No, Ms. Montgomery, I happened to follow you the day you were going to get those files you'd conveniently left at your place. You stopped at Ms. Sanders house and left the note. I read it before Carmen did."

Lisa's face turned pale. "I never saw you."

"I'm trained in surveillance. Now, why don't you level with me on the problem between you and your coworker?"

She glared at him. "Mr. Casey, our personal problems have nothing to do with your investigation. I don't think I have to answer such a question."

"I'm afraid you do. Anything involving Morning Glory Haven is a concern to the police and this investigation. Since you don't want to cooperate, I'd advise you to get a lawyer."

She jumped up from her chair. "What are you telling me? Am I a suspect?"

"Afraid so, Ms. Montgomery. Not only for Gladys Owens' death, but if the woman who died this morning didn't succumb from natural causes, you can add her to the list."

"Mr. Casey, I'm not responsible for anyone's dying in this place. For God's sake, I work here. I definitely don't want to go to prison."

"Then you better get your act together before Monday. Detective Williams will want to talk to you."

He turned and left her standing with fear in her eyes. When he stepped into the hallway, he met Carmen Sanders at her office door. She looked up at him with tears flowing down her cheeks.

"Mr. Casey, Hazel was the dearest friend I had in this home. I loved her like my own mother. I'd go by and visit her every evening after work. Last night Don had the duty. I so wish I'd been here." Her voice cracked as she wiped away the tears from her face. She sucked in a breath. "I couldn't believe it when Mr. Foster called this morning. Everyone loved Hazel." She glanced up with a pleading expression. "How did she die?"

"We won't know for a few days."

"She seemed in such excellent health for her age."

"Why don't you go on into your office and pull yourself together. I'm sure Mr. Foster is going to need you to work with the residents. The word has already spread and the police have come and gone. So the people are going to be edgy. They'll need you."

She nodded, unlocked her office and went inside.

He meandered down the corridor and Don Jackson came hurrying into the building from the door leading into the garden. "Hi, Mr. Casey. Is Mr. Foster in his office?"

"Yes."

"Man, I can't believe what's going on here. It gives me the willies."

"Why do you say that? A woman died. Don't you expect death in an old people's home?"

"Well, yeah, but Mr. Foster said the police were swarming the place and he wanted us all here early to help ease the residents' nerves."

"True, but it's mostly because of the questionable death of Gladys Owens. This woman could have died of natural causes. Did you know Hazel?"

"Yes, a very personable person. I'd chat with her in the dining room, if she sat alone." His gaze darted toward the office area. "I better get my butt in there and find out what my boss wants me to do."

"By the way, what time did you leave the building last night?"

"I received a call from Ms. Montgomery about eight o'clock. She told me I could leave, because she was coming in with May to visit some friends and they'd stay through my shift."

"She do this often?"

"No, but it's great when she does."

"How do you work these long shifts?"

"They're really just an eight hour day. We come in at one, unless we've made an appointment to show someone around, or need to catch up on some work in the office. We usually like to show people around the home at eleven-thirty because we take them to lunch in the dining room. If the visit spills over into our normal schedule that's okay. We have the six o'clock dinner break and usually eat here because we can get our meals free. Then we leave around ten or a little earlier if things are quiet."

"That schedule sounds good to me."

Don smiled. "I like it." He moved away from Hawkman. "I better go check with Mr. Foster."

"I'll talk with you later."

He sure didn't seem bothered about the woman's death, Hawkman thought, as he walked toward the elevator. When he passed the recreation room, the tension tingled his bones. People stared at him, as if he should have prevented Hazel's demise. He rode up to the second floor and headed for Maggie's apartment.

George let him in and leaned on his cane as he stared at the floor. "This is horrible. Another death."

Maggie pointed a finger at Hawkman and screeched. "You can't let it happen again. This has got to stop. George is going to take me out of here if you don't find the killer."

Hawkman put up his hands in defense. "We don't even know if foul play is involved. Once they do the autopsy, we'll know something from the preliminary report; but until then, we've got to look at her death as caused by natural means."

She slammed her small fist into the cushions of the couch. "You know she didn't die naturally. Hazel was in excellent health."

Hawkman walked over and put his hand on her shoulder. "Be calm, Maggie. We should know something by Monday or Tuesday. In the meantime, I'm on patrol."

chapter

FORTY-THREE

Hawkman left the Hamptons, journeyed down to the recreation room, and mingled with the residents. He ended up holding a mini-forum full of questions and answers, assuring his captive audience that Hazel Spencer's death could have been from natural causes. Many were shocked as she'd appeared in good health, and everyone thought highly of her. No one living in the adjacent apartments to Ms. Spencer had seen any strangers in the halls, but most were inside their own quarters by ten on the night of her demise.

Several asked about his relationship with the police. He explained how he had worked with the detective on solving many cases. They'd become good friends through the years, and worked together often. However, he said, "I never get paid."

The comment brought several chuckles.

"Sure glad the patrol cars aren't lining the street outside," one of the men said. "It doesn't look good for others to think there's something unlawful going on, even if there is. It's really not any outsider's business. We'd much rather have just one man nosing around."

Hawkman raised a hand. "Don't get your hopes up, as the police may be back next week. It all depends on what we find out about Ms. Spencer's death. Rest assured, we'll be doing everything we can to keep the place safe. I want you to continue your normal everyday activities. If you remember seeing anything unusual or something that bothered you the night in question, please feel free to come to me."

Once he ended the small meeting, he seemed satisfied people felt a bit more comfortable. When he turned around, Perry Foster approached him from the side.

"Thank you, Mr. Casey. Your talk seemed to have put the residents at ease."

"It does seem like the tension subsided a bit. Maybe if any of them have information, they'll come forward."

Out of the corner of his eye, he spotted Don Jackson go out the entry leading to the garden. "Excuse me, Mr. Foster."

Hawkman took long strides, and pushed open the door in time to see Jackson go into the other building. "Now where's he going?" he mumbled as he trailed the man into the assisted living area, then observed him going out their main entrance. Hawkman peered through the glass, and watched him trot to an older model, silver gray Honda Accord in the parking lot. Jackson unlocked the door, fetched a clipboard from the back seat, and headed back.

Quickly crossing the room, Hawkman stepped into the elevator and pushed the close button. He stood in the cubicle for a few seconds before tapping the open door knob. When it slid ajar, he spotted Jackson moving toward the independent living side.

Hawkman strolled outside to the Honda. He glanced in the window of the car, and noticed several medium sized boxes cluttering the back seat. He couldn't quite make out the printing, so he took out his small portable camera from his jeans jacket pocket, snapped some pictures, then took a photo of the car and the license plate.

Going back into the building, he moseyed through the garden, noticed a beautiful jasmine plant against the wall, and imagined the fragrance it would throw while in bloom. A cool breeze gusted around him, so he pulled open the glass doors and stepped inside. He observed Jackson speaking with a family of newcomers, and Carmen Sanders who'd joined a group of people in the recreation room, chatting and trying to make them feel comfortable.

Things appeared calm, giving him the opportunity to leave for a while. He wanted to pay May Montgomery a visit, but after seeing the items in the back seat of the Honda, he wanted to make a secret rendezvous to Don Jackson's place. He left Morning Glory Haven and climbed into his vehicle. Reaching under the passenger seat, he removed the briefcase, pulled out Jackson's folder, and wrote down the address. Replacing the file, he slipped the case back under the seat and drove away.

Hawkman found Jackson's apartment complex and classified it as mediocre. The rent probably agreed with his salary. He parked in a visitor's slot, then climbed out of his vehicle. Opening the back door, he rummaged through the duffel bag he always carried, and pulled out a pair of latex gloves, along with a lock pick set. He shoved them into his jacket pocket and locked the 4X4. No security guard appeared on the premises, and he scouted the area as he went inside. The building seemed unusually quiet, but he figured most people were still at their jobs. He'd better put a move on it as it wouldn't be long before the work day ended. Figuring apartment fourteen would be on the first floor, he moved along the corridor and came upon it immediately. Checking both ways to make sure he was alone, he slipped on the gloves, and gave a soft knock. When he received no answer, he maneuvered the lock pick into the key hole and had the door open in a matter of seconds. So far, no one had entered the building, so he slipped inside.

Hawkman stood in a small living room with plenty of sunlight coming through the West window so he could make out a sofa, which had newspapers cluttered across the cushions and several pieces had slipped to the floor. A shirt dangled off the back of a chair and a pair of slacks on a hanger hung from a hook on the wall. He shook his head as he moved across the room. A kitchenette occupied one side of the apartment, and a door stood open on the opposite wall. He figured it led to the bedroom and headed in that direction. Covers were tossed in a pile on the mattress, several pillows were stacked at the head of the bed, along with detective magazines strewn across the covers. He noticed a computer on a table and fingered through several sordid murder game CDs alongside the machine. He took his camera and shot several pictures, then went into the bathroom. Shutting the door, he flipped on the light switch and opened the medicine cabinet. He took several more photos, then made his way to the front door. Placing his ear across the wood, he could hear footsteps in the hallway. When they faded, he peered out, stepped into the corridor and closed the door which automatically locked. He hurried out of the building to his vehicle, jumped into the driver's side and quickly left the area.

When he pulled up to the front of the Montgomery's house, the drapes were open and May's car sat in the open garage. He removed the latex gloves and placed them along with the lock pick on the floorboard of the passenger side, climbed out of the 4X4 and strolled up the sidewalk. After he rang the bell, he reached into his pocket and flipped on the recorder.

May opened the door and stepped back startled. "Well, hello, Mr. Casey. This is quite a surprise. If you're looking for Lisa, she's at work."

"Yes, I know. I came to talk with you."

"Oh? What about?"

"Carmen Sanders."

May put a hand to her neck. "I see." She opened the door wider and gestured for him to enter. "You might as well come inside; no sense in your standing on the porch in the cold."

Hawkman entered a small, but cozy room. A yellow parakeet paced its bar and nodded its head in an elaborate wrought iron cage in the corner. A couch upholstered in a floral pastel green material sat against one wall and two matching chairs faced it, with a small glass topped coffee table in the middle. A tall bronze lamp with a gold shade stood between the two chairs. One large watercolor print of a forest hung above the fireplace.

"Make yourself comfortable. Can I get you something to drink?"

"No, thanks," he said, sitting down at the end of the sofa. "You have a lovely home."

"Thank you," May said, taking the chair across from him. "What is it you want to know about Carmen Sanders?"

"I understand you were close friends with her mother, Abby."

May shrugged. "We were friends. Not sure the word 'close' fits our relationship. She was not the type of woman I took to public gatherings."

Hawkman frowned. "Why not?"

"She knew nothing about the arts. Taking her to a museum or opera would not have fit well in her life."

"I see. What did you think about Carmen?"

"Quite a little brat growing up. However, I must admit she's turned out okay. However, she's not qualified to work at Morning Glory Haven."

"Oh?"

"Good grief, the child doesn't have any formal education. Many of those folks living there are college graduates, with master's and doctor's degrees. Morning Glory Haven is a high class place."

"What does that have to do with Carmen working there, if she's doing the job?"

May stiffened and harrumphed. "She can't even carry on a knowledgeable conversation."

"I'm sure the residents don't rely on her to let them know where the latest musical is playing. They seem to like her just fine."

"Carmen does tend to mingle with the few more simple minded ones. They giggle and act silly like school girls. For instance, Hazel Spencer." She raised a hand. "Forgive me for speaking badly of the dead, but it's true."

"I understand Ms. Spencer was well liked."

"She made people laugh." May put a finger to her temple and shook her head. "She didn't have it up here where it counts."

"I see. Did you know Gladys Owens?"

"Gladys Owens," she muttered. "No, I don't recall the name. Does she live at Morning Glory Haven?"

"Not anymore. She passed away."

"I'm sorry. A friend of yours?"

"No. Tell me about the relationship between your daughter and Carmen Sanders."

She opened her eyes wide. "There isn't one."

"Why? They grew up together."

"Not really; there's an age gap and Lisa never cared for Carmen."

"How come?"

"They weren't in the same social class."

Hawkman stood. "Thank you for your time, Mrs. Montgomery. It's been interesting."

She saw him to the door. As he drove back to Morning Glory Haven, he flipped off the recorder and could feel the steam churning inside his head. "What a snob," he mumbled. He could definitely see where Lisa got her haughty attitude.

He parked, but before leaving his vehicle he called Jennifer and told her he'd probably be working all night, so not to worry if he didn't show up. Then he opened the briefcase to make sure he had the connecting cord for his camera. He'd use Morning Glory Haven's computer room later tonight and check out the pictures he'd taken.

When he went inside, he noticed the recreation room was void of residents, but filled with workers putting a stage at one end, adjusting a ceiling spot light and moving chairs into rows. He watched for several minutes, as he'd seen the magician show after all this work had been completed, and wondered how they put it together. Quite a transformation took place before his eyes. Then it dawned on him, he'd seen on the bulletin where a comedian was due to appear tonight. Good, he thought. It will help get the people's minds off of murder.

chapter

FORTY-FOUR

Hawkman took the elevator up to Hazel Spencer's room, and found the lab team wrapping things up. He talked to them from the doorway. "Find anything out of the ordinary?"

One of the technicians glanced up. "Hi, Casey. We've gone through everything in this room. From what we can tell right now, it appears the fingerprints we've found belong to the individual who lived here."

"Isn't that odd? What about the cleaning crew?"

"We wondered too, so I went down and spoke with the head housekeeper. Their people wear gloves. All I can say is, if someone was in this room with her before she died, they also wore some sort of protection, or did a good job of rubbing everything down. We'll go through the vacuum when we get to the lab, and check the drink residues in the glass next to her bed. We'll know more tomorrow."

"You say there was a glass next to her bed? What kind?"

"Drink type. It contained some sort of liquor, you could tell by the smell. The fingerprints on the outside were very smudged and a napkin was wrapped around it."

Moving out of the way, he watched the lab crew close the door and press yellow security tape from one side to the other in a crisscross fashion.

"Don't want anyone in here before we've run the tests on the rest of the stuff we've collected," the technician said.

Hawkman strolled along with them, making small talk as they carried their equipment down to the lab van. He waved as they drove off, then decided he'd run into town and grab a sandwich. It was mid-afternoon, and he hadn't had a bite to eat all day. It would be a long night and a thermos of coffee would be good to have available. He hated to go to the dining room, as he knew they wouldn't charge him for a meal or drink, and that just didn't seem right.

He hopped into his 4X4 and took off. While glancing up at the darkening sky and feeling the wind blow against his vehicle in sharp gusts, he almost passed a Togo's. He quickly made a U-turn and pulled into their parking lot. When he got out, he had to grab his hat to keep it from whipping off his head.

Hurrying inside, he ordered a foot long sandwich and had them cut it in half. This way he'd save part for later. He ordered a soda to go with what he'd eat now, and had them fill the thermos. Sitting at one of the small tables, he enjoyed the six inch sandwich, then drove back to Morning Glory Haven. Placing his future meal and his briefcase behind a chair at the far end of the recreation room where it would be safe, he journeyed toward Carmen Sanders' office.

He knocked lightly on the door, then stuck his head inside. "Hello, Ms. Sanders, do you have a minute?"

"Sure, come on in."

"How's it going with the residents?"

She made a face and wiggled a hand in front of her. "So, so. They're very nervous. Thank goodness we have a good program scheduled for tonight."

"I saw it on the bulletin board. It should help relieve the tension."

"What can I do for you?"

"I'd imagine you'd have a list of all the apartments and who lives in each one. Is there a possibility I could get a copy?"

"Sure." She opened a folder on her desk, removed a couple sheets of paper, and stepped back to the copying machine. Then she handed him the duplicates. "The information is short coded, but it tells you if the person is a widower or widow, also the floor number and if the person is living here without the spouse."

Hawkman quickly scanned the names. "Perfect. Thank you."

"Is there anything else I can do to help you?"

"No." He glanced at her. "How long will you be working tonight?"

"Not sure. This is an unusual day and Mr. Foster will let us know when we can go home." She grimaced. "Hopefully, before midnight."

"This was your weekend off, if I remember right."

"Yes, but I don't mind coming in. Helps my days pass faster and I had nothing planned for this weekend."

"I haven't seen Mr. Jackson since morning."

"He's around. Sometimes, he'll walk over to the shopping mall with one of the older seniors, and carry back their purchases. Most of them have baskets on their walkers, but others don't."

"Does he have many favorite residents?"

Carmen shrugged. "I have no idea. He doesn't talk much to me unless it's duty related, like our work schedules or such."

"Does he always park his car in front of the assisted living building?"

She laughed. "He did gripe one day about not having a place to park nearby. I told him to use the employees' parking lot, but he said there was never a space available."

"It does appear there are more slots on the front side of the facility."

"That's because many of the people in the independent side have their own cars."

"I won't take up any more of your time. Thanks for the list."

When he stepped out of her office and moved down the hallway. Lisa Montgomery came out of her office.

"Mr. Casey, I'd like to speak with you."

Hawkman stopped in his tracks. "Yes."

Her eyes flared with angry fire. "How dare you go talk to my mother. You have no right to involve her in the affairs of Morning Glory Haven."

"What makes you think she's immune to questioning?"

"She doesn't work here."

Hawkman stared into her face. "Ms. Montgomery, you and your mother were two of the last persons to leave this building the night Ms. Spencer died. I'm investigating a possible murder and there are few holds barred. So don't tell me who I have the right to question."

She turned on her heel, stalked back into her office, and slammed the door.

Hawkman stared after her for a few seconds, then continued down the corridor mumbling, "Like mother, like daughter."

He sat down on the couch in the large sitting room and read through the papers Carmen had copied for him. Taking a pen from his pocket, he circled four names. Two he recognized, one being Maggie and the other, a male he'd met in the recreation room. The other two women he didn't know and would need to have them pointed out to him. Maybe Foster could help. The thoughts going through his mind bothered him. Things were beginning to fit into a weird pattern.

Rising from the sofa, he made a trek down the first floor corridor and spotted two of the apartments he planned to watch. He ran up the steps of the stairwell exit to the second floor, and searched for the apartment occupied by the male, since he already knew Maggie's location. Once he found it, he took the stairs back down to the main floor and journeyed into the dining room where people were starting to gather for an early dinner, as the show would start at eight.

He left there and went back to the recreation area where he retrieved his briefcase, then went up to the second floor, entered the computer room, and closed the door. Everyone would be concentrating on the upcoming show and he'd have plenty of privacy.

Taking the small camera from his pocket, he pushed in the connecting cord, and plugged it into the computer. Once the photos were transferred onto the monitor, Hawkman zoomed in on each picture. He leaned back in the chair, and stared at the screen.

Hearing a familiar voice in the hallway, he quickly closed down the snapshots, disconnected the cord, and turned off the machine. Don Jackson opened the door.

"Oh, excuse me, Mr. Casey. I expected an empty room, since everyone would be preparing for the entertainment tonight." He ushered in an older couple. "I'm showing off the perks of our facility to these guests before show time."

"No, problem. I'm just leaving." Hawkman nodded at the man and woman as he picked up his valise and left.

Perry Foster's door stood open and Hawkman tapped on the door jamb. Foster glanced up and waved for him to enter.

"Man, what a day."

"I can imagine. I need a favor and hope it won't be too much out of your way. I'd like you to point out two of your residents."

Perry rose from his chair and stretched. "Sure, it will be a welcomed break. I need to get up and move around. Who are the people you'd like to meet."

"Ms. Rose Fletcher and Ms. Patti Cline."

"Any special reason why you've picked those two?"

"I'd rather not say."

"They're a couple of our original residents and are usually at the events early. They like to mingle and socialize." Perry slipped on his suit jacket, which he'd thrown across the back of the chair, then ran his hands over his hair as he came from around the desk.

"I appreciate it," Hawkman said.

The two men walked into the recreation area. Foster shook hands with several of the men and greeted many of the women. He then turned and took Hawkman by the arm. "Mr. Casey, I'd like you to meet one of our charter residents. This is Ms. Patti Cline."

Hawkman touched his hat. "My pleasure."

She put out a frail, small hand. A big smile lit up her face. "Oh, my, you're the private investigator I've heard so much about. Aren't you one handsome, sexy brute."

Hawkman felt the heat in his cheeks. "Thank you. I'm lost for words."

"No need to talk, I'll just stare at you."

Perry called out and waved. "Rose, come here. I want you to meet someone."

A woman very different from Ms. Cline waddled over, pushing a walker. She had several chins, but twinkling blue eyes. Perry made the introduction and Rose elbowed Patti. "Is he not the best-looking guy we've seen around here?"

"I already told him; now you're embarrassing him more."

"You ladies are more than kind. I hope you enjoy the show tonight."

"Are you hanging around?"

"It's possible, but you won't know me, because I'll be undercover."

The two women erupted in peals of laughter.

"He has a sense of humor too," Patti said.

Hawkman observed both women held beverages. He glanced up at the bar in the entry alcove where two men were mixing drinks. Glancing around the room, he noted almost everyone had a glass. No wonder they were here early.

He strolled back toward the office with Foster. "Is your bar open every evening?"

"No, usually just Fridays, and occasionally on special nights like this one. I figured with all the stuff going on, the residents needed a little pick-me-up.

They stopped at the door of the office.

"Thanks for your time. I won't bother you any longer. Those were two delightful women."

Perry grinned. "They'd like for you to come back and chat with them. I could see it in their eyes."

Hawkman rubbed his sideburn. "Uh, I think I'll keep my distance."

chapter

FORTY-FIVE

Hawkman stood back in a shadowed corner as he watched the residents take their seats for the show. The Hamptons had arrived earlier and took occupancy in the second row. Maggie glistened in her turquoise sequined pant suit and freshly done hairdo. Carmen Sanders made her way into the crowd, and a few of the women waved their hands, motioning for her to come where they'd saved a chair. She looked radiant as she made her way to the vacant seat between Ms. Cline and Ms. Fletcher.

Lisa Montgomery came out of her office and strolled to the back of the room where she scooted a couple of last row chairs further back. She sat down on one, then placed her handbag on the other. Hawkman expected to see May come in the front door any moment, but to his surprise, Don Jackson took the seat, and placed an arm around the back of Lisa's chair. Hawkman thought this to be a very interesting discovery.

The lights dimmed and the small spotlight from the ceiling came on bright as Perry Foster stepped up to the microphone. He thanked the people for attending, then introduced the entertainer. When the comedian took the stage, a clap of thunder shook the walls and the spotlight flickered. The wind driven rain rattled against the glass panes in a torrential downpour.

"Wow, what a welcome," the comedian said. The crowd broke out in peals of laughter.

He kept the audience in a humorous uproar for an hour and a half. Even Hawkman found himself chuckling several times. The guy is good, he thought.

Keeping an eye on the staff, he noticed Jackson had removed his arm from around Lisa, and placed a hand on her thigh. She didn't bother to move it. When the entertainer told his last joke, the lights came back up, and the crowd hailed the entertainer with a standing ovation. Don stood and clapped.

Hawkman noticed Jackson immediately went to the bar, then with a drink in hand mingled with the crowd while Lisa headed back to her office. Perry stopped her midway and they conversed for a few minutes; then she went into her cubicle. Hawkman leaned against the wall, as Perry came down the hallway.

"Hi, Mr. Casey. I'm going to let my employees go home. Mr. Mackle called and he'll be here tomorrow morning. He's flying in tonight."

"Good move on his part." Hawkman pointed toward the stage. "I thoroughly enjoyed the entertainment. The comedian did an excellent job of relaxing the residents. He kept them in a good mood."

"Yes, he's very talented." Perry cocked his head and looked at Hawkman. "What are your plans?"

"I'm going to stand guard during the night, but I'd like the freedom of moving in and out of the building. Is there a possibility I could get one of those cards so I could get in without having to disturb anyone?"

"Sure." He reached in his pocket, and handed one to Hawkman. "Take mine. I'll make another when I get back to the office. Right now, I want to touch base with Carmen and Don."

"Thanks, I'll return it when I'm through."

Perry nodded and took off, looking for his two employees. He caught Jackson with Ms. Cline and Ms. Fletcher at the end of the hall.

Hawkman tucked the card in his back jeans pocket and meandered into the recreation room where the workers were dismantling the small stage and putting everything back in order. The wind howled through the trees outside and an occasional lightning bolt lit up the interior. He crossed over to the far end of the recreation room and checked his lunch and briefcase. The items were all accounted for in the corner where he'd placed them. Plopping down on the overstuffed chair, he unscrewed the thermos and poured himself a half cup of coffee. The liquid, still hot enough to burn his tongue, tasted good.

It didn't take long before the room appeared as before. You'd never have guessed it had resembled an auditorium half an hour ago. Perry and Jackson came down the corridor, while Carmen trailed behind. Hawkman noticed Jackson was empty handed, and he wondered where the drink went.

They all looked tired from the long day, and didn't even glance his way as they trudged down the hallway toward their offices. Lisa Montgomery hadn't left yet, unless she went out some back door Hawkman didn't know existed.

When the corridor lights dimmed, he heard the click of the automatic door locks. The overhead fluorescents went off, casting him into almost total darkness, except for the occasional lightning flash and dimmed hallway. He glanced toward the elevator when he heard it open. George stepped out and limped toward the front. Hawkman didn't say anything, as the man looked exhausted. He watched him open the door, then suddenly close it. George stepped back, buttoned up his sweater, removed a soft hat from the pocket and shoved it on his head, then ventured out into the weather. It baffled Hawkman why the old fellow didn't move in with his wife. This coming and going must get awfully tedious.

Shortly, Carmen came through the room, a huge purse slung over her shoulder, her lips drawn tight across her teeth as if she had something heavy on her mind. She opened an umbrella, and hurried out the door, letting it slam hard, as she disappeared into the darkness. Several of the kitchen and cleaning staff meandered into the recreation room. Some wore rain slickers, while others had confiscated plastic bags they tied around their heads or put across their shoulders. They chatted and laughed with one another as they exited.

Soon, Perry Foster, made his way through the dimness. His shoulders slumped, and his clothes looked more rumpled than earlier. He trudged along as if he had a hard time putting one foot in front of the other. It had been a rough day for him, carrying the burden of today's events alone.

Hawkman glanced toward the corridor. "Where the hell are Jackson and Montgomery?" he mumbled.

Several minutes passed before he heard a door open and shut; then a soft knock resounded.

"Are you ready?" he heard Lisa say.

"Be right there," said the unmistakable voice of Don Jackson.

Crunching down in the chair, Hawkman tried to make himself invisible. To his surprise, when the two emerged from the dimmed hallway, they headed toward the door leading into the garden. He waited until they'd stepped outside before he left his secluded corner. Hightailing it toward the entry, he made it just in time to see Lisa lower the umbrella as they entered the other building.

Grabbing his lunch, thermos and briefcase, he hurried out the recreation entry and jogged to his vehicle. The rain had slowed down and he threw the items on the passenger seat, inserted the key, and drove slowly around to the assisted living front. He made it just in time to see Don Jackson's car pull out of the lot. The silhouettes of two people in the front seat stood out as they passed under the glow of the street light.

Hawkman followed at a distance and parked at the curb when the car pulled into the apartment complex where Jackson lived. When the two climbed out of the vehicle, the rain started coming down in sheets. Lisa quickly raised the umbrella and they dashed toward the door. As they entered the building, Don gave her a pat on the butt.

"Man, I didn't expect this," Hawkman said aloud. "No sense in hanging around here while they have their rendezvous." He started the 4X4 and drove back to Morning Glory Haven. Driving through the employees' lot, he spotted Lisa's car, and figured Jackson would bring her back, or she'd spend the night with him. It dawned on Hawkman, she may not have to come in, since it would be Sunday, but he knew Don had the duty. However, Perry might want them all present when Mackle arrived. He chuckled at the vision of May's reaction if he approached her about her high society daughter spending the night with a man.

He pulled into Hampton's empty parking slot near the door. Leaving his briefcase in the vehicle, he grabbed his sandwich and thermos with one hand, held his hat with the other, then ran for the door through the pouring rain. Using the card Perry had given him, he entered the building. He removed his coat and hung it on the tree horn near the door, then went to the seat in the corner where he'd been earlier. His view covered the entries, elevator and corridor which would serve his purpose. Holding his wristwatch up so it would catch the light, he noted it was midnight. There were long hours ahead, and he wasn't sure anything would occur. However, his gut told him not to drop off to sleep. These murders had been happening closer and closer together.

After finishing his sandwich and drinking half the coffee, he decided to walk around, as a full tummy would probably make him drowsy. His sight had grown accustomed to the darkness, so he found it easy to maneuver in the surroundings without bumping into tables. He moved down the hallway trying the office doors, and found them locked, which didn't surprise him. Then he traveled the opposite direction, and looked in the exercise room full of very expensive machines, which didn't cease to amaze him. The first floor corridor appeared quiet, so he rode the elevator to the second. When he passed some of the doors, the sounds of sleep made its way through the panels. He smiled as he listened, and figured in twenty years he'd probably make enough noise to run Jennifer out of bed.

Maggie's apartment appeared quiet. More than likely, George's snoring might have been one of the reasons she liked it here so well. He checked the computer room, the pool table area, and the large movie alcove with a big screen, then stopped to examine a half done jigsaw puzzle in one of the leisure niches.

All seemed serene as he headed back to the elevator. Suddenly, he stopped in his tracks as he heard the hum of the pulleys. He quickly ducked behind the wall of the game center, reached inside his shirt, and loosened the Velcro flap on the shoulder holster that protected his gun.

chapter

FORTY-SIX

Hawkman heard the clank of walker wheels hit the bump leading out of the elevator. He stole a peek around the door jamb and couldn't believe his sight. What the hell was Maggie doing up at this hour? When he stepped out of the shadows, she jumped and almost dropped the item she held in her hand.

"Mr. Casey, you scared the living daylights out of me. Why are you hiding in there?"

"Watching to see who came out of the elevator. I sure didn't expect you. What are you doing roaming around at this hour?"

"I couldn't sleep. Guess I've had too much excitement. Decided to go down to the kitchen and see if there were any goodies left." She held up a small plastic bag half full of cookies. "I lucked out. There were a few left on a platter. Would you like to come to my place and share them with me?"

"No, thanks, but I'll accompany you."

When they reached her apartment, she turned the handle, and pushed open the door. Hawkman immediately moved in front of her.

"Hold on. Why didn't you lock up while you went downstairs rummaging for treats?"

She glanced up at him with wide eyes. "I didn't think it necessary since I'd only be gone a few minutes."

"You wait here, and I'll check inside before you enter."

He stepped over the threshold, pulled his gun, and walked through each room. After examining the closets, and under the bed, he holstered his weapon, and called for her to come on in. He pointed a finger. "Don't leave again without locking your door."

She stared at him with concern. "You're frightening me. I probably won't go to sleep at all now."

"Sorry, but right now I want you to be very alert." He reached for the door knob. "I need to leave so I can patrol the halls. Will you be all right?"

Maggie waved him out. "I'll be fine. Get out there so you can protect us."

Hawkman left a very nervous woman, and heard the lock click as he walked down the corridor. He hoped he hadn't missed anything while taking the few minutes with her. Hurrying down the hallway, he checked the man's apartment, then headed downstairs by way of the stairwell.

This would bring him right in front of the two women's quarters.

The floor appeared quiet. He went back to the recreation room and his stake out chair. He rubbed his chin trying to analyze how he'd not seen Maggie going down to the dining room, and figured he must have missed her when he was examining the extra rooms. Since her apartment wasn't far from the elevator, it would've been easy not to see or hear her with the carpeted hallway. Not wanting it to happen again, he decided his best bet was to remain in one spot where he could see the comings and goings from all directions.

The minutes seemed to drag as the night grew longer. Hawkman rubbed his face several times and wiggled in the chair trying to find a position where he wouldn't get too comfortable. He didn't dare get up and move around, afraid he'd give himself away to anyone coming into the building. The room had taken on a chill and he noticed the shadows of the plants in the garden area whipping back and forth in the wind. The storm he'd heard about on the weather forecast had hit. His tall body ached in the soft chair and he had to stand up. Checking for the darkest area, he moved toward the corner and leaned against the wall, where he could still see the entries.

He figured it must be close to three in the morning, and angled his watch so it caught the reflection of the dimmed hallway lights. It surprised him to see it was only a little before two. His intuition had made him stay here tonight and it seldom proved wrong.

The deaths were happening closer together. However, there was always the possibility nothing would occur, and he'd have to stay another twenty-four hours. He'd need some shuteye sometime or he'd not last through another long night.

Suddenly, a noise at the front door caught his attention. He quickly dropped behind the couch and peeked around the edge as he watched the door slowly open. May Montgomery stepped inside, closed her umbrella, and stood it beside the jamb. She cautiously crossed the room, then turned down the corridor toward Lisa's office. He could no longer see her, but heard her try the door, then knock softly.

"Lisa, are you there?"

He stayed behind the couch not wanting to spoil his cover. He doubted May was the murderer, but what she was doing here at this early hour, and why is she knocking at her daughter's office? Surely she knows she's not there. Then he remembered Lisa's car parked in the lot. He wondered how May got the card to get in the building?

About that time, he heard the door leading to the garden area open. Lisa Montgomery stepped inside, closed her umbrella, and stomped down the hallway.

"Mother, what the hell are you doing?"

"Looking for you."

"I told you I'd be working late."

"How come your office is locked?"

"Because I'm in the other building helping out a new girl. When I went to my car, I saw yours parked next to mine. Now let's get home. I've got to be back here in the morning."

Hawkman hunkered down behind the couch and remained motionless as he watched Lisa lead her mother by the arm. May picked up her umbrella, as Lisa opened hers outside the door, then the two walked out into the rain. Once the door clicked shut, Hawkman waited a few seconds before he stood and went back to the dark corner.

It felt like an hour had passed when suddenly a cool breeze hit him in the face. He jerked around to see a shadowy figure enter the building through the garden, and again he dropped behind the couch. A bright lightning flash coming through the windows gave him full view of the person and the glistening syringe he held in a latex covered hand. Hawkman edged out from behind the sofa, took his gun from the holster, and silently followed the intruder down the corridor.

When the man reached the door of Patti Cline, he stuck his master key into the hole. Hawkman stepped from the shadows and aimed the gun. "Hold it right there."

Don Jackson whirled around. His eyes flashed and his mouth contorted into a nasty grimace. "What are you doing here?"

"Waiting for you."

"Ms. Cline invited me up."

"Why didn't you knock instead of using your master key? I'll tell you why. You drugged her drink with Halcion and know she's in a deep sleep. Now you're going to go pump her full of insulin."

Jackson gripped the syringe like a knife, then in a quick movement, swung his arm above his head, lurched at Hawkman and brought the needle down on his gun hand, planting it deeply into his arm. Stumbling backwards against a heavy metal trash can, Hawkman snatched the syringe from his flesh and threw it aside. Not wanting to fire his gun within the confines of the building for fear of hurting a resident, he regained his balance, and took after Don down the hallway.

Jackson had a couple of seconds head start and made it out the door leading into the garden. By the time Hawkman reached the landscaped area, he'd slammed the seldom used wrought iron gate shut. Hawkman struggled to unlatch it and grabbed the card from his back pocket as the door to the other building closed. He jammed the card into the slot and threw open the door. As he passed a wide eyed nurse watching the chase, Hawkman yelled, "Call 911"

The woman hurried to the reception desk and picked up the phone.

He ran out the other door, just as Jackson jumped into his car. He aimed his gun at one of the back tires and fired. It immediately went flat, but it didn't prevent Jackson from trying to steer the vehicle toward Hawkman. Taking aim at the front end, Hawkman fired, which forced the car to spin around on the wet pavement, stopping with Jackson looking down the barrel of his .45 pistol.

"Get out," Hawkman said.

Jackson opened the door and slowly moved from under the steering wheel, holding his hands in the air. "How did you know?"

"You shouldn't leave your murder paraphernalia in plain view in the backseat of your car."

About that time two patrol cars, sirens blaring and lights flashing, bounced into the parking lot, and rolled in at an angle in front of the two standing men. The officers jumped out with guns drawn as Jackson yelled, "Don't shoot."

"I'm making a citizen's arrest," Hawkman said. "I want this man booked for attempted murder."

One of the officers pushed Jackson against the car and threw on the handcuffs. After reading him the Miranda rights, they shoved him into the back seat of the police car.

Hawkman holstered his gun, then pointed at the Honda. The lab needs to go through this vehicle, so you better call a tow truck and get it to the police yard. There's a lot of evidence inside. Also, you need to get to his apartment where you'll find other incriminating items."

Soon, an unmarked car rounded the corner and Detective Williams climbed out.

"Looks like you caught our villain?"

"I'm sure of it. You got a plastic bag on you?"

"Yeah. Why?"

"He tried to hit me with a syringe. I need to go retrieve it out of the hallway."

Hawkman took the evidence bag and jogged through the assisted living area, then into the independent living building. He found the needle on the floor of the corridor where he'd tossed it, picked it up by the sharp end and dropped it into the sack. A man opened the door of one of the rooms.

"What's going on out here?"

"Nothing for you to be concerned about. It's over and you can go back to bed."

Returning to the parking lot, Hawkman handed the plastic container to the detective. "Careful of the needle. My fingerprints are going to be on that too, as he jabbed me good and I had to pull it out."

Williams frowned. "What's in it?"

"Insulin, I'm sure. It's not going to hurt me, as it's still almost full. He didn't have time to plunge much."

The detective carefully took the syringe and placed it in his vehicle. "How did you know this guy was your man?"

"I really got suspicious after I followed him to his car one evening and took a gander at what he had in the back seat. Then I checked out his apartment."

"Oh, so I won't be able to use you in court without getting you arrested for breaking and entering."

Hawkman scratched his sideburn. "Something like that. However, the evidence is still there without any of my fingerprints."

Williams grinned. "Figures. What'd you find?"

He pointed to the car. "In the Honda you'll find a couple of boxes of syringes, carton of latex gloves and a small ice chest, which I assume holds the insulin."

"Yeah, but if he's a diabetic, wouldn't that be normal?"

"Not when he's wearing an insulin pump. He has no need for so many needles. It's possible he might carry an extra syringe if his pump malfunctioned, but not boxes full."

"In his apartment?"

"Several prescriptions of Halcion are in the bathroom medicine cabinet."

"Ooh, sweet."

"I imagine, if you can get a hold of Ms. Cline's glass before she washes it you'll find residue of the sleep medication.

"I'll get right on it. Do you have any idea of a motive?"

"I'm leaving it up to you to find out. His past record is sort of weird. It appears he's messed up. After he got out of the service he got slapped with charges of sexually harassing women at three jobs. Maybe you can question him about why he went after older women in particular."

The detective nodded. "No sense in us standing out in this rain any longer. Come with me and we'll check on Ms. Cline before I head for the station to book Jackson."

"Hope we can arouse her."

chapter

FORTY-SEVEN

Hawkman and the detective hurried to Ms. Cline's room. When they couldn't get a response, they pounded louder on the door and called her name, causing the residents to come out of their apartments. Hawkman then pointed to an object on the floor.

"I wonder if Jackson lost his master key?"

Williams pulled an evidence bag out of his pocket, picked it up by the tip, and dropped it inside. "I can use this, but will probably rub off his prints."

About that time, Rose Fletcher scooted up on her walker. "Patti and I share keys to our quarters in case of an emergency."

"Thanks," Hawkman said, taking the key and inserting it.

Shoving the door open, the two men dashed to Ms. Cline's bedside. Hawkman called her name many times and Williams tried shaking her. They knew she was alive, but no matter how much they tried, they couldn't awaken the woman.

"I'm calling 911," the detective said.

After the paramedics arrived, and Williams told them he suspected she'd been overdosed with Halcion, they hoisted her onto a gurney and took Ms. Cline to the hospital. Hawkman and the detective checked the room and found an empty drink glass at her bedside. Williams carefully put it in a plastic evidence bag.

"This will tell us what she had to drink."

When they left the apartment, the residents were huddled around the door and bombarded them with questions.

The detective raised his hand. "She's alive and will be fine. We just want her checked out."

After all the excitement, Hawkman could feel exhaustion setting in. He trudged to the recreation room, retrieved his thermos from the corner, left through the front door and climbed into his vehicle. He knew he didn't have time to go home, grab some winks and return by eight, so he drove to his office. Checking the needle jab in his arm, he washed it with a disinfectant, but didn't see any symptoms of infection, and felt no alarming disturbances in his body.

He crashed on the small couch, but his legs dangled over the end, causing him to thrash about. Finally, he managed to get a couple of hours sleep by curling into a fetus position.

At seven-thirty, he staggered to the bathroom, washed his face in cold water, brushed his teeth and ran a comb through his mussed hair. He always kept an extra set of clothes in the office, so he changed into a fresh shirt and jeans, then placed the wrinkled clothes into a plastic bag to take home.

He called Jennifer, but received no answer. Leaving a message, he assured her he was fine and they'd talk tonight. He left the office, and thought about what faced the people at Morning Glory Haven. Lisa Montgomery's reaction would be interesting. George and Maggie would breath sighs of relief the mess had ended, probably along with many of the other residents. He also had the sordid job ahead of calling the relatives he'd talked to about their deceased loved ones, also to notify the doctors. They would have to decide whether they wanted to pursue charges to find out if their relatives or patients had died of natural causes. Not an easy decision.

When he pulled into the parking lot of Morning Glory Haven, he saw two police cars and Detective Williams unmarked vehicle parked in the front. Reporters had already gathered and shouted questions at Hawkman as he entered the building. Inside, Julie, at the reception desk, directed him to the conference area where Mr. Mackle was holding a staff meeting. He slipped inside the room, took a seat at the back, and listened to Williams explaining what had happened last night.

Hawkman watched Lisa Montgomery's body language when the detective mentioned Don Jackson had been arrested for attempted murder. A hand went to her mouth, she turned pale, pursed her lips, and a look of fear crossed her face. Several gasps were heard around the room as people learned one of their own had more than likely committed a horrible crime. Mr. Mackle's expression appeared drawn and serious. Carmen Sanders dropped her head into her hands and softly sobbed.

When Detective Williams finished, he left the room, leaving Mr. Mackle to conduct his business. Hawkman followed him out.

"Did you get anything out of Jackson?"

"Not really. I think he's slipped over the edge. He kept babbling about how women could say sexual things to men and never get in trouble, but males always got thrown to the buzzards. I could never get any sense out of him. I think he's nuts. I have him on suicidal watch because he rattled on about how life isn't worth living now that the cops know he's killed. I've got a psychologist coming in this afternoon. We'll see what sort of results we get from his report."

"I might warn you, the reporters are converging on the place."

Williams stopped and put his fist on his hips. "Damn, I hate to meet with a bunch of vultures right now." He strolled over to the two officers waiting on the inside of the front door. "I want you two to stay and keep out the reporters. If they try to force themselves in, arrest their butts. These people are going to have enough to deal with, they don't need harassment too." He turned to Hawkman. "I'm going to need your statement. Can you come in this afternoon?"

"Yes, I'll be there."

George Hampton limped in the door, looking bewildered. He glanced at Hawkman as he ran his fingers through his unruly hair. "What the hell's going on?"

"Let's go up to Maggie's apartment and I'll explain."

The detective waved as he pushed open the door. "I'll see you later."

Hawkman saw the microphones shoved into William's face as the reporters swarmed around him. George leaned on his cane as he watched the scene unfold, shaking his head. The two men rode up the elevator to Maggie's apartment.

George opened the door and poked his head inside. "You presentable? Got Hawkman with me."

"Yes, yes, get yourselves in here and tell me what's going on. My word, sirens, police cars all over the place, shots fired during the night, and officers again this morning. I'm dying to know the story."

The Hamptons listened in awe as Hawkman related the events. "Unfortunately, the murderer happened to be someone on the staff. I'm sure this worries Mackle, as he's afraid some people will move out."

"I'm very surprised it turned out to be Don Jackson." Maggie reached over and patted George's hand. "You thought he was okay."

He cocked his head. "I really didn't know him well. Only chatted with the guy a couple of times, but he seemed pleasant enough."

Maggie raised a finger in the air. "Mr. Mackle might be pleasantly surprised. He might lose one or two residents, but I truly doubt it. Many will be so happy this whole mess is over and the culprit caught, they won't leave. Older people realize a basket of apples usually has a rotten one in the bunch. As long as it's removed, the rest will be fine."

"I hope you're right, Maggie," Hawkman said, rising. "I'm going down to talk with some of the staff and see if I can be of any help."

"Guess you're happy to know George and I didn't kill anyone," she said, grinning.

Hawkman laughed. "You know, Maggie, I never truly suspected either of you."

He left the apartment and went down to the staff offices. Noting Don Jackson's room had the yellow crime scene tape across the door, he peeked inside and saw the lab boys clearing out drawers, files and wastebaskets. He walked on down to Foster's office, but he wasn't in. Hawkman figured Perry and his boss had to plan a strategy to keep the residents from moving out. Knocking on Lisa Montgomery's door, he heard her invitation to enter and stepped inside.

She glanced up. "I hope you're not going to question me anymore."

"No, it won't be me, but I'm sure the police will make an appearance once they get my report."

"What do you mean?" she asked, frowning.

"They always investigate the culprit's lover."

She stared at him wide-eyed. "I don't know what you're talking about."

Hawkman put his hands on her desk and leaned forward. "Ms. Montgomery, don't play games with me. I followed you and Jackson to his apartment last night. You were very, should I say, friendly with each other. Obviously, your mother didn't know you were having an affair, as I witnessed the two of you talking in the wee hours of the morning in front of your office. My being there and hearing you two will probably save you from being arrested."

Tears welled in her eyes as she stared at the top of her desk. "Then I'm glad you were eavesdropping. Don seemed so sweet and kind. I've never been so shocked in my life to hear the news this morning."

"I don't suspect you of any wrong doing, but be prepared to be questioned by the police. I'd also suggest you come clean with your mother. She's going to be mighty upset when the police come to search your home."

Lisa wiped the tears from her cheeks with a tissue. "This is going to kill her."

"You're both adult women, surely you can solve the problem."

She nodded. "Thank you for your warning. I appreciate it. I just pray I don't lose my job."

"That's between you and Mr. Mackle. I think if you'll be kinder to Carmen Sanders, things might go easier on you concerning your boss. By the way, how did your mother get a card to get into the building after hours?"

She glanced up at him and sighed. "Please, don't mention it to Mr. Mackle. I don't want Mr. Foster to get into trouble. I talked him into giving me one for mother, since she's a regular volunteer and has also enticed many residents to move in. I also promise to be more cordial to Carmen."

"I wish you luck."

When he left her office, he met Carmen in the hallway. "Hello, Ms. Sanders. I noticed you were quite upset at the meeting this morning."

"Oh, Mr. Casey, I cried for my uncle. He's worked so hard to make this place outstanding, and now this horrible thing has happened. It must hurt him deeply."

He patted her on the shoulder. "Your uncle is a strong man and will recover fine. You just keep up your good work."

She smiled. "Thank you. I will."

As she turned to go into her office, Mr. Mackle's receptionist approached him.

"Mr. Casey, Mr. Mackle would like to see you in his office."

Hawkman followed her and when he stepped inside, he nodded at Perry Foster sitting on one of the chairs. Mr. Mackle stood, came around the desk and extended his hand.

"I want to thank you for ending this horrible nightmare. It still puts a strain on us to think one of our own staff may have murdered more than one of our residents."

"I'm glad it's over too, and I do suspect Jackson killed more. Some bodies may have to be exhumed to prove it. Depends on how many relatives of past residents will want to bring charges. I'm sorry it had to be one of your staff, but at least he's out of here now. I wish you all the luck in the world on keeping your people. It may take some time to regain your excellent reputation, but it will happen."

Mackle nodded, his expression sober. "We have our work cut out to restore the good name of Morning Glory Haven. I can also guarantee I will take a much closer look at the resumes I receive to fill his vacancy."

"Good idea," Hawkman said.

"What was Jackson's motive?" Perry asked.

Hawkman shook his head. "At this time we don't know, other than he is mentally ill."

Perry rose and shook Hawkman's hand. "Thank you for everything, Mr. Casey."

"You're more than welcome. I wish all of you the best."

Hawkman left the two men and decided to go home. When he approached the recreation room, it was filled to capacity with the residents. To his amazement, as he walked through, they gave him a standing ovation. Maggie and George stood on one end of the room holding a huge hand written banner which read: 'Thank you, Private Investigator, Tom Casey'.

THE END

3988552

Made in the USA